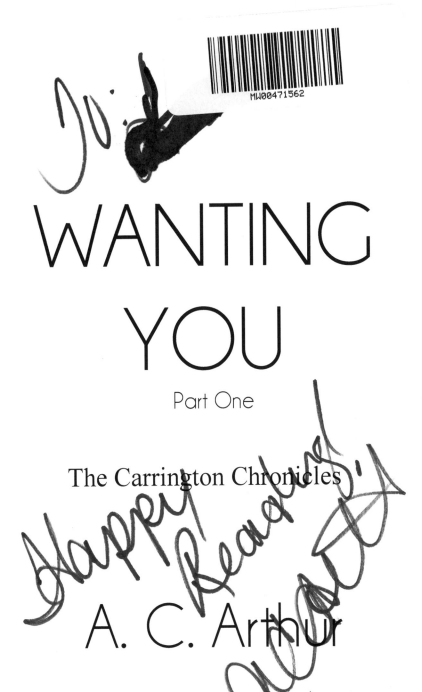

To: [redacted]

WANTING YOU

Part One

The Carrington Chronicles

Happy Reading!

A. C. Arthur

AN ARTISTRY PU███████G BOOK

WANTING YOU Copyright ███████ A.C. Arthur
First Edition: 2013
Print Edition: 2015

www.acarthur.net

Cover Design by Croco Designs

Interior format by The Killion Group
http://thekilliongroupinc.com

Sex is emotion in motion.
~Mae West

OTHER BOOKS BY A.C. ARTHUR

PROLOGUE

Six Months Ago

I am not a prude. I can do this.
There was that voice inside my head, reminding me of what I could do, what I could endure. I didn't need this reminder all the time, just when he looked at me that way. When his eyes glazed over with hunger and I began to feel like the selected feast.

He moved toward me in his slow, purposeful gait, his tailored suit hanging expertly on his tall, lean body. At one point—in the very beginning—I remember wanting him. There had been a slow spiral of heat that entered the pit of my stomach the moment he walked into a room. My heart had raced with the possibility that my presence garnered a mutual response. The first touch of his mouth to mine had been like a door opening and blinding light shining on the other side. I really had no choice but to walk through, to take the steps necessary to get to the other side, to be with this man.

Now, a year later, I know this look like I know my name. It's as familiar to me as what will undoubtedly come next.

"Come to me," he said in that deep rasped voice, the one that could only belong to him.

I took the first step and then a second, all the while a war was brewing within.

"Don't tease me," he warned, fingers clenching at his sides. "I want you to come here."

"Yes," I whispered because I knew what he expected.

It wasn't a command, I tried to tell myself, but a request, because he wanted me so desperately. I was sick to death of his commands and the great expectation he had of me following them.

Unfortunately, my feet had another idea, their speed working in direct contrast to his words. When I thought he would react with the petulant disappointment he had before, he smiled. A slow gleam that bordered on being wicked. My heart rate increased sending an instant message to my feet to get going.

In seconds I was before him and his hands were on me. My body knew his touch, each inch of my skin in tune with the heat from his fingertips. I gasped, because this time was different. There was a singeing heat as his fingers wrapped around my neck, squeezing gently, but with enough force to spike white hot fear at the base of my spine.

"I don't like to wait," he said his gaze intent on mine. "You know that, don't you?"

I wanted to speak, truly I did, but there came a point in life when one had to accept their limitations. So I nodded instead—an act that did not please him. My clothes were off in seconds, my naked body bared for his scrutiny. Traitorous nipples hardened and I took a retreating step.

"I've toyed with you long enough. It's time you understand your position."

Every word he said was a warning, tinged with the promise of retaliation. His hands went to his belt buckle, slowly, because his appearance meant everything. The most expensive clothes, the best cars, food, everything in Nigel Bingham's life was top of the line—including his woman.

When his belt was undone, his pants unzipped and the head of his dick revealed, understanding dawned and I went to him. I fell to my knees dutifully, using shaking fingers to completely expose him. I leaned in closer, inhaling the cologne he seemed to bathe in on a daily basis and had to swallow deeply to staunch the wave of nausea.

He'd grabbed me by the hair, pulling so hard tears immediately sprung to my eyes. Tilting my head back until I could look up into his face I tried desperately to hold onto myself, to the woman I knew I was somewhere deep inside.

"Give me what I want, when I want. That is how it is to be between us."

A part of me knew that was a stupid command, it was selfish and high-handed and I should have rebelled at the very notion that I would be his beck-and-call girl forevermore. Still, for the sake of peace—which I needed like my next breath—I nodded.

"Deny me and the end will justify the means." He taunted with his intent gaze and heavy accent.

The end being the moment he pushed my face into his groin and thrust his hips forward. The woman within, the one that I'd been keeping on a very short leash, broke said leash and bit down with just enough strength to send Nigel rearing back, yelling so loud the neighbors were sure to hear.

I didn't care. This wanting game was a two-way street. Nigel wanted things and so did I. And at this point we'd either have to find some common ground or this union was doomed. I grabbed my clothes and my purse, pulling the dress over my head and stuffing my underwear in my bag. I was at the door when he called my name.

"Celise.   You   are   my   fiancée.   You cannot...walk...away," he groaned from crouched down on the floor. "What will your father say?"

I turned away, touched my hand to the knob and stilled. He was right, I couldn't walk away.

CHAPTER ONE

She set her Louis Vuitton luggage down beside her leg, reached into her matching purse and pulled out her wallet. Delicate hands retrieved a credit card, and she waited while Marsha passed it through the machine.

Jason Carrington had been coming off the elevator, about to go into a meeting in the Apollo conference room when he saw her. In all honesty, he had to admit, it was like a scene out of one of those chick flicks his mother watched all the time. The man enters the room, the female appears, and the connection is made. They stand staring at each other, entranced, enamored...CUT! CUT! CUT!

He closed his eyes, opened them and refocused. She couldn't be as beautiful as he first thought. She couldn't possibly be appealing to him this way from clear across the room. But when she pushed her long, straight, coal-black hair over her shoulder and leaned down to sign her name to the room receipt, his stomach plummeted, and he felt like he had the week before when Clive had elbowed him during their weekly basketball game. Only this time the pain was replaced by longing, a sensation he hadn't felt in years, but recognized as something that would not be ignored. He moved slowly, deliberately, because if not he'd break out into a run to get to her before she vanished. Surely she was a dream, a figment of his imagination.

Oh no, those long legs—bare if he wasn't mistaken—that short skirt, with the flirty little split up the side, the fitting white blouse that was just transparent enough to give a glimpse of plump breasts were very real. He grew hard instantly.

Then she spoke. Jason was close enough to hear her voice.

"Thank you," she said as she replaced her credit card into her wallet and repositioned her purse on her shoulder. She bent slightly to pick up her bag, but was stopped before she could lift it completely.

"Let me get that for you," Jason spoke before he could help himself. He was a reputed ladies' man with an image to uphold. Only those close to him knew how he carefully considered any woman before approaching her. Just this once, however, he'd have to concede to the rumors. He wasn't about to let her get away without finding out who she was and how soon he could have her in his bed.

She looked up at him and froze. For an endless moment she simply stared into his eyes, as if there was something there she couldn't quite decipher. She had thick eyebrows that slanted seductively over intriguing hazel-colored eyes. Her high cheekbones and full, luscious mouth created an exotic look, like one of those models in a magazine. Jason tried not to get lost in those eyes filled with so much emotion, something unexplainable clogged his throat. He should look away. But he couldn't. She had a startling kind of beauty, the kind that instantly took a man's breath away with her buttery skin tone and innocent, but sexy demeanor.

"Thank you," she finally replied in a breathy voice.

Jason swallowed deeply. "Do you have your room key?" he asked while lifting her bag.

She raised her hand, the white key card clenched between her fingers.

He smiled. "The elevator's this way."

This was no ordinary meeting because she was no ordinary woman. Jason knew that without any doubt. He'd met more women than any one man should ever be able to brag about, he'd assessed them and decided which ones were worth it and which ones were not. The number he eventually asked out would also be a surprise, especially to the tabloids.

She, however, this lovely female walking beside him with sure steps, perfect posture and an air of confidence, was beyond anyone he'd ever come in contact with before. That probably seemed like overkill, but as they came to a stop in front of the elevators and he glanced at her once more, he confirmed it wasn't. She was fine.

"Thanks, again. I think I can handle it from here," she said when the elevator doors opened.

Jason didn't move. In fact, he pulled her bag just out of reach. "You shouldn't have to carry your own bags. I'll be happy to escort you to your room."

She raised an eyebrow. "Do I need an escort?"

Before the door could close, Jason eased her inside. "Yes, you do."

Because without an escort a woman this attractive would surely catch the eye of every eligible bachelor in this hotel, and Jason wasn't pleased with that thought. Not pleased at all.

"What floor?" he asked when they were closed inside the elevator together.

Intrigued by his casual answer and admittedly, this entire episode, Celise rattled off the number, then asked for clarification, "Did you say I do need an escort?"

He stared at her a moment then seemed to gather his thoughts before replying. "Yes, you definitely need an escort."

Celise watched him watching her through the mirrored doors and felt waves of heat moving from her ankles—where his gaze started—all the way up to her bared neck, where he was staring. Impressive did not seem to accurately describe him. The way he wore that black suit, starched white shirt and bright yellow silk tie said debonair. He'd approached and walked beside her with more swag than she'd ever encountered in a man. He was bald. That alone she found terribly enticing. His creamy complexion highlighted only by the dark hair of his goatee was wreaking havoc on her already frayed senses.

"Why would I need an escort?" she finally managed to stammer.

He grinned, as if he too were feeling the undeniable heat simmering between them. "There are a lot of men in this hotel. I'd hate for there to be a stampede."

Celise laughed. "Okay, as lines go, that has to be the worst I've heard in a long time."

He turned to her then, moving forward until her back was up against the wall. "Why? You don't think men would fall over themselves for you?"

He was so close, barely a breath away, in that space reserved only for a...lover. He smelled so good, her mouth watered, her body responding instantly to his proximity. It was insane, she didn't know this man from Adam and yet she was letting him invade her personal space as if she'd invited him to do so.

Celise tried to clear her mind, she was definitely not in the market for a lover. Not after what she'd just been through.

"I didn't say that, but I'd like to think the men in this hotel have a little more decorum than that," was her reply.

He looked at her as if he were contemplating his next move. Maybe a kiss? That would certainly lead to more, she thought letting her gaze fall to his mouth. Full lips, a perfectly trimmed mustache and goatee were more than alluring. She could tell he would be a great kisser. The pulsating between her legs only confirmed that fact.

"You would tempt even the most mild-mannered man," he told her. Then he stepped to the side, and with a sweep of his arm let her exit the elevator first.

Celise tried to walk normally even though she knew he was staring at her butt as she did. That thought made her mildly uncomfortable. She didn't like being watched. Then again, no man had ever looked at her the way this man did. His gaze made her feel something she wasn't familiar with. It wasn't a bad feeling. No, she was actually a little worried about how good it did feel.

Common sense made a brief appearance and Celise wondered if she should be allowing this stranger to walk her to her room.

"Here we are," she said, stopping in front of the first door to which they came. She'd just take her bag, and when he walked down the hall she'd hurry to her real room.

He smiled down at her again, reached for her wrist and turned her hand palm up. "Your card says 413. This is 417." He turned and walked toward the correct room.

She wasn't embarrassed, but she was rattled. She didn't especially like that feeling. Still Celise stepped lively behind him, noting that he even looked good from behind. How weird was that? Just a few seconds ago she was sure he was watching her butt, now she was watching his.

"Alright, we're here. You've walked me to my room, saved me from a stampede and carried my bag. I'd say you win the chivalry award of the day. Now, you can go."

The look he was giving her said leaving wasn't exactly what he had in mind. That look alone should have frightened her, should have pushed her right into the defensive mode—in which case she would be reaching into her purse for her can of Mace so she'd be ready when he made a move. And yet, she simply stood there, unable or unwilling to stop staring at him, she wasn't sure which one she was ready to claim.

"Yes, I've done all those things and can think of so many more I'd still like to do," he said in a tone as smooth as fine wine.

Heat swirled throughout her body, finding a home right between her legs, releasing moisture until she felt wetness on her thighs. "What's your name?" she asked breathily.

He laid his palms flat on the door behind her, moving closer so that the tips of her breasts grazed his chest.

"Jason," he murmured in a husky voice.

Celise licked her lips, fighting the urge to stand on tiptoe and lick his as well.

"Hello, Jason. I'm Celise. With regard to those other things you'd like to do to me," she said, inhaling a deep, refreshing breath, "I'll have to take a rain check." Jason was damned fine but this trip wasn't about a romantic interlude. It was about finally getting her life together.

"Celise," he said her name again.

Damn she liked how he said that.

"I can give you a rain check, but it expires tonight," he told her seriously.

Oh yeah, he was turning her on. Her nipples had hardened, her body was humming with awareness, and at any moment she was going to wrap her arms around him and pull him into her room. But that wasn't possible, being with him wasn't possible, she'd sworn never to go through that disappointment again. With one finger Jason traced her moist bottom lip until she could see by the quick rise and fall of his shoulders that his own breath hitched just a bit.

"I'll pick you up for dinner around seven," he told her in a quiet whisper that made her knees shake.

He was teasing her. It aroused her. She hadn't been aroused in a long time, and the last time had ended disastrously. It wasn't worth it, a part of her brain warned. The other part was entranced by his good looks and this sexy-as-hell vibe that seemed to vibrate from him like a sensual melody. She wondered…thought about trying…maybe this time would be different…maybe it would be…

Before she could change her mind, Celise quickly extended her tongue capturing the smooth tip of his finger just as he was about to pull it away. A flash of pure lust flickered in his eyes, and she smiled in triumph.

"I haven't accepted your invitation," she whispered when he pulled his finger away.

He put the same finger to his own lips and licked it slowly as if savoring the brief taste of her. "You will."

And then he was gone.

Celise watched him walk away, then with her hormones in an uproar and her heart beating wildly, fumbling fingers finally managed to open the door.

"So we're definitely seeing a profit, just not the kind we originally predicted," Clive Murdock, Jason's accountant/business partner and long-time friend, told him as they sat across the table from each other.

The Carrington Resorts' board of directors meeting had just ended, and Jason was now feeling the heat of three male and two female patriarchs of Monterey. The hotel, formerly known as the Regency, had been slowly dwindling when he'd seen it and decided he could make it three times as nice. He'd researched for an entire year, mapping out his plans, noting just how much money he would need and how much he'd make. He was that type of person, a meticulous planner who took his time making his dreams come to fruition. Owning his own hotel was definitely one of Jason's biggest dreams.

Unlike his family, he didn't want to be holed up in an office all day long, studying transactions, profit margins and benefits. His father, Jeffrey Carrington, was in mergers and acquisitions. The only company he spent time building and maintaining was Carrington Enterprises—everything else was simply a paycheck. Jackson, the oldest Carrington heir, had been groomed to work alongside his father and did so proudly. The middle brother, Jerald, loved to gamble with other people's money, so he'd been the official family investor since he'd graduated from college. Jason had been the only one to completely stray from the bunch.

When Jason had announced he wanted to take his own money, a trust fund left to him by his grandfather, and buy himself a hotel, his father had been outraged. In the last year as Jason poured his heart and soul into making Carrington Resorts a profitable and luxurious hotel, his father had eased up a bit, supposedly bidding his time until Jason got tired of this foolish venture. He'd even offered to buy it from Jason, giving him a tidy profit when he did.

But Jason wasn't about to sell—not to his father or anybody else. The Regency was a sound investment if not for the fact that it was a historic building, but because of the reputed riches stashed somewhere on the premises. Jason didn't buy into that old myth, but knew that there were some who did.

"So if we're not in the red, what the hell is their problem?" Jason asked.

Clive chuckled and closed his file. "They're old and set in their ways, you know that. You're shaking things up around here, and they don't know how to deal with that, so they've got to find something to complain about."

"This whole county is changing with the times. Have you seen all the new shops on Cannery Row? Five years ago we didn't have half this much culture in Monterey. Now, tourists are flocking here all year long. In another three or four years we'll be making more money than they'll know what to do with." Jason was angry that the board still saw him as an inexperienced businessman who was going to renege on his promise to make them all a fortune.

"I know. You don't have to sell me on the idea, but remember, you only own forty-nine percent of the stock in this place. All I'm saying is they want something big—now—and it has to be something substantial that will show them you're on the right track. Weren't you thinking of opening a restaurant on the penthouse level? Why don't you get that moving? At least then they'll have something to look forward to," Clive suggested.

Jason did have some preliminary ideas about what he'd like to do with the space on the top floor, but the mention of restaurants had his mind returning to the sexy little woman he'd met earlier and his unusual hunger for her. Celise was her name. It floated through his mind like a feather on the wind as he thought of that scrumptious body and all the wicked things he'd like to do to it. That in itself was strange. Jason never met and decided to sleep with a woman in the span of ten minutes.

"Hellooo?" Clive waved his hand in front of Jason's face.

"What?" Jason blinked and looked at his friend. "Were you saying something?"

"Yeah, I was saying you need to get something done to shut them up, but then you spaced out on me. Care to share what put that silly look on your face?" Clive began tossing papers into his briefcase.

"I don't have a silly look on my face." Jason stood, adjusting his tie. He hoped the heated sensations that went through his body each time he thought of Celise weren't showing on his face.

"Whatever you say, Jase. Just come up with something, and do it quickly. The next meeting's in three months, and if you don't have something major to report, they're going to start looking to sell again."

Jason had moved toward one of the windows looking out at the Monterey Harbor. Sailboats occupied the water space like cars in a parking garage. Tourists and natives walked along the streets on the beautiful June day. Eyeing the beach, he wondered what it would be like to make love to Celise with the waves crashing behind them, the breeze rustling over their naked bodies.

"Jason?" Clive raised his voice.

"Yeah?"

Clive sighed. "Who is she?"

Turning, Jason stared at Clive quizzically. "Who is who?"

"The woman who has your mind all twisted. You're a million miles away, and I know for a fact that the only thing that interests you more than business is women. So who is she?"

She was nobody, Jason told himself. Just a sexy woman with whom he planned to have dinner and most likely spend the night. Then she'd be out of his mind, out of his system, and he could concentrate on his hotel again. "Nobody. Don't worry about it. You and I will meet next week to go over the preliminary numbers for the restaurant. It's a good idea to go ahead and get that started right away."

"Uh-huh." Clive nodded. "If you say so. Just remember what I taught you."

Jason laughed and walked toward the door. "What you taught me? I think I've always been the teacher between the two of us."

"Please. I've taught you every rule in the playa handbook, and you know it." Clive laughed behind him.

Jason looked over his shoulder with a smirk. "Yeah, all the ones that don't work. I've made up my own rules, and the last time I checked, you were copying those."

CHAPTER TWO

Celise had taken a long, hot bath; moisturized her body; and pulled her hair up into a neat chignon. She lay across the massive canopied bed in her suite, clad only in her underwear staring up at the ceiling, wondering what the hell she was doing.

The last year of her life had been one hell of a ride. She'd been engaged; graduated tops in her class at NYU, obtained her master's degree in culinary arts; and was busily planning her future when all her dreams had come crashing down. For some reason she'd thought Nigel loved her, but all too quickly she realized he loved her father's company more. And that wasn't the only thing that had changed with Nigel. Pinching her arm, she reminded herself that she'd sworn not to think of Nigel and his foolish scheme to marry her or the pain she endured because of it.

Making the cross-country trek home to San Francisco had been the only high point. She'd traveled by train, stopping in cities and enjoying their culture before finally ending up at her family home. Her mother had been happy to see her, her brothers, DJ and Kyle, were cool and ready to pick up where they'd left off with their ominous teasing and bantering. Her father, David Markam, however, was hardly pleased with his daughter and didn't bother to conceal that fact.

Her first two nights at home had been spent arguing over her choices, her "scatterbrained decisions" as her father called them. She was impulsive and irresponsible. She always leaped before she looked. Her mind hadn't matured as much as the rest of her obviously had. These were the things he'd said to her. Celise was crushed by his assessment of her after all the hard work she'd done in school to impress him, but even that wasn't the right choice in his eyes. He wanted her to receive a college degree, but really didn't care in what. His idea for his daughter's happiness was to marry well and live the life he'd given her mother.

Madeline Markam did have a good life. She had a big, beautiful home in San Francisco as well as one in Florida, and by the end of the year she would have one in Greece. She was the dutiful socialite, the perfect showpiece on her husband's arm, and the best mother for whom a little girl could have asked.

But that wasn't the life Celise wanted for herself.

Never having been one to bite her tongue, Celise stood up to her father, telling him her desires, her plans for the rest of her life. When he'd laughed at her, telling her she was being ridiculous, she told him to go to hell. It was disrespectful, she knew, and in a few days when she had calmed down, she'd called him and apologized—for cursing, that is—because everything else she said, she meant. She was not going to sit at home while some man—Nigel Bingham—went out and made all the money for her to spend. She had her own dreams, her own aspirations, and she knew she wouldn't be content unless she followed them through.

And that didn't even graze the emotional turmoil she chose to endure on her own.

So with the money she'd saved and the savings account her mother had kept for her, she was determined to make her dreams come true. The quaint little town of Monterey was exactly where she needed to be.

That was her thought until that gorgeous but cocky man carried her luggage for her that morning.

Through all she had on her mind, she hadn't been able to stop thinking about him. Jason. He'd said his name in a deep, enticing voice, and every pore in her body went on alert. He'd appeared gentlemanly although the moment he lifted her suitcase from her grasp and their hands had briefly touched, she'd felt that bolt of desire and knew without a doubt he'd felt it too.

Initially she'd thought that was a fluke, but then her desire had grown as if it had been planted inside her all along, waiting for the right person to awaken it. She had rested in the tub thinking about him. As the warm water caressed her skin, she'd imagined it was Jason's hands, moving sinuously over her, finding all her hidden secrets and fears, exposing and conquering them. He was like those Greek statues her mother had all around the house, tall, foreboding and sexy as hell. She remembered in her younger years looking at the scantily clad gods and thinking how every woman in their time must have been completely satisfied. She, however, had not found that type of gratification.

Her thighs had begun to quiver so she'd gotten out of the tub. Her skin remained ultrasensitive while she covered herself with lotion. Slipping into her underwear she felt sexier than ever before in her meager twenty-seven years as she remembered the way Jason had looked at her. Smoldering dark eyes caressed her fully clothed as if he could see right through the garments. Her hands moved over her slick skin once more as she thought of Jason's heated gaze stroking her body, touching her, revealing things she hadn't even known were there. Her nipples hardened, and her breathing hitched.

Clamping her knees together, she scolded herself. "Girl, you've got to get some and get it quick."

Nigel had been the last man with whom she'd slept, two days before she'd tried to castrate him and one day before finding out his true plan where she was concerned. Sex with Nigel had not been what she would have expected from an older, more experienced man. It had been unexplainable. He'd done things and wanted her to do things that had both repulsed and scared her, until finally she'd had enough.

She'd wondered if she'd ever find real passion, a true intimate connection and ultimately genuine satisfaction with another lover. Now her body hummed with sexual awareness the likes of which she'd never before experienced. And she hadn't even slept with Jason.

That fact, however, would soon change.

Celise stood after having decided what she needed to do first. The one lesson she'd taken from her time in New York and her brief stint with therapy was that the only way to rid yourself of fear was to confront what frightened you. She moved to the closet where she'd hung her clothes, found a red dress, pulled it out and placed it in front of her body. "Oh yeah, this'll work."

For a moment she paused, her father's words ringing in her head. Maybe she was being impetuous. No. She was doing what she needed to do to finally put her past with Nigel behind her. Jason stirred something inside of her. Something she hadn't felt in a long time and was told she didn't have. Celise had always liked sex—at least she had before Nigel. She desperately needed to confirm that what happened between them wasn't entirely her fault.

Jason had invited her to dinner. He'd told her there were other things he wanted to do to her. Well, she could think of a few things she'd like to do to him as well. For a moment, doubt in her own ability crept over her, but she quickly pushed it away. Every man was not like Nigel. She had to remember that.

Jason frowned as he pulled the slip of hotel stationery from the door. *I needed a drink,* was all it read. *Was she serious?*

He crumpled the paper and made his way to the elevator. He'd thought about her all day—her smile, her lips, her legs. He hadn't been able to concentrate on anything else. He'd expected her to be there waiting for him, but she was gone. He couldn't resist a smile as he stepped into the elevator, remembering the way she looked at him when he said he'd pick her up. Shock, then that "who does he think he is" look took over. She had spunk that was for sure.

Jason was used to women throwing themselves at him. It was part of the Carrington curse he and his brothers always joked about. Dashing good looks and smooth-as-velvet charm was passed down through the blood of the Carrington men, and they all used their lineage to their advantage. Jason received his playboy status by default. It was assumed that if the older Carrington's were promiscuous, he was too. For the most part, the reputation didn't bother him, except for the fact that he did plan to marry and have kids someday. In fact, he'd been pretty close to doing just that before he'd seen through the charade. Now, he was being even more selective.

Celise, on the other hand, was not a choice. She was inevitable.

He took long strides toward the Pompeii Lounge, the hotel's small bar and lounge. That was undoubtedly where she was indulging in her much-needed drink. He entered the room and once again admired the tall pillars and recessed lighting he'd made sure the designer did not disturb when they'd renovated the space. Floor-to-ceiling windows were in every room on the first level. That was another original element he'd been sure to keep. He wanted the guests to see the waterfront, to view the town and all it had to offer, all while sitting comfortably in his hotel. It was a good effect, he noted as he walked through seeing that most of the tables were full. Business was good. It was the beginning of summer, tourist season, and he expected things to pick up even more. The new full scale restaurant he'd discussed with Clive, would be a welcomed addition.

Then he spotted her and paused momentarily to catch his breath. It simply wasn't possible. A matter of hours could not have made her more beautiful.

She sat at the bar, those long legs crossed, her short dress riding even higher up toned thighs, giving him and every other man in the room a clear view of what she had to offer. For a second he grimaced at the thought of the other men looking at her.

The dress was red. Hot, insatiable, take-me-I'm-yours red, and she wore it well. When his feet could move again, he progressed toward her, noting that she'd pulled up her hair. All that luxurious length had been twisted and swirled until it sat in a neat little bun at the base of her neck. Two long wisps hung past her ears down to brush over her breasts. Breasts, he noticed, bulging and fighting to escape the tight bodice.

He was hard as a teenager with a room full of *Playboy* magazines and cursed himself for not having more restraint. Slipping his hands in the pockets of his slacks with the hopes of keeping his blatant arousal to himself, Jason stood directly behind her. "Are you enjoying your drink?"

She didn't turn, didn't do a thing to acknowledge his arrival. Instead she remained seated and posed as she sipped from her glass once more. Sassy and sexy, his pulse quickened.

"The first drink was fine. The second will be even better," she finally replied. Then she crossed her legs and set down her glass, letting her hands rest at her knee.

Jason followed her movements, his gaze stopping momentarily on her crossed legs before moving slowly to her face. "Why is that?"

Celise grinned. "Because you're buying."

"Come on. Let's get a seat." Jason chuckled.

He watched as she slid gracefully from the stool and stood in front of him. He put a hand to the small of her back and led her to a table close to the window. Like a smitten schoolboy, his gaze followed the sway of her hips through the body-molding material. But Jason was a man, sure of what he could do to her and those hips, and continued to boldly assess the goodies in front of him.

That was a lecherous thought, he figured, but it was honest. From the first moment he'd seen her he'd wanted nothing more than to rip off her clothes and have her naked beneath him—no, on top of him with all that hair draping them both. He was a dreamer, and she was a fantasy come true.

She sat, and he pushed in her chair then took the seat across from her. For a moment they both simply stared at each other, then he broke the silence.

"What are we doing?" he asked quietly.

"We're having dinner, aren't we?" she asked.

On the surface, that's what it appeared, but this feeling between them was unfathomable. It didn't feel like a first date, but a beginning. And that was a frightening thought to a man like Jason Carrington.

"Is that all?"

Instead of answering, she immediately looked away. Jason wondered what she was thinking.

Then she signaled for a waiter, asking, "Can I have another strawberry daiquiri, please?"

He could play this one of two ways: push her to admit that there was something intense going on between them and possibly discuss that fact to death, or simply let go and see where they would end up. The latter sounded better since his questions had already put her on edge enough to order another drink.

"That's the drink you needed so badly? A daiquiri? It's probably virgin, isn't it?" he joked.

"So what if it is?" Celise gave him a sultry look. "There's nothing wrong with a virgin every once in a while."

The air around them crackled with sexual energy. A few moments ago he'd swear he saw a flash of leeriness in her, as if maybe she wasn't sure she should be there. Now, she was looking at him with the allure of a practiced seductress. The contradiction only intrigued Jason more.

"I didn't say there was." He motioned to the same waiter before he could walk away. "I'll have vodka." He cleared his throat. "Straight."

Celise sat back in her chair, grateful that the conversation about where this thing between them might be going had been successfully alluded. He was questioning this feeling between them, this sense of sexual urgency that seemed to feed everything they did and said. She'd been thinking the exact same thing. They looked at each other like long-lost lovers, she knew because her feelings were mirrored in his eyes. The attraction was undeniable, and even though she'd had every intention of sleeping with this man, at the moment, she wasn't so sure that was a good idea.

"You're wondering if I'm a virgin, aren't you?" she asked after his drink order.

Celise couldn't help but stare at him, as rude or assertive as it may seem. He wore all black—pleated slacks, a black T-shirt that looked as if he were born with it attached to his skin and a black jacket that gave an air of cool sophistication. His shoes—because she was a shoe guru as her mother always teased—she knew were of excellent quality, a dressy loafer either Kenneth Cole or Dolce & Gabanna. The dark clothes seemed to illuminate his light skin, making his eyes appear even more ominous, if that were possible.

He watched her closely, maybe contemplating his response. Her body tensed then warmed as if being wrapped in heated silk.

"You could say I'm curious," was his response.

Their drinks arrived before she could reply. Jason lifted his glass first, took a guarded sip while keeping his gaze fixed on her. Even though her throat had gone dry she was determined not to show her nervousness. Instead, she toyed with the umbrella straw in her glass, then speared the cherry and lifted it to her lips.

She extended her tongue, spun the cherry around on the tip, and then popped it out of her mouth. "How curious?"

That might not have been such a good idea.

He reached across the table, grabbed her wrist and pulled until the cherry hovered over his own mouth. "Very," he replied.

Before she could answer, his teeth grasped the fruit, and he crunched.

Celise removed her hand from his grasp and sat back in her chair. "Can't you tell a virgin when you see one?" She was baiting him, she knew, but it felt so good. This enticing tug-of-war they were playing was so much better than the man assuming the teaching role with her as the slow-to-learn student.

"I can tell you're enjoying yourself," he said in a gruff whisper.

Slowly he eased his way out of his chair to sit in the chair next to her. Dropping a hand to her knee, he squeezed gently. "If you have a boyfriend, now is the time to tell me."

His hand on her knee, his close proximity, the erotic scent of his cologne and the vodka in her not-so-virgin daiquiri had her head spinning. She blinked before answering. "What?"

"Your boyfriend? Where is he?"

"I don't have one," she replied in as steady a voice as she could manage.

He didn't speak.

"Should we expect your wife soon?" was her comeback.

It was his turn to lick his lips and her turn to watch with anticipation. "No wife. No girlfriend."

"Good. Then you buying me dinner isn't a problem." She reached across the table for the menu, trying to keep from squirming. She desperately needed to remain in control of this situation, but his hand had just moved from her knee to her thigh.

"Are you hungry?" It was a low growl.

One she was certain he'd used on plenty of women before her. Celise took a deep breath. It was obvious that Jason was very experienced with women. His good looks and candid charm were evidence of that fact. She prayed her lack of experience wasn't as transparent. Still, she felt like she should stop him, after all they were in a public place and this was only their first date. But she didn't. The warmth spreading throughout her body at his touch easily won over logic.

"I'm starved. I hope you don't mind that I have a big appetite." She really hoped he didn't pick up on the fact that she wasn't just talking about an appetite for food.

"So do I," was his quick reply, followed by a sexy smile.

He'd picked up on it.

"Great," she said going with the flow. "Then we're going to get along just fine."

They ordered, and Celise decided to check the place out while they waited. Considering she was thinking of opening her own restaurant, it made sense that she'd take mental notes. And she needed a distraction from her handsome dinner partner.

She'd already taken in the décor, the dark heavy black and gold drapes, candles on each covered table and dim lighting providing a very romantic atmosphere. She was excited when the food arrived to see if the restaurant would come full circle.

"So what brings you to Carrington Resorts, Celise?" Jason asked a few seconds after the waiter had left them alone.

She'd just finished blessing her food and was now setting her napkin in her lap. The menu featured a variety of appetizers but no main entrees. That was logical since it was designed more like a bar/lounge than a full scale restaurant. The Tuscan chicken skewers she'd ordered smelled divine.

"I'm taking a short hiatus," she told him, deciding an abbreviated version of the last year in her life was definitely in order.

Jason had ordered the Teriyaki steak skewers that also looked very appetizing.

"A hiatus from what?" he inquired.

She should have known he wouldn't take that answer at face value and move on. "Excuse me?"

"People normally take a hiatus from something. Like work or school."

She'd just finished chewing her first bite of chicken. The mushrooms were flavorful, the tomatoes, Roma, if she was correct, were fresh and juicy. Lifting her napkin she dabbed at her lips, then replied, "I graduated in December."

"Really? From where, and what did you study?"

Celise figured this was pretty harmless conversation and could probably pass for normal first date, getting-to-know-you sort of thing. On another note, it was the first time anybody had really seemed interested in her and what she was doing with her life. That, garnered a few cool points in Jason's corner.

"I graduated from NYU with a master's in culinary arts." She took another bite of chicken.

He watched her chew for a minute then shook his head and dragged his eyes away from her mouth. "So how is it? Since you're a master and all, you can probably tell me if the chef's any good."

"Mmmm, this is fabulous. The basil and oregano are a perfect blend and aren't overshadowed by the mushrooms. And these vegetables...steamed to perfection," she told him with a little more excitement than a person probably have when talking about food.

She chewed another bite and had to close her eyes it was so good. A small moan escaped and her eyes shot open, hoping he hadn't heard. The darkening of his eyes and the quick drink he took from his glass told her he had.

"You're from New York?" he asked after clearing his throat.

"No, I'm from San Francisco. I have family in New York, and I wanted a change of scenery, so I went to school there."

"Do you always travel alone?"

Celise paused and cocked her head to the side. He sounded like her older brother, DJ, with that question. "I was born alone," she quipped.

He smiled and took a bite of his steak.

"What about you? Why don't you have a girlfriend?" she asked.

Jason choked, using his napkin to quickly cover his mouth while he recovered. "I thought we were talking about school," he said.

"I don't want to know what school you went to. I want to know why you don't have a girlfriend."

"Why don't you have a man?" Jason rebutted.

Celise simply shook her head and pointed her fork at him. "Too late. You had your chance to ask questions."

"Fine," Jason said, giving in. "I had a girlfriend, and things didn't work out. Satisfied?"

"Why didn't it work out, and how long ago did you have this girlfriend?"

"You're full of questions, aren't you?"

"How else do you learn? Now stop stalling and answer me." She moved her brows up and down as she forked vegetables into her mouth and smiled. Talking with him was just as entertaining as looking at him. More cool points were racking up in his favor.

He smiled politely even though she'd already sensed he didn't want to talk about his ex. Celise could completely understand that but her curiosity overruled.

"Two months ago, and it didn't work because we wanted different things," he answered.

"Let me guess: She wanted to get married, and you didn't want a commitment."

Jason smoothed down his goatee, an act that was a lot sexier than it should have been. "It's not that I didn't want a commitment. I just didn't want it with her."

"Oh." Celise stopped chewing, probably trying to figure out if he were telling the truth or not.

"Now, how about you? Are you looking for a commitment?" he asked pointedly.

She cleared her throat, absolutely sure of her answer. "I'm committed to starting my career. Whatever happens in between is totally up to fate."

Once more, he nodded. "So having dinner with me was fate?"

"Something like that," she replied with a shrug.

"Then having dessert in my suite must be our ultimate destiny," he replied with a smile that made her thighs tremble.

CHAPTER THREE

"She's not answering her phone, Uncle David." Sharrell Markam switched her cell phone off after only the second ring. She'd already tried to call two times before. Her uncle was furious. They were leaving for Monterey that night, and nobody knew where Celise was. Sharrell almost smiled. Her cousin and best friend was always doing something. Throughout their teenage years, Sharrell had always longed to be more carefree and vivacious like Celise, but she'd been cursed with her mother's patience and her father's cool head for business, so she lived vicariously through her cousin and had a feeling that wherever Celise was at that very moment, she was having much more fun than the rest of them.

"That girl's going to be the death of me," David Markam mumbled as he pulled his signature fedora down onto his head.

"I'm sure wherever she is, she's just fine, Uncle David. Celise is very capable of taking care of herself." Sharrell spoke and dropped her cell phone back into her purse before moving toward the door.

"Celise only thinks of herself, that's always been her problem," David argued. "Here I am about to make a huge acquisition, and she's causing an uproar. I swear that girl has been disrupting this household since the day Maddy gave birth to her."

"And she's been the apple of your eye since exactly two minutes after that." Madeline Markam appeared in the foyer just as her husband of thirty-two years finished his sentence. "She'll be fine, David. She's simply growing up."

David opened the door and held it while the two women passed him. He stopped his wife, kissed her gently on the forehead and grumbled again, "She's acting out—something I've been trying to put a stop to for a long time now."

Maddy tapped his shoulder. "You can't tame a restless spirit, dear."

David sighed. There was no use discussing his youngest child with his wife. She always defended her, he suspected because Celise was the only girl. Still, he'd worked hard all his life to assure his children had a good life. His sons were following in his footsteps, and for the life of him he couldn't figure out why his daughter couldn't do what was expected of her. He'd received a particularly upsetting phone call just moments before she'd arrived home a few weeks ago, then she'd breezed into his office dressed to kill with a smile that would light up the darkest night and acted as if nothing had happened. She'd probably destroyed one of the biggest deals he'd ever had going, and she didn't seem to give a damn.

He vowed that the moment he came back from sealing this deal in Monterey he was going to deal with Miss Celise. She was going to straighten up and fly right if it was the last thing he did.

In the elevator this time, Jason stood so close to her their arms touched lightly. His body was all too aware of her closeness though, having felt the warm flush of desire since seeing her in the restaurant. It occurred to him that taking her to his personal suite might not be a good idea. Yet there'd never been a doubt in his mind that Celise and her luscious body would end up in his bed. The erection that had been with him since the moment his gaze set upon that red dress, throbbed against his thigh and he reached for her hand.

Upon his touch she looked up at him and smiled. In all his years, comments on his good looks and/or his prowess in bed had never made him big headed or overly egotistical, but with that one smile, that one look from her, he'd felt like he was larger than life, like he could conquer the world.

"You must be some big shot having the keys to the penthouse suite," she said.

Jason paused, wondering for a brief moment if he should tell her he owned the hotel. Would that make a difference? She didn't strike him as a gold digger. On the contrary, her stylish dress and oblivious attitude toward the luxurious atmosphere he knew his hotel boasted made him think she was well off on her own. He'd had his share of women out for the Carrington money and was thoroughly tired of them all, but something told him he didn't have to worry about that with her.

"I have a few privileges around here," he replied.

He opened the door, stepped to the side so she could go in first. As she walked past, Jason found himself watching her walk once more. He groaned inwardly, the round lushness of her bottom calling to him. After closing the door, he removed his jacket and tossed it on the back of the sofa.

"Can I get you another drink?" he asked. Moving to the bar he noticed how she checked out the apartment.

The door opened to a sitting room where Jason had installed a top notch bar and deep cushioned mahogany suede chairs that offset the cinnamon toned carpet. She moved inside with a sort of knowing ease. Looking, but not gawking, assessing but not judging, facts that affirmed she was used to the finer things. Now, whether or not she had those finer things on her own or if she made a habit of being surrounded by them on the lookout for bigger and better, he simply wouldn't allow himself to consider. For now, all he could do was watch and anticipate.

She dropped her purse on a suede recliner then let her hands roam over the soft material. "If I didn't know any better I'd swear you were trying to get me drunk." She didn't turn to him, but went toward the balcony just beyond the bar. Flicking the lock, she opened the patio doors and stepped outside into the warm breeze. She didn't stop until her thighs hit the railing then she tilted her head back, closed her eyes and inhaled the scent of salty seawater.

Something thick and warm clogged Jason's throat as he'd fixed their drinks and now stood in the doorway watching. She seemed completely at home, none of that practiced shyness or overstated boldness. She'd simply entered his realm and made herself comfortable. That warmth moved slowly, sinisterly, down his chest, spreading like wildfire. Downing the brandy he'd poured, Jason reminded himself that he'd only met this woman that morning. He didn't know much about her, except that her body had awakened things in him he hadn't felt...ever.

He shook his head to bring some sort of reasoning to what was happening. Maybe he was the one who needed to get drunk. He'd fixed her something lighter, something to make sure she stayed levelheaded. Whatever they did that night needed to be consensual. He didn't roll any other way.

When he stepped outside, she was still enjoying the view looking out over the harbor as if it were her first time seeing it. The balcony was large. It wrapped around to the front of the building and had enough furniture so that he could have taken a seat a good distance away from her. But she was magnetic and he, hard as steel, was drawn to her instantly. He stood close behind her until the soft curve of her bottom rubbed against his thigh.

"I promise you won't get drunk," he said reaching around her, handing her a flute of champagne and dropping an open-mouthed kiss to her bare shoulder. "Not by alcohol at least," he whispered against her smooth skin.

Accepting the glass she turned to face him. "Do you sweet talk all the women you meet in hotel lobbies?"

She'd asked the question in a light, almost coy tone, but one look into her eyes told him she was serious and that his answer meant a lot to her. He slid a finger seductively along her collarbone.

"I haven't met a woman in the lobby in quite some time."

He hadn't met a woman of whom he was ready to sink himself inside so quickly before either. Her skin was so soft, he knew without a doubt she'd be sweet and suddenly felt an overwhelming urge to taste her.

"I wonder why I'm inclined to believe you," she said bringing the glass to her lips to take a sip.

"I don't lie. It's much too complicated." His eyes fell to the glass. He watched as the liquid slipped between her lips. In his mind she was licking him, starting at his pectorals, then moving to his tight abdomen, feeling his muscles quiver beneath her lips as she did.

When her glass was empty, her tongue removed the remaining moisture from her lips. She had a beauty mark just beneath her bottom lip, on the right side. Her tongue flicked over the mark effectively sealing Jason's fate.

The rampant arousal in his pants strained against his zipper, and his heart hammered in his chest. Without another word he lowered his head, let his tongue roam over the small, dark mark at the corner of her mouth. She gasped, parting her lips slightly. He continued with a warm trail over those lightly glazed lips, teasing her with what he hoped was a mutual desire. Her fingers clenched his shirt, her nails biting softly into the skin beneath. When he couldn't stand his own torture any longer Jason thrust his tongue into her waiting mouth.

The glass in her hand fell to the ground, but neither of them noticed. Her free hand cupped the back of his head. She pulled him down, deepening the kiss. He moaned again as her mouth opened wider offering her tongue which he suckled hungrily. Her hands shifted on his chest, moving up to clasp his shoulders.

Jason pulled her closer, until her breasts were molded to his chest, his fingers moving in her hair. With savage motions, he pulled at the bun, felt the pins falling and groaned. Tearing his mouth away from hers for a brief second, he looked into her eyes. "I like it down."

Then he was ravaging her mouth again while she whimpered in concession. She ground her hips against his as if she were as desperate to feel more of his rigid erection pressing into her, as he was. Slipping a hand between them, she grabbed his engorged sex, squeezing it in the palm of her hand. Jason almost choked on a moan of pleasure so intense his entire body reacted. Their kiss immediately shifted from simple desire to a deep demand for more, tongues clashing and thrusting with persistence.

Normally, Jason was a very contemplative person, not reacting rashly to anything, carefully considering the pros and cons of each situation. At this moment, however, all he could manage was the thought of her naked and writhing beneath him, her legs clamped around him as he brought her to one climax after another. Jason feared he'd never have another rational thought until he'd made that happen.

"You know it's too late to stop this, don't you?" he growled into her neck before nipping the smooth skin there.

Celise let her head lull back and stroked his hot length again. "I don't think I'm putting up a fight." She gasped.

Her hand on his penis felt like a blessing the moment she grabbed him, claimed him, a perfect piece of heaven. Bending slightly, he lifted her legs until she clasped them around his waist. "Good, because it would be pointless." He ground his mouth down on hers again, hot and fierce as he stalked back into his suite toward the bedroom.

Jason set her on the bed as gently as he could. Her arms remained entwined around his neck and she pulled him down with her. Her hips undulated frantically, her breath coming in deep gasps.

"I know, baby," he whispered, untangling her legs from his waist.

He knew exactly how desperate and hungry she was feeling because he was experiencing the same rush of desire. His chest heaved with the effort of holding back, trying to do this with some semblance of maturity, when what he really wanted was to simply rip both their cloths off and dive in.

Jason took a deep breath and gently pulled her arms from around his neck, then he stared down at her. She lay back against the pillows, her dark hair fanned around her face. He traced the pad of his thumb over her swollen lips and thought he'd come instantly when her tongue snaked out and she sucked him.

"We're going to be so damn good together," he whispered.

She looked at him as if she were searching for something. When she seemed satisfied, she moved his hand from her mouth, to her breast and said, "I concur."

All thoughts sane or otherwise were quickly abandoned as Jason's hands moved all over her body. He pulled her dress over her head, released the hook of her bra, and went beneath the band of her panty hose, ready to rip them free. Then he stopped...looked down at her feet and back up to her face, considering. For a moment—one fleeting second—he thought he saw panic in her eyes. He opened his mouth to ask her about it then she smiled, and he let his gaze fall back to her feet again.

She was driving him crazy. He'd noticed her shoes that morning, black pumps—come-and-get-me-pumps, he corrected. That night they were red, a satiny type with a huge bow that tied around her ankle. He kissed her thigh, pushed her panty hose down a little farther, kissed the backs of both knees as she lifted her legs slightly off the bed, pushed down the panty hose some more and kissed her calves. He paused just above the bows at her ankles and smiled. Had a bow ever been so arousing to him before? With a deep growl, he attacked the satin material with his teeth, undoing each bow so that his hands could slide the shoe from her foot. He removed the panty hose and stared down at perfectly manicured feet, a fetish that up until then he'd kept undercover.

He took her first toe into his mouth, heard her moan, and then slid his tongue along the backs of all the others, all the while kneading the sensitive center of her foot. For endless moments he kissed and teased and massaged her feet. Celise writhed and whimpered his name.

Thoroughly pleased with her feet and making a mental note to pay more attention to them the next time, Jason moved back up to remove her underwear. She'd worn red underwear—coordination was important to her he could see. The bra had barely contained her heavy breasts while her thong tempted and teased him mercilessly. He pulled it down her legs then could do nothing else but stare.

Had he ever seen anything as beautiful in all his life? While his dick bulged and demanded release, Jason's mind took in the total picture: a gorgeous woman with a quick mind, smart eyes that assessed a person even when she didn't speak, beguiling lips that seduced whether someone was willing or not and a smile that rivaled the sunshine. Where had she been all his life, and what was he going to do now that he'd found her?

Pushing her legs apart, he watched her watching him and could think of several answers to his question.

His perusal must have taken too long for her because in the next instant she'd come up onto her knees in front of him.

"I want you naked. Now," she told him, even as her fingers deftly undid his belt and zipper.

Pushing his slacks and underwear down hastily, she cupped his hardness in both hands, stroking slow from base to tip, then with more strength.

More than anything, he wanted her to take him into her hot mouth. He wanted to pump while she sucked. His balls tightened with the very thought. There would be time for that later. He pulled his shirt over his head then let his hands fall to her shoulders, kneading them like she was handling him.

"I believe I must have fallen into some kind of luck to have met you today."

Celise let her hands fall to the base of his shaft, then moved up his length slowly, applying gentle pressure.

She rubbed the now moist tip with her thumb and when he sucked in a breath asked, "Are you sure this doesn't belong to anybody?" She looked up at him, then back down to his thick shaft.

"For tonight, it's all yours," was his reply.

Jason palmed her breasts and squeezed, and she moaned. He pushed her back onto the bed, crushing his mouth down on hers with the fierce intensity he felt ripping through his body. He wanted her, needed her, like he'd never needed another woman in his life, and that night—if only for that night—he was going to have all of her.

He sucked on her nipples, rolled the hardened buds between his teeth as he squeezed the heavy globes. She arched her back, and he gorged himself. Because she was writhing beneath him, because her warm mound was incessantly rubbing against his thigh, he slipped one hand between her legs and sighed.

"You...are...so...wet." He spoke each word with deliberate restraint as the sound of his finger moving against her moistness filled the room.

"Mmmmm, Jason," Celise murmured between gritted teeth.

He stroked her clit loving the feel of the hardened bud as his finger flicked over it back and forth. Then he dipped a finger inside her center and felt her muscles tighten around him. She shivered, mumbling his name as her head thrashed from side to side against the pillow. He inserted another finger and watched with elation as she tensed and moaned deeply, tumbling right over the edge into the prettiest climax he'd ever witnessed.

She was so responsive to his touch, even as he lifted her legs, spread them apart and looked down at her pulsating womanhood. He could swear he saw her essence flowing stronger, welcoming him, calling to him. Her scent permeated his senses, and he bent his head, licked her from top to bottom in one long, luxurious stroke—another first for him. This part of sex was definitely intimate, something he didn't share with many. Yet he couldn't resist her, couldn't stop himself from tasting her sweetness. She bucked beneath him, and he cupped her bottom to better position her for the onslaught.

In childhood Jason remembered summers filled with watermelon—ripe, fresh, pink watermelon. He'd hold his slice and immediately sink his teeth into the sweet flesh. He devoured Celise with the same fierceness, the same pleasure-filled enthusiasm. He licked and suckled, dipping inside her center then moving to capture her tender bud between his lips. Her juices flowed like an endless river, moistening his chin, his cheeks and his nose. She moaned and moved her hips in accordance to the rhythm his mouth set. When she grabbed his head and steadied him over her tightened bud, he thought he'd come all over that bed. She tasted so good, so intoxicatingly sweet. He slurped and sucked her until her thighs quaked. Sometime between that morning when he'd rolled out of bed and the moment his lips first touched hers, he could swear he'd died and gone to heaven.

His goal was to always please his women first, but he couldn't hold on any longer. Pulling out the nightstand drawer, he retrieved a condom and slipped it on. He rose over her, positioned himself between her legs and pressed the tip of his dick to her opening. Moving it up and down along her slit, he coated it with her essence then tried to push the tip in.

"Jason," she said on a long, low whisper. Her legs shook, her insides quivered. His tongue had mastered her, branded her, and Celise knew she'd never feel this way with anyone else again. That thought was problematic considering his earlier remark about him belonging to her just for tonight. Those words had bothered her, maybe hurt just a bit, even though she'd sworn to never let another man hurt her.

And right at this moment, Jason was doing anything but. Need drummed inside her fiercely, and for once in her life, she entertained the idea of doing things she'd only read about. It was unexplainable, this desire she was feeling, this need to explore and be explored. As impulsive and liberated as she liked to believe she was she had reason to doubt herself when it came to sex. That didn't really seem to matter now. At this moment, she needed him completely. She needed him deep inside her until he filled her body as well as her mind.

"Please, Jason," she just about whimpered.

And even though she was slick and ready for him, when he tried to adhere to her request and push gently inside her, it was a tight fit.

"Mmmmm, baby. Let me in," he sighed, still moving his hips slowly, saturating his shaft with her secretions once more.

For her part, Celise tried to relax, tried to release the performance apprehension she knew her body was reacting to. She could do this, she told herself while focusing on breathing slowly in and out, willing every muscle in her body to relax and enjoy.

Finally her body welcomed him and he sank deep into her, stretching and filling her with a completeness she'd longed for. Elated with this seemingly small feat she gasped.

"Are you okay?" he asked with concern.

Celise took a deep breath. "Mmmm, perfect." She rotated her hips, loving the pressure against her center. "Just perfect."

Jason moved with her. "Open your eyes. I want you to see everything I do to you. I want to see how I make you feel." He pulled out then thrust his entire length into her again.

Her eyes shot open, and she bit her bottom lip. "Yes, Jason. Yes!"

He pressed her to the bed, lifting her bottom to meet him. Celise grabbed her breasts and pinched her nipples knowing that this action would intensify her pleasure.

They held each other's gaze as he moved in and out of her. She met him stroke for stroke, and when he put his hand between them to find her sweet spot again, she moaned and climaxed once more.

So far the score was 2 to 0 and she felt like crap. Actually, the waves of guilt began to roll in. This wasn't happening to her again, she refused to let it happen again. With a quick movement they tumbled across the bed, and she was on top of him.

"It's my turn." She pushed her hair back over her shoulders and straddled him.

Jason grinned up at her. "You're bossy, aren't you?"

She ground her hips down on him, and Jason let out a whoosh of air. "I wouldn't dream of depriving you, baby."

Celise began with a slow, precise rhythm, rocking them both back and forth. His entire length was inside her, pressing against a particularly good spot. She bucked and moved up and down, letting that feeling build and build until she wanted to scream. Beneath her, Jason's face contorted as his fingers dug into the skin of her hips, lifting her up then dropping her down on his shaft with quick, fluid motions. Her breasts were bouncing, her hair flinging wildly against her back. "Oh, Jason. Jason!"

She repeated his name, kept moaning it and chanting it like he was the only man in the world. He thrust inside of her like he was just that—the only man in *her* world. Jason rubbed her buttocks and fingered her anus as she bucked violently. He eased a finger in slightly, and she cried out loudly.

It wasn't painful physically, but the quick flash of memory that assails her at the pressure almost takes her breath away. That feeling is quickly replaced by a wicked pleasure that ripples up her spine, encouraging her motions to quicken. Her hips thrusting back and forth to create an arousing suction sound between their bodies. She worked her hips over him, and he lifted her and slammed her down hard on top of his erection. She screamed…he repeated the motion again…she came.

"Ooooohhh, Jason."

She held onto his shoulders looking down at him as her entire body convulsed. He stared back up to her and it almost seemed like he was just seeing her. It was an eerie feeling to have him looking at her so strangely while they were in such an intimate position. Then his grip on her hips tightened and he pumped quickly into her, their gazes still intact. He stilled and she knew he'd found his release.

Soon after he moved her off him, Celise's heart took one final plummet. Why these messy emotions were tangling with the most intensely gratifying sexual experience she'd ever had, she had no idea. And just when she was about to put on her big-girl panties and go back to her room, he pulled her close, wrapping his arms around her front and spooned against her back.

It took her a second to nestle into him and to hide the smile that had immediately spread across her face. "Mmmm, I guess we were both right," she murmured.

"Right about what?" he asked after a couple of seconds.

"We were good together."

CHAPTER FOUR

Celise watched him sleep. Dark eyelashes fanned across butter-smooth skin, his strong jaw and perfect lips parted slightly as he lay in deep slumber. The sheet twisted around his waist, leaving that marvelously sculpted chest bare for all to see. She sighed with the memory of her hands gliding over the taut skin and rigid muscles.

The night before had been beyond anything she could have imagined. Jason had touched her in places she'd never dreamed existed. While his magnificent hands had moved possessively over her body, Celise couldn't dismiss the deeper reality. Again, she felt a connection to Jason, which she was incapable of understanding this early in the morning. Yet, there was a keen awareness that he was now a part of her whether or not she wanted him to be.

With another deep sigh, she moved away from the bed. Pulling her now wrinkled dress over her head, she attempted to grab her shoes and tip out of the room when she heard him stir in the bed. She stood still as a statue, hoping he didn't wake up. She'd planned a quick getaway. No conversation, no questions. That was the easy way. The best way.

Jason had only stirred and lay on his back, a low snore echoing through the room. Celise looked at him again, her thoughts drifting back to the physical pleasure they'd shared. She remembered riding him as he lay in a similar position—of course he was fully awake and fully cooperative at the time. She remembered how he filled her, how the sound of her name in his voice had stoked the fire inside of her. Then she remembered the sweet comfort of him holding her through the night—the warmth of his front against her back. And the insane wish that she could sleep that way forever. She remembered the release and the glorious climaxes he'd brought her.

Okay, so those weren't entirely physical memories, and this was supposed to be a purely physical act. She blamed that on too many daiquiris.

Her focus had to be on her future. She needed to scout out locations for her restaurant, work on menus, think about staff, zoning and equipment and stuff like that.

She didn't need her thoughts consumed by this man.

He stirred again, and Celise figured she wouldn't be getting off as easy a second time, so she hastily grabbed the knob and slipped out the door. She didn't stop again until she was out of his suite and on the elevator toward her own room.

Jason rolled over, spreading his legs and stretching his arm to the right where Celise should have been. He felt the emptiness then cracked open an eye to see it for himself. Sitting upright so fast he felt a wave of dizziness, he rubbed his eyes then looked down at the bed again.

She wasn't there.

Tossing the sheets aside, he climbed out of the bed and went to check the bathroom. She wasn't there. Completely oblivious to the fact that he was naked, Jason went into the living room and checked out on the terrace. Nothing. His one-night stand had officially left the building.

"Dammit!" Running his hands down his face, he walked back into the bedroom. He'd been dreaming of her, dreaming of sinking deep inside her warmth again that morning. That dream had lulled him so completely he hadn't heard her leave.

He looked down at his erection and frowned. "Good going."

Heading straight into the shower he didn't calm down until the warm water sprayed against his body. Then his calmness turned into contemplative thought. And those thoughts, of course, centered on Celise.

She'd been everything he imagined and then some. The gorgeous body he'd imagined through her clothes had rated far more than a ten, and the way she'd used it against him had to have broken all kinds of records in his book. She'd given just as much as she'd taken, and as a result he desired her even more. Finding someone sexually compatible when a person possessed an insatiable appetite was rare but he sensed he'd found just that in Celise.

She was beautiful. She was smart. She was sexy. She was limber as hell. He'd entered her from so many directions he'd lost count, but the memory of each one remained emblazoned in his mind. The warm water, the soap he lathered onto his body, the still-throbbing erection and the salacious thoughts of Celise had him ready to find his release any way possible, but he refrained. He hadn't resorted to that method of satisfaction in a very long time, and as long as Celise was still a guest in his hotel, he wouldn't revert.

Stepping out of the shower he thought of what he had planned for the day and how he could incorporate time with Celise into those plans. He had a meeting at nine with David Markam. He frowned as he moved to his closet, thinking of all the calls he'd received in the last months from a Nigel Bingham at Markam Inns and Suites. He had to give it to the man, he was relentless in his pursuit of the hotel. Too bad he'd have to let him down that morning once and for all.

Jason was almost completely dressed and was pulling a gray tie from the rack when thoughts of Celise returned. He draped the silk material around his neck along the collar of his white dress shirt. Turning to the full-length mirror inside the closet door, he held the material in place, orchestrating a perfect Windsor knot, then smiled at himself. The night before had been one for the record books.

In his mind he'd planned one night of glorious sex. He'd known it would be good. But somewhere between strokes he'd decided that wasn't going to be enough. He hadn't counted on it being magical. After all, he'd had casual affairs before. Most of his female involvement had consisted of them—until Pamela, but even thoughts of her weren't going to spoil this.

Something unexpected happened the night before. She'd touched him with her brashness, her candor, her smile. When he'd seen her at the bar he felt desire, then jealousy. When he talked to her, he felt intrigue and adoration. When he'd kissed her, his whole world had shifted. While all that still amazed him, Jason accepted it along with the decision to spend more nights with her in the same fashion.

The one problem was that he didn't know much about the woman. Sure, he knew her body now better than he knew his own. He knew just where to touch, where to kiss, where to nip that would make her go crazy. But he had no idea what her favorite color was, what her aspirations in life were. Hell, he didn't even know her last name.

From the desk in the other room the alarm on his cell phone sounded, and he knew that meant he was on the verge of being late for his meeting. So with quick strides into the living room to retrieve it and his briefcase, Jason tucked thoughts of the sexy vixen in the back of his mind. There she would have to stay, at least until he finished with this meeting.

Freshly showered and dressed Celise headed down the hall to the elevators, toward the buffet breakfast in the Pompeii Lounge. She was ravenous. Having sated one appetite seemed to neglect the other. She planned to remedy that right away. Pressing the button, she found herself humming as she waited for the doors to open.

Her mood was gay, her step light as she recalled the events of the previous evening. While she'd showered she'd indulged in the idea of seeing Jason again. But once she was out, she thought better of that idea. He was good in bed—he was great in bed—and that was it. She didn't need or want anything else.

Her restaurant had to take precedence over any fanciful thoughts of love and commitment. She hadn't decided on a name yet, but figured that could wait. Her financial plan was in place, her money waiting in the bank, ideas tripping over themselves in her mind. All she needed was a place to start building.

She decided to tour Monterey, starting with Cannery Row where all the exclusive restaurants and nightlife hangouts were. She wanted to be in the midst of the party. Then she'd have lunch at one of them, trying out the local cuisine, getting to know the people and what they liked to eat. This was all research and would pay off in the end.

Her humming continued as the elevator chimed and the doors opened. Then her blissful melody was interrupted.

"Celise."

"Mama?"

Madeline Markam stepped off the elevator dressed in a pink Chanel suit and stunning pink-and-lime pumps. A smile graced her lightly glossed lips, but didn't quite meet her eyes. Celise took a protective step back.

"What...um...what are you doing here?" This was the last place she'd expected them to find her—after all Carrington Resorts was the enemy. At every possible opportunity David Markam and his family stayed in Markam Inns and Suites or one of its affiliates. Staying under the roof of the competitor was a no-no.

Madeline's eyes narrowed as she reached for her daughter. Grabbing her by the shoulders, she pulled Celise to her for a tight hug. "I was so worried about you," she whispered in her ear before pushing her away gently. "Now, tell me why my almost thirty-year-old daughter is still running away from her problems instead of facing them head-on?"

Celise wanted to roll her eyes, but thanks to her mother, remembered her age. "I'm not almost thirty," she said in a sulky tone.

"You can hold on to those three years for dear life if you want, but sure as the sun will rise and set each day, you'll be turning thirty eventually."

"Not if I die first," Celise quipped.

And she felt just like that at the moment. Her blissfully happy mood had been banished by the sight of one of the most important people in her life. If Madeline Markam was here at the Carrington, she could rest assured that David Markam was too.

Madeline waved a hand. "Don't be morbid. Now, answer my question. Why did you run? And why did you run here?" She looked around her as if the hotel really did leave a lot to be desired.

Celise felt differently. Because she'd been brought up in the hotel business, she knew class when she saw it, and Carrington Resorts was definitely four-star material. It could use a facelift here and there, and the menu at the lounge could stand an update, but overall it was a nice place to stay.

"I like this hotel," she said defiantly.

"We'll deal with logistics later. Right now I'm more interested in the child I raised. I didn't raise a quitter, nor did I raise a child to back down from a fight, even if the fight is with her parents."

"I don't want to fight with Daddy," Celise said simply. And that was the honest truth. She didn't like fighting with her father. She loved him above all others and respected him almost more than she respected herself. That's why going against him was so hard for her, but it was what she had to do.

"But you knew that once you made your little announcement that was exactly what would happen," Madeline continued.

She took a deep breath and exhaled slowly. *You can run but you can't hide.* "Yes, ma'am, I knew."

"And yet you made the announcement anyway?"

"I did."

Her mother sighed. "My point is, if you knew it was going to lead to a disagreement yet you told him anyway, you should have had the courage to stand up to him."

Celise felt like a child being bitterly chastised, and it demeaned her. She was a grown woman, able to make her own decisions, and it was past time her family started respecting that fact.

"You're right, Mama. I did know how Daddy would react, and I should have stayed there to stand my ground. But the fact is, I'm going to open my own restaurant, and it will be successful. Whether he decides to support me is his decision."

Madeline Markam smiled then lifted Celise's chin like she'd done so many times before. "That's exactly what I wanted to hear. You've made a decision, and I expect you to stick to it. As for your father, he'll have to get over it. Now come on downstairs and tell him that yourself."

Celise could officially kiss the happy mood good-bye as she prepared to face her father. Boarding the elevator, she turned to her mother. "What are you guys doing here anyway?"

Madeline shrugged. "You know your father, he's been trying to get his hooks into this hotel for months now. The owner just won't budge. And since you've all but disposed of Nigel, he felt like he had to come and close the deal himself."

Celise cringed and stiffened at the name. "I do *not* want to discuss Nigel."

Madeline raised a brow in question.

"Neither does your father. All he really wants to hear now is the owner of Carrington Resorts saying, 'Yes, Mr. Markam, I'll be happy to sell this hotel to you.' "

The elevator door opened, and the two women stepped off. "And the odds of that happening after all these months are?" Celise asked blandly.

"Slim to none." Madeline chuckled. "But according to your father, 'it ain't over 'til it's over.' "

They laughed and were still laughing when they entered the conference room where her father; her cousin, Sharrell; and her oldest brother, DJ, were already seated at the table.

David was out of his seat in an instant.

"Celise?" Sharrell gasped.

"Where did you find her, Maddy?" David spoke with his eyes glued to his daughter.

"I'm staying at the hotel," Celise answered.

Her father was a big man, over six feet tall with skin the color of perfectly creamed and sugared coffee. The hard lines of his face gave way to soothing brown eyes that at the moment had darkened considerably as they glared at her.

"You're staying at *this* hotel?"

Again, Celise resisted the urge to roll her eyes. "Yes, Daddy."

David opened his mouth then hastily closed it again, taking a few deep breaths before his next words. "Fine. Go on up to your room and get your things packed. This meeting won't take long, then we'll be on our way."

He'd turned and was walking back toward his seat at the head of the conference table when Celise stopped him. "I'm not going back to San Francisco with you."

Out of the corner of her eye, Celise could see that her mother watched the situation carefully. Celise wondered if things really got ugly on which side her mother would remain. Upstairs she'd seemed in Celise's corner, but now in the room with her father and brother she wasn't quite sure. Sharrell would always agree with Celise, just not openly in front of David.

"I came to Monterey to scout locations for my restaurant. I plan on finding an apartment and making my home here."

She didn't fidget like she had when she'd gone to her family home and stood in the den breaking this same news. Her back was straight, her eyes focused and her mind clear of any guilt that may have lingered there. This was her life. Her decision.

David turned slowly, looking at this youngest child questioningly. "Celise, I have business to take care of today. Now is not the time to discuss your latest flight of fancy."

"That's not what this is, Daddy. This is what I've decided to do with my life. This is my dream." She took a bold step closer to him. "You remember what dreams are, don't you, Daddy? They're the things that drive you to be all you can be in life. The ideas that mold and shape you into the adult you will become. You told me that when I was eight years old."

"Ah, Dad, maybe we should table this conversation until after the meeting," DJ interrupted looking down at his watch.

Sharrell had quietly appeared at Celise's side. "Yeah, why don't you and I go and get some coffee while your father has his meeting, Celise?"

Celise ignored them both. "This is what I want to do. Why can't you accept that?" she asked her father.

"This is what you want to do?" David laughed. "When you were sixteen you decided you wanted to be a professional jockey. And at seventeen, when you were a senior in high school, you were going to study to become a doctor." He wiped a hand over his forehead, his eyes still on his daughter. "Then you get in your second year of college and decide that cooking is the flavor of the month. Now I'll hand it to you, you stuck with that a little longer than I expected. This restaurant thing is just too much. Celise, it's the last straw."

"But Daddy," she interrupted, but David held up a hand halting her words.

"No! You will listen to me because I'm your father and I know what's best for you. You're engaged to Nigel Bingham. You're going to marry him and build a home and have me some grandbabies, and I don't want to hear another word about this ridiculous restaurant idea."

His words vibrated through the room, leaving everyone in dead silence as they waited to see what would happen next.

The Markams were so intent on their own family drama that none of them saw the entrance of the owner of Carrington Resorts.

Her heart seemed to break into a million pieces, but the heavens would open up and swallow them all before she let her father see it. Her father had no idea what Nigel Bingham really was or what he'd done to her.

For a second she thought of telling her father just to have that one small victory over him, but she didn't.

"No, Daddy. That's not what I'm going to do. I'm an adult, and I'll make my own decisions from now on. If those decisions don't coincide with your visions for my life, then that's just too bad."

Her father stumbled back a step at her words, and DJ grabbed his arm, giving Celise a heated look.

"I'm sorry if this hurts you or the rest of the family, but I have a right to find my own happiness, and that's what I plan to do," she finished feeling a tremendous weight lift from her shoulders.

Before David could say another word and with Madeline hiding a small smile behind her manicured hands, Celise turned to leave. Tears burned her eyes, but she dared them to fall. They wouldn't see her cry. Nobody would ever see her cry. She was strong. She was determined. And she was going to make this work all by herself. Her steps were momentarily halted by the sight of Jason standing in the doorway. She couldn't figure out why he was there, but didn't have the energy to ask. Instead, she pushed past him and ran down the hall to the elevators.

With a nod from Madeline, Sharrell made her way toward the door. "Excuse me," she murmured to Jason then took off down the hall to find Celise.

CHAPTER FIVE

She was David Markam's daughter?

"No! You will listen to me because I'm your father and I know what's best for you. You're engaged to Nigel Bingham. You're going to marry him and build a home and have me some grandbabies, and I don't want to hear another word about this ridiculous restaurant idea."

Jason had just walked into the conference room, prepared to let David Markam down easily then offer the man his best suite for the week. He would finish this meeting as soon as possible then he'd meet with Clive about restaurant plans and have the rest of the day free to continue getting to know Celise better. Imagine his surprise when the first person he noticed in the conference room was *her*.

She wore a white pantsuit, and her hair was down, hanging around her shoulders alluringly. Then the words he'd overheard registered. David Markam was talking to her. All thoughts ceased, and Jason halted with the man's words.

She was engaged to Nigel Bingham?

Nigel Bingham who had called him nonstop for the last six months. Nigel Bingham who was arrogant and self-centered and believed that a hostile takeover was imminent in the future of Carrington Resorts. Celise had told him she didn't have a boyfriend. A boyfriend, he reminded himself. He'd never asked if she had a fiancé.

His hands fisted at his sides. Had she set him up? Had she checked in before the meeting to purposely blindside him? Was this all a part of David Markam's plan to get his hotel?

Then Celise spoke. She appeared calm, but he heard the undertones of hurt and disappointment. She wasn't agreeing with David Markam. Her shoulders drooped just a little but not enough to admit defeat. She'd turned, and he glimpsed the pain etched along her face and felt a tug at his heart.

He blocked her path, and for a moment thought she would run to him, seek comfort from him. Something he would have gladly given. Instead, she ignored their intimate knowledge of each other and bolted from the room, another female quickly following her. Now he stood there, in the middle of what he could only surmise as a family feud, and wondered what the hell his next line was supposed to be.

This was the part in the movie where a good actor was expected to ad-lib, to keep the tape rolling and the show going. Only he'd been at a disadvantage. He didn't know all the cast and wasn't quite sure what the ending of this story would be.

Clearing his throat, Jason pretended to straighten his tie as he walked toward David Markam. A strange mixture of contempt and respect swirled in the pit of his stomach as he prepared to meet the man whose reputation had preceded him in the hotel industry.

"Mr. Markam, I'm sorry if I'm interrupting something personal," Jason said, extending his hand. "I'm Jason Carrington."

David immediately straightened all evidence of the previous argument gone from his face as he pumped Jason's hand.

"Nonsense, Mr. Carrington. Please let me apologize for the scene. We can get down to business now."

Jason couldn't believe the man wasn't going after her—that he was her father and he didn't care that he'd just crushed his child's spirits. That didn't sit well with him, at all, but it was none of his business.

"This is my son, David Markam, Jr. My wife, Madeline Markam." He paused and looked toward the door. "My niece, Sharrell. She runs Markam Inns and Suites in New York. I invited her along to strengthen our position, but she had something to...ah...tend to." David took a seat and waited for Jason to do the same.

Jason presumed that was the young woman who'd slipped past him right after Celise. He'd read about David Markam, Jr., and his success. Madeline Markam appeared to be the epitome of style and grace and a woman who obviously loved her daughter. This was evident by her concerned look as Celise left the room.

Taking a seat, he vowed not to think of Celise again until this meeting was over. Then he would deal with her and the few facts she'd neglected to mention before they'd made love.

With purposeful strides, Jason left the conference room an hour later and boarded the elevator. His destination: room 417.

David Markam had had the audacity to sit in that room and tell him how he was wasting his time trying to contend with the big hoteliers. With Hilton and Marriott within a block of him, and Sheraton two blocks away, the competition was surely closing him in. All of this Jason knew before purchasing the hotel but hadn't cared. Carrington Resorts was just as good, if not better, than all of those hotel powerhouses. Apparently David Markam didn't think so.

DJ Markam offered advice on Jason staying a silent partner and how good an investment that would be for him as a young man. Jason was outraged but had managed to remain the confident businessman he called himself. He declined their offers over and over until finally, in a move that had shocked all the men in the room, Madeline Markam announced it was time to go.

There was something about that woman he liked. He wasn't sure if it was the fact that she'd given birth to such a lovely specimen as Celise or that she had a very motherly way about her that forced memories of his own childhood to surface. Whatever it was, he was grateful.

They'd been in the Apollo conference room on the first floor. He needed the elevator to stop on the fourth floor. But on the third floor, Lucy Delaney rushed into the compartment, her sea-green eyes as big as saucers.

"Oh, Mr. C, there you are," she exclaimed. "I've been on every floor looking for you."

Noting her very excitable mood, Jason put his hands on the young girl's shoulders. "Calm down, Lucy. I was in a meeting. Why were you looking for me?"

"In the kitchen. There's something you need to see in the kitchen. Dad's in an outrage and your man—that Clive person—he's down there trying to calm him down. But...um...it's not working."

Lucy had flaming red hair to go with her Irish green eyes. Her entire family worked at the hotel and had for the past twenty years. They knew more about this building and its history than Jason did, so he had decided it was wise to keep them in his employ.

Dragging his hands down his face, Jason held back the urge to yell. Confronting Celise would have to wait again. How could last night have been so beautiful, full of so many options and then this morning—he looked down at his watch, yeah, it was still morning—be going so badly so quickly?

"Let's go see what the problem is," he said and jammed his finger into the down button. Glancing at the number four that had been lit but now remained uncolored on the floorboard he made a silent promise, "I'll deal with you later, Celise Markam."

"So what do you want to tell me first? Why you would pick this hotel of all the ones in Monterey to stay in or how you know that gorgeous man who looked at you as if you and he shared a secret downstairs?" Sharrell plopped down onto the couch and stared up at her cousin who was still pacing the room.

"What?" Celise asked with obvious distraction.

"Okay, let's try it this way," Sharrell continued. "How do you know the guy who interrupted our family feud?"

Celise paused a moment, then vaguely remembered Jason appearing and wondered how to explain to her cousin that she'd slept with a stranger and now he'd apparently been following her around the hotel. Would that seem like another wrong turn made by the infamous Celise Markam, the troublemaker of the Markam clan? She had no idea. All she knew for sure at that moment was that her father had no respect for her as an adult. That thought hurt a lot—more than she'd ever allowed herself to believe. But she absolutely would not back down. Now, more than ever, she was determined to do her own thing and to make it work.

"Celise?"

She'd been twirling a strand of hair, in deep thought about her future, when Sharrell's voice interrupted her. "What?"

Sharrell walked to her cousin and placed her hands on her shoulders. She guided her to the couch, then sat her down none too gently. Taking a seat next to her, she clasped Celise's hands in hers. "Talk to me, Celise. What's going on with you?"

Celise looked at Sharrell and realized with painful clarity that she needed to talk to someone. The past few months she'd been holding in all her confusion, all her doubts, and now she felt like she was going to burst. After all, Sharrell was not only family, she was her very best friend. She was also the manager of Markam New York, which meant her first concern was for the very company on which Celise was turning her back.

"I'm really stressed over this decision and my dad's reaction, that's all," she admitted.

"I don't believe you," Sharrell replied quickly. "I've known you all your life, and you've never been stressed like this. There's something else going on. You never explained to me what really happened with Nigel."

Celise groaned, her head falling to the back of the couch. "I don't want to talk about that slime Nigel Bingham."

"Ooooh, he's slime. Tell me how you came to such a conclusion."

Celise shook her head. "In essence, I guess he's a man. He's the type of man who doubles as a four-legged creature." When Sharrell didn't seem to follow, she clarified. "He's a dog in an expensive suit. I'd suspected it for a while but then like all dogs, even the trained ones, he pissed on the floor and got caught," she said dryly.

Sharrell actually looked shocked. "He cheated on you?"

"That's putting it lightly. He used me *and* cheated on me." And that was only part of what he'd done to her.

"That tacky bastard," Sharrell spat vehemently.

"Yeah, my sentiments exactly. I didn't tell Daddy because he never asked me what happened with Nigel. He just assumed it was something I'd done."

"You have to tell him, Celise. He needs to fire him. Hell, when Uncle David finds out he cheated on you, he might kill him." Sharrell chuckled.

Celise frowned. "But I can't talk to him now. You saw how he looked at me down there, as if I were two seconds away from being cut out of his will."

Sharrell waved a hand. "Girl, you know Uncle David loves you more than his hotels. He's just angry right now, but he'll get over it. Aunt Maddy will make sure he does."

Celise wondered if her mother could pull off a feat that big. She admitted that her mother seemed to have some sort of spell over her father but wasn't sure that applied with his own flesh and blood betraying him.

"You know what, Sharrell? I'm not going to be sad. I did what I had to do. I went to him like an adult and told him my plans. It's not my fault he refuses to accept them. There's nothing else I can do until he finds a way to deal with it."

"You're right. He has to deal with your decision. I just want first dibs on the newest, hottest restaurant on the West Coast coming to my hotel."

Celise finally smiled. She could always count on Sharrell to be in her corner, even if it was as a silent supporter. "You better believe it. Once I open the doors to *Chances* and build up my clientele, I'll definitely be looking to expand to hotel chains. I know where the money is."

"*Chances*? That's what you're going to call it? The last time we talked you hadn't decided on a name."

She was right, and up until that morning she still hadn't decided. But between the confrontation with her father and talking with her cousin and of course, sleeping with Jason, Celise realized that was the perfect name. She was taking chances. It was a big step, yet she was doing it without question. Yes, *Chances*, was the right name. "I know. Do you like it?"

Sharrell smiled. "I love it."

Celise returned her smile, her mind now more focused on opening *Chances* than ever.

"Now that that's out of the way, tell me about the man. And don't even try to tell me you don't know who he is."

"What..." Celise started to say then paused. "Oh, Jason? He's just a guy I met yesterday, that's all. I really don't know what he was doing in that conference room this morning." But she did wonder.

Sharrell stared at her strangely. "You're kidding, right?"

Celise looked confused. "Kidding about what? I did meet him yesterday, when I checked in, as a matter of fact. We had dinner and—" She debated just how much she should tell her at the moment. "And we talked."

"Uh-huh, did you happen to talk about the fact that he's the owner of the one hotel your father is trying to buy?"

A heated sensation swirled in the pit of her stomach at Sharrell's words. This could not be happening to her twice in one lifetime. "You know Jason?" she asked in a shaky voice.

"Know him? He's Jason Carrington, owner of Carrington Resorts." Sharrell made a wide motion with her arms. "Owner of this fine hotel you've chosen to lay your head in."

Celise felt dizzy.

"Oh God, Celise, tell me you knew that. Tell me you didn't do what I think you did," Sharrell insisted, all the while shaking her head as if she already knew the answer.

Celise's head lulled on the back of the couch again. This time the groan coming louder, more painful than the previous one.

Pushing through the swinging doors covered in the same salmon wallpaper as the rest of the east hallway Jason wasn't prepared for what he saw or what he felt. Coolness hit his ankles, his feet moving just a bit slower than they had been when he'd been in the elevator. Looking down he wasn't pleased to find his three-hundred-dollar Kenneth Coles covered while the cuffed hem of his pants floated in a swirl of water.

"What the—" he exclaimed seconds before he scanned the room to find pots and pans, spoons and other kitchen paraphernalia bobbing atop the water as well. The rage he'd felt earlier in no way compared to the heat flaming through his head now. "I know there's an explanation for this."

Clive gave a half smile and sloshed his way from where he stood near the deep ovens toward Jason.

"Sure there's an explanation. I'm just not sure you want to hear it," he said wryly.

Clive had been Jason's friend for a very long time. As such, he knew how much this hotel meant to Jason. In fact, Clive had invested in the hotel as a silent partner, so he had a personal stake in it as well. Jason was the calm one. Clive, the realist. Right now, Jason didn't like the real look of concern on Clive's face.

"My feet are soaked, and I'm not on the beach. Humor me," Jason said. The last strands of his patience were wearing thin.

"Funny thing, it 'tis. That pipe looked fit enough the day before. This morning it up and explodes all over the place." Chef Paul rubbed the top of his head, the spot where hair used to be, and continued to stare puzzled at the pipe. " 'Tis a right funny thing, I say."

Paul was a great chef, and he was Lucy's father. His wife, Netta, who was of African-American decent, had taught him some soul food secrets to go along with his Irish menu, and wham, Jason's Greek-themed lounge had a new flare all its own. He liked the eclectic mix, and so did his customers. But for the moment, as he wiggled his toes to that annoying squishiness, he pictured the room full of angry customers at dinner that night and frowned.

"Did anybody call a plumber?" He sucked up the outrage and the slight chill moving through his body as his feet tread deeper into the water. He wanted to check the damage of the ovens and to get a closer look at the pipe in question. Unfortunately most of Paul's pots and pans were now floating throughout the kitchen, hampering his trek across the room. Stooping to pick one up, he dropped it unceremoniously onto the cutting table and continued.

"Plumber's already here. He wanted to take a look down in the basement first to see if there was a bigger problem," Clive offered, trying not to laugh at the sour expression on Jason's face and the trail of fruit and veggies that seemed to follow him like a parade of sorts.

"There's nothing wrong with the plumbing in the basement. We just had that checked earlier this year," Jason said.

Clive shrugged. "That's what I told him, but he said he still wanted to check it out."

"These pipes were fit as a fiddle yesterday," Paul offered dryly.

Jason looked in his direction. He'd known the man for well over a year, and in that time had figured out some of his moods. Paul was thinking something wasn't right about his kitchen filling up with a good portion of the Monterey Bay, and Jason was curious to hear what that was. "What do you think—" he started to say.

"Ah, Mr. Carrington, you've arrived."

Jason turned to see the man he remembered as the plumber from just a few months ago. He extended his hand. "Sir, what's the damage?"

"Call me Stan." Taking Jason's hand, the short, stout man gave a wan smile. "Like I told you before, you're in great shape in the basement."

Jason's frown deepened. "Then what the hell is this?" He kicked out a leg and sent water splashing. Lucy yelped and took a step back. "Sorry," he offered dismally.

"This—" Stan motioned toward an overhead pipe with a huge gash in it— "is the result of I'd say a sledgehammer."

Both Jason and Clive looked incredulous. "What?" they replied in unison.

"Somebody did this on purpose." Stan moved to the other side of the kitchen, knelt beneath one of the deep sinks and turned a valve. The steady stream of water stopped until it was a slow trickle and then nothing. "These are two-year-old pipes. There's no way a gash that big and deep could have just appeared in that short amount of time without a smaller leak occurring first."

Paul slicked back the three strands of hair on the top of his head. " 'Tis a funny thing," he murmured once more.

CHAPTER SIX

It was almost noon, and Jason had showered and changed, letting the events of the morning wash over him. The night before he'd slept with Celise Markam, the daughter of David Markam, the man who wanted very badly to buy his hotel. In a nutshell, he'd slept with the enemy.

But that morning when he awoke, it was to a loneliness that threatened to suffocate him. She'd left him in that bed—the bed in which they had loved each other so well. At that moment he'd wanted nothing more than to find her and bring her back.

Not an hour later he'd walked in on her arguing with her father about an engagement and a career that she was hell bent on pursuing. Two hours after that he'd seen his lunch special float across the floor of his kitchen and discovered that someone was sabotaging his hotel. The throbbing at his temples increased.

Dressed in clean dress pants, shirt and tie and dry shoes Jason was determined to get a drink and be on his way. The sight of Clive stopped him. "You're still here?"

"Yup," Clive said cheerfully.

"Why?"

He shrugged. "I had a few questions I thought you might be able to answer."

Jason poured a finger of brandy then gulped it down. "Not right now. I have something to take care of."

"Would that something be the little hottie I saw you leave the restaurant with last night?"

Jason's forehead knotted. No wonder he had a headache. He hadn't frowned this much since he'd been a boy. "Are you spying on me now?"

"Please. I was having a leisurely drink before going home for the night when I saw you two. Actually, I felt you. The heat radiating from that table in the corner was enough to scorch the entire room. It's a wonder we weren't dealing with a fire last night and then a flood this morning."

Grabbing his suit jacket, Jason walked toward the door, intending to ignore Clive and the direction he was sure this conversation was going. "Very funny."

"Not as funny as the fact that you were panting over David Markam's baby girl."

That halted him. Jason turned, faced his friend. "You knew who she was?"

Clive recognized the look and held his hands up in surrender. "Nah, man. At least not until this morning. There's a huge article in today's paper about Markam's arrival in town and the reason for it."

Jason crossed the room, took the paper Clive held toward him. "Son of a bitch," he roared.

"That's what I said when I made the connection." Clive sat back in the chair. "So tell me, Casanova, is she as ambitious as her father?"

"Shut up," Jason said, tossing the paper back at Clive then stalking out of the room.

Ten minutes later he stood at the door of room 417, Clive at his side. He tossed him a questioning glance.

Clive chuckled. "I'm here for support."

"Mine or hers?" Jason lifted a hand and knocked, fully aware that he could have just gotten a key and entered on his own.

A tall, leggy, mocha-complexioned beauty pulled the door open. "Hello," she said brightly.

Clive looked at the woman then looked at Jason. "Hers."

Celise and Sharrell had talked this situation up and down and still came to the same conclusion. She'd walked herself right into the fire pit. The moment she stepped into his hotel, into his room. Her father would most likely forgive her career betrayal, in a year or possibly ten, but he'd never, ever forgive her for sleeping with the enemy.

Besides being a staunch businessman and an honest man period, David Markam prided himself on one other thing: loyalty. And in the span of two weeks, Celise had proven—three times—that her loyalty to her family came second to her own whims and demands. With a heavy sigh, she rested her head on the glass patio door.

"What's the matter? Your plan to sleep with me didn't work? Are you thinking of another way you can slip my hotel from under me and hand it to dear old dad?"

Like tiny darts against her skin, Jason's words slammed into her, and she turned slowly. "What are you doing here?" *And why do you still look so damned good?*

"I own this hotel. I can go anywhere I please in it. Or did you conveniently forget that fact already?" he asked.

She'd changed her clothes as well. Gone was the flimsy but sexy sundress she'd worn that morning. Now she wore a skirt and blouse, still a thin material, this time of deep pink with a sleeveless shirt baring her bronze-toned arms. Her hair was in a ponytail, not his favorite style on her, but still appealing. She looked stressed but still very much in control. His gut clenched.

"Did you bring backup to throw me out?" Celise nodded toward Clive who stood behind Jason.

For a minute her words were lost on him as he was lost in the perfection of her. He turned to Clive then back to Celise. "This is my partner and accountant, Clive Murdock."

"Well, partner, accountant and hotel owner," she said snidely, "I'll be out of your hair by the end of the day." Jason felt a slither of panic. He took another step closer to her. "I didn't come here to put you out."

"Then what did you come here for, Jason? I would think that after this morning—after the revelations of this morning—we'd have nothing else to say to each other."

As he grew closer, he noticed the erratic jump of her pulse at the hollow of her neck. He'd kissed her there. His tongue had tasted the sweetness of that very spot, and he longed to do it again. "And after last night? What do we have to say about last night?"

She looked, for about twenty long seconds, embarrassed and Jason decided to back track. They were in mixed company and he was asking her something personal, very personal. But he was feeling desperate, very desperate. The last thing he wanted was for her to walk out of this hotel and he never see her again. No, that was definitely not an option.

"Clive?" Jason called without taking his eyes off Celise.

"Ah, yeah?" Clive said sounding as if he'd been far away, but now appeared at Jason's side.

"Leave us," Jason said simply.

Clive hesitated, then Jason heard him ask the female who had answered the door. "Would you like a tour of the hotel?"

She was Celise's cousin, Sharrell. Jason remembered her from this morning's meeting.

There was no such hesitation on Sharrell's part, "Sure," she replied to Clive.

Celise shifted, then squared her shoulders as if ready for battle. She moistened her lips, and heat soared through his body. The clenching of his gut had turned into desire spreading toward his groin, stiffening his manhood until he could think of nothing else but planting himself deeply inside of her, no matter whose daughter she was. This wasn't how the confrontation had played out in his mind, but Jason's body overruled.

"About last night..." she began.

He took another step toward her. "It was wonderful."

"It was a mistake."

He arched a brow. "Was it?"

She backed up and connected with the patio door soundly. "It was..."

"Phenomenal." He reached out, hooked his arm around her waist and pulled her to him. There had to be another explanation. How could she have slept with him so willingly if she were engaged to another man? And could she have done this just to get the hotel for her father?

She shook her head. "It was wrong. We didn't know each other," she insisted.

With all the questions running through his mind, Jason struggled with the physical impact she had on him. He lowered his head, nipped her earlobe. "And yet we fit perfectly. Just tell me you weren't with me because of your father."

If she said it, he would believe her. Last night when she'd responded to him so passionately, they'd made a connection. She couldn't have faked that. And if that was real then the possibility that she hadn't used him was real too.

"My father didn't even know I was here." She kept her hands at her sides. "But last night, we didn't know who we were...what we were." She sighed as his tongue continued to move slowly over her skin.

"And it didn't matter." Last night it didn't matter, and today? He was nibbling along her jaw line, his arousal pressing deeply into her stomach. "All that mattered was us. Me and you and what was happening between us. What will your fiancé think about that?"

She opened her mouth to speak, and his tongue slithered inside, capturing hers in a sensuous duel. On a ragged moan her arms came up and around his neck, her head tilting into the kiss.

Jason fell deeply into the kiss with her, focusing completely on the orchestration of his tongue, the melodic way it danced with hers, the sweet entanglement of mouths and moans. She gripped his shoulders, held the back of his head, and then simply melted against him.

"I'm not engaged anymore," she whispered when she'd finally pulled her mouth away from his.

She didn't look at him, but held her head down slightly.

His hands moved up and down her waist, from the rounds of her breasts, down to the curve of her buttocks where he grabbed and pressed hungrily. He heard her clearly even through the thumping of his blood in his veins. She wasn't engaged; she belonged to no other man. He didn't give a damn what her name was or who her parents were. All he knew was that she drove him insane with wanting, and he had no intention of giving that up—yet.

"I want you. Now," he declared.

It was ridiculous how everything he wore seemed to hang on him perfectly. This suit was navy blue with the thinnest stripe. His shirt was a lighter shade of blue, crisp with a blue and white paisley tie. His ensemble was professional. The serious set of his jaw, intense dark brown eyes and unwavering set of his shoulders was intimidating to say the very least. The complete package made her heart hammer wildly.

Celise was helpless against him, a fact she didn't relish but could no longer deny. Jason had a way of touching her. It aroused instead of frightened, something she wasn't quite used to. He told her exactly what he wanted in a demanding fashion that strangely still allowed her the choice of whether to proceed.

"Then take me," she whispered against his lips.

That wasn't something she had to say twice. With lightning-fast efficiency, his hands were up her skirt pulling down her panties. As she stepped out of them, he pulled a condom from his back pocket and undid his pants. Sheathing himself quickly, he grabbed her at the waist, lifted her until her legs wrapped dutifully around him, and then positioned himself to enter.

His lips captured hers again, and she happily obliged, pulling him closer, centering herself over his erection.

Jason moaned and thrust forward, entering her completely. He held perfectly still for one second, as if savoring the moment, then he began to move inside of her, and everything else became a blur. Her muscles grasped his thick length, slick with arousal as he pounded soundly in and out. Her breasts rubbed against his chest, and he bent his head to bite one distended nipple through her blouse. She gasped, and he pumped harder.

"I don't care who you are. This is where you belong," he declared in a raspy voice.

Celise heard his words, heard the truth in them and whimpered. God help her, he was right, and she couldn't deny it. They did fit perfectly—too perfectly. She'd waited a long time to be desired like this, to be pleasured like this and was amazed that she was allowing it to happen so soon.

Not too long ago she'd doubted if she could ever share this type of intimacy with another man. There seemed to be so much between her and Jason, so much at stake with this joining, but at the moment she just didn't care. All she cared about was the wave she now rode, the sweet sensation of him moving deep inside of her, pressing against that spot that would release a tidal wave of satisfaction.

"Jason," she whispered.

He buried his fingers in her hair, and with his other arm held her close while he moved them slowly to the couch where he lay her down gently. Still inside of her he placed her legs on his shoulders and thrust into her passionately.

"That's it, baby. Give it to me. Give it all to me," he instructed.

Aroused beyond belief, her hands moved to her breasts, toying with her hardened nipples with urgency. She was right there, right at the precipice, waiting, wanting, needing to be pushed further.

Jason could see it in her face, his dick growing even harder at the sight of her playing with her breasts. Licking two fingers before placing them over the bud of her center, he rubbed. She moaned and bucked off the couch.

"Come for me," he whispered and increased the motion of his fingers as well as the deepness of his thrusts. Her head thrashed on the cushions, her panting intensifying even as her essence poured over him.

He was dangerously close to losing it himself. The mere sound of her wetness connecting with his hardness had him counting the seconds until eruption. Flattening the pad of his thumb on her nub, he plunged deeply and felt the reward of her thighs tightening and her legs shaking with her release.

"Jason," she sighed.

"Mmmm, yes, Celise. Yes!"

"Won't it look suspicious with us both sharing a room at Carrington Resorts?" Pamela asked. They were sitting inside the limo parked in front of the hotel, his hand on her knee, inching its way up to her thigh.

Just the sight of him made her wet. His tall stature and broad build only the tip of the iceberg. The combination of dark brown hair and deep green eyes, the rugged low cut beard and the alluring Irish accent, were a total package for her. Pamela loved Nigel Bingham—or rather she loved the things he could do for her. The rest, she simply endured. She saw the lust in his eyes the moment he turned to her. On command, her body responded, her breasts swelling beneath his perusal.

"I've booked us separate rooms, in different names. Nobody will know we're there until we're ready for them to know."

His hand inched up further until he was between her thighs, just a breath away from her womanhood.

Pamela purred. "Do you think he'll sell to you?"

Nigel barely reacted to her question. He was like that, all rigid control boxed into a body that looked like it should belong to a thirty year old man instead of a fifty year old one. His maturity had been another draw to Pamela. There'd never been a man in her life like Nigel Bingham.

"David Markam has made his best offer. I, however, know what it is that Carrington is looking for, and that gives me the upper hand. I am positive he will sell to me."

Squirming beneath his roaming fingers, Pamela licked her lips. Initially they were trying to get Jason to sell to Markam Inns and Suites. Nigel was going to marry the princess of the empire and make loads of money. A year later he would divorce the spoiled little rich girl, but by that time he'd have made the company so much money that he'd own controlling stock and would then take over the family-owned business. He would be a very rich man, and Pamela would be by his side. But the spoiled little rich girl had come to a revelation while she was in college and had broken the engagement. Nigel had been outraged.

Pamela's part in the plan was to get in good with Jason Carrington—to marry him if possible. This would give her rights to his money and possibly some of Carrington Resorts stock. When she divorced him, she and Nigel would complete the ultimate merger and live happy and wealthy together.

Now that neither one of them had the marriage factor with which to contend anymore, it was simply a matter of getting Jason to sell the hotel. And Nigel was determined to make that happen.

"And Carrington won't be able to resist you," Nigel told her.

Pamela wasn't a fan of the new plan where she would go back and attempt to seduce Jason once more. She'd thought that she and Nigel were over having other people in their lives and that as soon as this purchase was made they would concentrate on their future together. It wasn't exactly the future Pamela had dreamed of, but it would keep her off the streets where Nigel had first found her.

"But he doesn't want anything to do with me," was her cool retort. She was always mindful of the way she responded to Nigel. He had a temper that she did not want to experience, not ever again.

"He doesn't want to marry you, darling, which is just fine. But he'll sleep with you." Slipping his hand past the rim of her thong, Nigel sank his finger deep inside of her. "No man can resist you. I just need you to keep him distracted while I make the deal."

Doubts and issues aside, Pamela melted against the seat as he continued to finger her. With his other hand, he grabbed her breast, squeezing until she gasped in pain. She bit down on her lip to keep from crying out. Nigel squeezed harder, his fingers digging through her blouse to her flesh. He loved to do this, loved to push her to the point of yelling in pain, of breaking. She knew that's the way he would see it. If she did not take whatever he did to her in stride, if she did not give every inch of herself to his commands, he would dump her and find someone who would.

Or, worse, he would intensify the pain until she passed out. That had happened once and she vowed it would never happen again.

So Pamela inhaled deeply. She willed the tears that sprang to her eyes not to fall and she let out a sound that resembled a pleasured sigh.

He leaned closer then, letting his hold on her breast slacken a little. He licked the tear that had traitorously slipped down her cheek. Then he took her mouth in a brutal kiss, biting her bottom lip until he drew blood. Pamela whimpered and quivered as a soul-shattering orgasm ripped through her.

Nigel smiled and licked the lip he'd bitten. Pressing her head into his shoulder, he cradled her until her orgasm ceased. "Now go in there and do exactly as I told you."

"Tell me why your father is so pissed about your career choice?" Jason asked Celise suddenly.

He'd carried her from the couch to the bedroom where he'd loved her yet again, their thirst for each other seemingly unquenchable. Celise sighed, completely comfortable with Jason, as if she'd known him for years instead of days. Thoughts of to whom they were related had been lost about an hour ago.

"As I told you, I studied culinary arts. I want to open my own restaurant. My father doesn't like that plan," she told him.

"What does he want you to do?"

Pillows had been propped and Jason lay back on them, his arms wrapped around her shoulders holding her close, his fingers forming lazy circles on her bare shoulder. While comforting, his touch was more than a little distracting, but Celise found herself enjoying this bit of intimacy.

"He wants me to marry well and be a trophy wife," was her eventual reply.

He chuckled. "And you're supposed to be Nigel Bingham's trophy?"

"Something like that. Do you know Nigel too?" she asked, not necessarily caring about Nigel either way, but curious as to Jason's possible business dealings with him.

"I haven't had the pleasure of meeting him personally, but we've spoken a lot in the last few months. He seems pretty, ah, how can I say it…"

"Old," she finished for him. "That's the only way to say it. He's twenty three years older than me. Most of the time he treated me like a child." Her tone was bitter and just a little sad.

"Why would your father want you to marry a man so much older?"

"Because he thinks I need to be tamed." Folding her arms over her chest, she rolled her eyes at the ceiling. "You see, I have this reputation of being impulsive and headstrong. My father doesn't like that. I should be more focused, more serious. He thought Nigel, in all his infinite wisdom, could change me."

"I think it's inherent that parents think they know what's best for their children. I've endured a lot of that myself," he told her, letting his hands rest over hers.

"At some point every child has to grow up and go their own way. I don't know how to make my father realize that," she said trying to hide her exasperation.

"It's easy, decide what you want to do and do it well. So what type of restaurant are you going to open?"

She smiled instantly, the thought of her future having that effect on her. "I want something chic, but affordable to the customers, and I want to have an international cuisine. I like variety—like your lounge serves. I noticed you only offer small items, but there were Italian and Greek offerings and then the Southern sweet potato fries. That's what I'm aiming for, small and eclectic."

"Yeah, I like that about Pompeii, but to tell the truth I'm thinking of reworking that entire menu and possibly opening a new full scale place."

"Really? Why?" She shifted, propping herself up on an elbow to stare down at him.

"I've always liked the lounge, the ambience, the location—but I'm trying to upgrade the hotel, to bring in something that will suit all the guests. I'm thinking about a skylight restaurant."

Celise thought for a moment, remembering the magnificent view from his penthouse suite. "That would be fantastic," she spoke from memory alone. "One side could be all windows, welcoming the guests to the gorgeous Monterey view. The décor could be a little less themed than Pompeii, representing the small-town ambience. But the menu...the menu should still be classy, upscale, yet affordable." She caught herself, then gave a bashful smile. "Sorry, I'm getting carried away with *your* restaurant idea."

"No. No. Go on. I don't mind at all," Jason encouraged her.

Her voice had changed from the sultry siren he'd taken in the living room to the distressed woman who'd talked about breaking her father's heart, to the now excited businesswoman about to embark on a fantastic journey. He admired her strength and tenacity. Just now, she'd gotten this glow in her eyes as she'd talked, and he could clearly envision the ideas as she spoke. He liked what she was saying, and he liked hearing her say it.

She shrugged. "They were just random thoughts. I'm sure you have ideas of your own and a team working on them. It'll be a great restaurant."

He looked at her quizzically, wondering how she could be so sure about this after knowing him such a short time. "How do you know it'll be great?"

She rested a hand on his chest. "Because you're a good businessman. This hotel was a great investment, and I can tell you take it seriously—that you take your career seriously. All you need for success is the drive to make it happen. I can see that in you."

He was honored. He was flabbergasted. Nobody had put it quite that way to him before. His parents reluctantly supported him, and his brothers were proud but stood on standby in case he should need bailing out.

But she, this woman he'd just met, looked at him and felt nothing but confidence in what he was doing and of what he was capable. That was amazing.

Lifting a hand, he cupped her cheek and pulled her down to him until his lips met hers. "I can see so much in you, Celise Markam."

His touch was gentle, his words so soft she almost melted. She wondered what he saw when he looked at her—what he really thought of her. She'd been honest with him—she saw his ambition and dedication clearly. And she believed in him. Carrington Resorts would be a renowned hotel in a short time. She was happy for Jason and his anticipated success.

In addition to being a great-looking man with his own money and his own business venture, Celise noticed something else about Jason Carrington. He was a good listener. He'd listened to her as she spoke the night before about school, and he'd listened attentively to her ideas about her restaurant. It was as if he actually cared about what she had to say. That was certainly new in her life. The acute awareness her body had to his was not lost on her. Nor was the fact that she enjoyed being with him entirely too much.

Too much, too soon. That couldn't be a good thing she thought dismally.

CHAPTER SEVEN

"She's a grown woman, David. There's not much we can do." Madeline flipped over another card in her game of solitaire. Her husband had been pacing the floor of their room at Carrington Resorts since they'd returned from the scenic tour and lunch she'd finally convinced him to take earlier. It was late afternoon, and DJ had gone to visit the gym and the rest of Carrington's facilities. Sharrell had checked in a little while ago then briefly explained something about a dinner date and was off.

So it was just the two of them, and Maddy desperately wanted to talk about something other than her daughter's decision and the loss of the deal for the hotel.

"Maddy, she's got to be made to see reason. It's a tough world out there, especially for someone like Celise."

Madeline paused, holding a card midway between the table and the air. "What does that mean? Celise is a very intelligent young woman, and it seems that she's finally found something to dedicate herself to. Why doesn't that make you happy?"

David dragged his hands down his face and finally plopped down into a chair. "I guess I'm just afraid."

Madeline abandoned her cards and went to kneel beside her husband. David Markam was never afraid. "Afraid of what, darling?"

He took a deep breath, loving the feel of his wife's hand in his. They'd been together for so long, her companionship and strength having gotten him through so many rough times. "That she'll be hurt. That the big ole world out there won't treat my baby right."

Madeline smiled up at him. For all his blustering and yelling, he was simply jealous. "She's been your baby for twenty-seven years now, David. Didn't you ever think she'd grow up? That she'd move on?"

"Sure I did. But not like this. She's growing away from me, Maddy, and I can't seem to stop it."

Madeline rubbed his hand. "No, dear, you can't stop it, but that doesn't mean that she'll stop loving you or needing you. You're her father. Nobody or nothing can ever take that place in her life. Do you know how much your disagreement is hurting her?"

"Then she should stop pressing this foolish idea," he roared.

Shaking her head, Madeline smiled. "But then she wouldn't be your daughter."

David was quiet while her words sank in. He was stubborn and ambitious. Wasn't that his reason for being in this very hotel? Jason Carrington had been turning down his offer to buy it for almost a year, yet he'd come there with the express intention of convincing the man to do otherwise. Celise was his only daughter. She was as stubborn and headstrong as he.

"Nigel Bingham did something to her," he said as an afterthought.

"Do you really think so?" She had wondered what had happened between Celise and Nigel, although she couldn't say she was upset about the outcome of that relationship. She'd always felt Nigel was too old, too staid and too much of a brown-noser for her daughter, but she'd let David have his way.

"I'm sure of it," David continued. "As soon as I find out what it was, I'm throwing him out on his ass."

"Dinner tonight?" Jason asked her as he stood with his back to Celise's room door.

He was holding her again, loving the feel of her in his arms.

"Hmmm, two nights in a row. We'd better be careful, people might start to think we're an item," she joked.

With a start, Jason realized that wasn't such a bad idea. "It's just dinner."

"You're right. This time I'll pick you up at seven." She gave his bottom lip a teasing nip.

"Hey, I'm all for women's lib." Squeezing her tempting bottom one last time, he took her lips, sank his tongue into her warm mouth and moaned. Man, did he love kissing this woman. She melded herself against him, giving him all of her once more. She always responded to his touch with complete abandon. He'd never had thoughts like that before and realized then that he needed to explore them a little more. He needed to explore her a little more. While they'd talked, he'd gotten the distinct impression that her focus on her career was based on so much more than simple ambition, and he was desperate to find out what.

Pulling away reluctantly, he stared down into her eyes. "Seven o'clock. Don't be late."

"I'm never late," she whispered, then watched him leave the room.

A merry little dance carried Celise back to her room where she searched for yet another outfit to wear. Her day had been mostly shot since she'd spent the bulk of it in bed. They'd spent the afternoon together, talking, getting to know each other. Jason was a conscientious businessman, a caring family member and a pretty cool guy to whom to talk. If she were looking for a boyfriend, he'd definitely be tops on her list.

But for the moment she'd settle for the great sex and easy conversation. He seemed to be at ease with that arrangement as well.

The sun was still shining bright—sunset only another hour or so away. She had time to go out and look around, and that's exactly what she planned to do.

A half hour later she was walking out of the hotel and onto the streets of Monterey. The very first thing she did was inhale the salty sea air. It made her feel like summer vacations spent on the Bay or that year her family had gone to Hawaii. A warm summer's breeze floated over her skin, and she slipped sunshades on her eyes and began walking.

She wasn't going any place in particular, just walking, and enjoying the scenes like any other tourist. Only she was looking for permanency. Her parents had made their home in San Francisco. They loved that city—loved everything about it—and it fit them perfectly. Celise wanted to find her own place, somewhere that fit her just as nicely. She had a hunch that Monterey was that place.

In an antique shop, she saw a miniature replica of the Carrington Resorts, when it used to be the Regency. It had a classic beauty even back then. Holding it in the palm of her hand, she felt something strong, something definitely potent and wondered at it. She was thinking about Jason again. As many times as she'd convinced herself that she wasn't going to think about that man, her thoughts continued to return to him.

Her body still tingled from his touch, his kiss. If she inhaled deeply enough she'd conjure up his scent. If she closed her eyes, she'd see his dark, entrancing eyes and hear his words clearly, telling her she was beautiful, that she was perfect and as of just a little while ago, that she was someone special. When he'd said that she'd playfully jabbed at him, but her heart had done a dainty flip at his words. Was she special to him? Surely Jason Carrington had a wealth of women chasing after him. And she, Celise Markam—his literal enemy, his new part-time lover—could not be classified as one of them.

She liked Jason, that was apparent, and she loved sleeping with him, but beyond that…was there something beyond that? Most definitely not. And it was better not to fool herself into believing otherwise. Besides, she was there to enjoy the scenery, to make her home, to build her business. She was not there to fall for Jason Carrington.

Even as she dug into her purse for her credit card to pay for the statue she still told herself they were just sleeping together, nothing more and nothing less.

"Like my hotel, do you, sweetie?"

The voice from behind startled Celise, causing her to jump from her daydreams. Turning she looked into the watery gray eyes of a woman clearly beyond her sixties. The woman was a few inches shorter than Celise, with a round cherub-like face and tight silver curls that peeked from beneath a very dated pill-box hat with a thin veil in the front. Despite the hat, Celise thought the woman was dressed extremely well. She noted the designer suit and Gucci handbag the woman held on her wrist. Pearls were at her neck and ears, and Celise would bet her life they were genuine. "Excuse me?"

"My hotel." The woman tapped the bag that now held Jason's gift. "You like it enough to buy a memento. Are you staying there?"

Celise smiled nervously. She'd been unaware that

her purchase was being monitored. "Ah, actually, yes. I am staying at Carrington Resorts. When I saw this, it made me think of a…a friend, and I knew he'd like it."

"Buying gifts for a man." The woman rolled her eyes. "In my day, Ralph bought me gifts. What is the world coming to?"

Celise tried not to laugh. "It's okay for a woman to buy something for a man, especially if it's just a friend."

"Is it his birthday?" she asked as if that were the only excuse for doing such a thing.

"No," Celise replied with a shake of her head. "At least I don't think it is."

The woman continued with an incredulous look. "Hmph. It's not Christmas."

"No. It's not," Celise replied.

"Then he must be more than a friend. You don't just buy gifts just because."

Feeling a little uncomfortable with the direction of this conversation, Celise thought it was best if she ended it and got away from this crabby old woman. She purchased the statue and attempted to leave the store. The woman blocked her retreat.

"Yes, you can buy a gift just because. And, no, the man doesn't have to be the only one giving in a relationship." But she wasn't in a relationship. Never mind, that woman didn't need to know all her business. "It was a pleasure speaking to you, but I have to go now," Celise told her.

The woman followed her out of the store with a man who Celise presumed was Ralph right behind her.

"I'm Myrtle Hampden," she said when they were outside.

Slightly exasperated, yet wanting to remain polite, Celise stopped and turned to the woman once more.

"Me and my Ralph own the Regency," she told Celise with a nod over to the man who was only about two inches taller than her with significantly less hair.

"I thought Carrington Resorts was owned by Jason Carrington," she stated slowly because she didn't want to offend the woman by correcting her.

Myrtle waved a hand. "That's the fresh young buck who tried to buy it from me and my Ralph, but we were smart. We kept our stock, and we still have some control over there. He can't just come in making a bunch of unnecessary changes and think that we'll stand for it."

Now Celise was curious. "Unnecessary changes? What is he doing that you don't like?" It was apparent that Mrs. Myrtle Hampden didn't like Jason Carrington.

Myrtle happily took Celise by the arm. "C'mon, we'll walk and talk. These old bones need all the exercise they can get."

Celise gave a polite smile and followed her lead. This was going to be interesting.

It was a little past six o'clock when Jason returned to his suite. Pulling off his clothes as he walked, he didn't stop until he was in the bathroom switching on the shower. The rest of his afternoon had been busy ensuring that the kitchen was in working order and checking on reservations and accommodations for a conference he had coming in the following week. The Food Festival's Annual Cook-off was being held in Monterey, and Carrington Resorts had been lucky enough to get the booking. This would give him national exposure, and everything had to be on point.

But he'd had enough of business for one day. A sexy hazel-eyed vixen had been steadily creeping into his thoughts, and he couldn't wait to see her again. She'd be there at seven, he thought as he stepped beneath the spray of hot water, and he'd be ready, willing and waiting.

Key cards were reprogrammed when guests turned them in at checkout. But Jason owned the hotel, the penthouse suite belonged to him, so his card did not change. Reaching into her purse, Pamela pulled out the copy she had made before she was unceremoniously thrown out of Carrington Resorts several months ago. Slipping it inside the gold door handle, she smiled when the light turned green and she was granted access.

Dropping her purse on the couch in the sitting area she removed her jacket, all the while noticing that nothing had changed in his suite since she'd been gone. From the expensive suede furniture, to the family photos lining the walls, and the fully stocked bar, everything was exactly the same. She heard a sound and followed it to the right, toward the bedroom.

She could smell him before she saw him. The memory of his cologne assailed her senses and her knees began to shake. There he stood, all six feet three inches of his honey-toned skin, naked for her to see. Muscled legs led to a tight butt, a strong back and broad shoulders.

She cleared her throat.

He turned.

A well-defined chest, six-pack abs and his greatest selling point, even in its relaxed state, had her heart hammering in her chest. "Hello, Jason."

Not the least bit embarrassed by his lack of attire but angrier at the person receiving this unsolicited view, Jason scowled. "Pamela. I'd ask what you're doing here but I'm more interested in whether you have bail money for when I call the police to report you're breaking and entering."

"Now is that any way to treat your ex-fiancée?" Pamela cooed and took a step closer, giving him an appreciative glance from head to toe. "I see you haven't changed much since I last saw you. Still fine as ever."

He grabbed his towel. Wrapping it around his waist, he kept his eyes on her. "We are no longer engaged, and you are no longer welcome here. I thought I made that perfectly clear to you before you left."

"You said something to that effect." She moved until they were face-to-face, toe-to-toe. "But I missed you, and I was wondering if you missed me too."

Jason despised this woman. He completely detested the person she was and the things of which she was capable. Unfortunately, his feelings did not change the fact that she was an attractive woman. Standing about five feet seven, her skin was the tone of dark chocolate, with hips that curved into a round ass and breasts that would make any man cross-eyed. Men had often been accused of thinking with the wrong head. Jason was sorry to say he couldn't dismiss that accusation. His erection was inevitable.

Pamela's gaze fell below his waist. "I see at least a part of you misses me."

"Too bad I'm old enough not to let that part control my actions. You've got five seconds to turn around and walk out of here," he warned her.

"Oh come on, Jason," she whispered, lifting a hand to his shoulder and squeezing. "We can at least be civil to each other."

Jason stepped out of her reach and walked into the sitting room, knowing she'd follow him. He opened the door to let her out. "I'm being civil since I haven't tossed you out on your ass. That's normally what I do with liars."

"That's not fair. I never lied to you," she said defensively. "You misunderstood what was going on."

Jason chuckled. "I didn't misunderstand you trying to seduce my manager or the confidential papers regarding Carrington Resorts I found in your suitcase."

What he did misunderstand was the terms of their relationship. For eight months he'd thought they were an item, in a committed relationship on its way to marriage and family. Boy, did he misunderstand that one.

"Don't be silly, Jason. You knew I loved you," she protested.

Moving closer Pamela put both hands on his bare chest, sliding them slowly over the muscled terrain.

"You don't know what love is," he said through gritted teeth. He knew exactly what she was doing. According to his reputation, this was what he wanted, what he regularly took from women, but that couldn't be further from the truth. Besides, after the night before and earlier that day, sex with Pamela just didn't seem all that appealing anymore, despite his body's reaction. He grasped her shoulders in an attempt to push her away.

Pamela obviously took that as a sign to proceed and let her hands slide farther down to his waist, her knees bending until they rested on the floor.

Celise was a few minutes early and readily admitted that she was anxious to see him again. Their morning together had been wonderful and then the afternoon's walk and talk with Mrs. Hampden had added so much more to her growing file on Jason Carrington.

The elderly woman and her husband seemed to think he was a good boy with good intentions, but that he was misguided by his already rich status. Jason's purchase of the hotel was like a passing hobby in their minds— one with which they were growing quite irritated.

However, Celise wasn't sure she shared the Hampdens' opinion of Jason. He appeared focused on making Carrington Resorts a success. His ideas and goals seemed well thought out and pretty damn good to her, so she had to wonder if the Hampdens had clear thoughts where the business was concerned. They were older and set in their ways, and if nothing else, Celise knew how a person set in their ways could act about change.

Stepping off the elevator on the top floor, she made the now familiar left turn and headed down the hall toward Jason's suite. She would mention the Hampdens at dinner and get a feel for his thoughts about the couple. She was also going to ask him about some of the local restaurants and get his views on her competition. He seemed impressed by her plans, and Celise found she really liked talking to him about them.

She was about to knock on the door when she noticed it was ajar. Then she heard voices coming from inside his suite. One voice was definitely female, and that aroused her curiosity. Now Jason wasn't her man. Hell, they hadn't even discussed where this thing between them was going. And to be honest, that was a topic of which she wanted to steer clear. She had enough going on in her life at the moment. Jason was fun, he listened to her, and the sex was good, that was all.

Still, she found herself pushing against the door and walking inside.

Okay, not a second ago she'd reminded herself that she and Jason weren't exclusive, that this was a passing fling, an affair that was giving them both some amount of satisfaction. All that nonsense flew right out the window as she watched a woman on her knees in front of him. He only wore a towel, and in a minute the woman's hands would see to it that he was rid of that.

Celise knew full well what was beneath that towel and felt rage slithering up her spine. With a hand on her hip and her eyes trained on the woman, she asked, "Am I interrupting?"

Jason turned in her direction just as Pamela's hand had reached beneath the towel to touch him. A moment before hearing the voice he'd clenched Pamela's shoulders about to finally push her away from him. Judging from the sound of the voice and the carefully controlled look on Celise's face, he surmised he'd been a moment too slow.

"Celise?" Pulling the towel around his waist tighter Jason stepped back and moved toward Celise who quickly stepped farther away.

Twisting her wrist, she looked at her watch, then back to him. "You did say seven, right?"

"Yes. I had sort of a surprise visitor and lost track of time."

Celise lifted a brow. "I can see that. Look, I'm not into threesomes, so I'll just let you get back to your business." She turned to walk away but Jason grabbed her arm.

"No. You stay." Then he turned to Pamela. "You leave."

He was irritated to see that Pamela had not only come to stand right beside him, but she was smiling at Celise as if this was exactly how she'd expected this episode to play out.

"I said, go. Now, Pamela," he reiterated in a voice that said he was definitely not playing with her. His next action would be to call security up here to haul her ass out the door.

He knew the shift in his tone had worked because Pamela turned to him, her smile faltering slightly.

"Fine. I'll go." Then with a heated glance toward Celise she added, "I'll be back."

"Don't push me, Pamela. The next time I *will* call the police," Jason spoke through clenched teeth.

Pamela's face hardened. "Don't threaten me, Jason. You might not like the results."

She was gone, and Celise was still standing there.

"You can let go of me now," she told him in a voice that was barely restraining its anger.

He wanted to say something, should try to explain, but Jason was no newbie when it came to women. The fact that most explanations only made things worse when a woman was looking at him like this was an undeniable one. Still, this particular woman was too important to simply brush off.

"Are you going to come in, or are we going to discuss this in the hallway?" he asked, his tone having shifted dramatically from when he'd spoken to Pamela.

"No. I'm not coming in, and there's nothing to discuss. Obviously I interrupted your quickie before dinner. I'd offer my apologies, but I'm a bit rude when it comes to catching my dinner dates with other women."

Right. She was definitely too upset to hear any explanations.

"Don't be childish, Celise. Come inside while I get ready for dinner," he told her seriously.

"No, Jason. You seem to have me confused with the previous chick. There's no telling me what to do and when to do it. I agreed to a date with you tonight, and now I'm breaking it. It's that simple." She turned and walked away.

Jason fumed. He was not used to women walking away from him, so he refused to follow her. But he did try to talk to her once again. "This is not the way to handle this."

Celise waved a hand without turning back. "Don't worry, there's nothing to handle."

Jason watched her step into the elevator then cursed and banged the door. Returning to the inside of his suite, he let the door slam behind him before stalking over to his desk and calling downstairs.

"How the hell did Pamela get back into this hotel?" he yelled at his administrative assistant whom he had purposely told that Pamela Walker was no longer allowed on the premises after he'd kicked her out eight months ago. "Get somebody up here to change my locks—now!"

Slamming down the phone, he stood there for a minute trying to calm the blood pumping fiercely through him. In his mind he saw two women, two totally different women who wielded the same power over him.

Dragging his hands down his face he realized the power wasn't the same. With Pamela, there had always been lust. Even if he couldn't talk to her about his hopes and dreams, he could make love to her and things would seem alright.

With Celise...he wasn't sure what it was with Celise. He had quickly become attached to her body and the sinful things she did with it, but then, for a moment he'd thought there was more. She looked upset at finding Pamela there. While he'd slipped into pants and a shirt, he realized he couldn't blame her for that. But she hadn't reacted the way he'd assumed she would, the way any other woman would.

Upon seeing her in the doorway he just knew it was about to be a scene. A cat fight perhaps? He smiled wryly. Yelling and arguing, accusations and curses, all of that would have been the norm for the situation. Instead she'd left. She'd simply broken their date. Leaving him basically naked and staring after her.

Damn, that intrigued him.

CHAPTER EIGHT

Whether she was running away from her parents or now running away from a man, it seemed to always be Celise's answer to a problem. Only this didn't really seem like running, it was more like self-preservation. If she could walk away from whatever this was between her and Jason before it became too emotional or too messy, that could only prove wise for both of them. And wasn't part of growing up and being mature, making wise decisions?

Letting herself into her room she'd already decided to pack and get out of Carrington Resorts. Where she was going was anybody's guess, but she had a credit card and two working legs, surely she'd find somewhere.

Jason hadn't promised her anything. He hadn't said he loved her then screwed any and everything with tits and ass in her father's business. He wasn't committed to marrying her just for the sake of gaining control of her father's company, and he hadn't demeaned her. So her anger was probably misplaced.

The one thing he did do was sleep with her only hours prior to accepting favors from another woman. That repulsed her and had almost brought her to the point of striking him. Instead she'd decided to take her knack for finding turmoil and get the hell out of dodge.

Jason Carrington could have all the favors he wanted from anyone else but her.

With her mind made up she'd already begun to pack when there was a knock at her door. As she walked to open it a part of her wondered if it were Jason, coming to explain what had been going on with him and that woman in his office. Another part, didn't really give a damn if it was him or not, she was still leaving. Not, running, just leaving on her own terms for once.

"Really, Celise, running away from your father is not the answer." Madeline sat on the edge of the bed picking up a blouse her daughter had folded incorrectly.

"I'm not running from him, mother," was her quiet reply.

Madeline arched a brow at her daughter's tone and contradicting actions as she tossed one thing into her suitcase after another.

"Oh? Then who are you running from?" She had an idea but wanted Celise to volunteer the information.

Celise sighed. "I'm not running from anyone."

Short, clipped answers and no eye contact. Madeline was amused. "So why are you packing?"

Celise pulled a red dress from the closet and yanked it from the hanger. Balling it up, she tossed it into the suitcase and turned to get something else. "I need to find another place to stay, that's all."

With each item Celise put in the bag, Madeline took it out and refolded it before laying it neatly in the suitcase. Her child was definitely upset about something. "And you just came to that decision suddenly?"

"No. I wouldn't say suddenly."

"Hmph. You're dressed to go out. It's almost eight-thirty at night and you're tossing clothes into a bag. I'd say it was sudden."

Celise scooped up shoes from the bottom of the closet and dropped them into the suitcase. Madeline yelped, and she turned in surprise.

"Shoes on top of your clothes. Now I know something is bothering you." She stood, grabbed her daughter's arm and pulled her down onto the bed. "Stop this nonsense and tell me what's going on."

Celise huffed. "Nothing is going on. I'm just going to stay at another hotel."

"Why?" Madeline persisted, Celise and her father weren't the only two in this family that could be stubborn.

"Mama, this really isn't about anyone in particular. I just think it's best that I find someplace else to stay. You and Daddy are here, and DJ and Sharrell. You're all doing business. I'm not a part of that business, so it would be less of a distraction if I left."

In that reply Madeline zoned in on one word: *distraction.* "Are we distracting you, baby?"

Celise blinked then ran her fingers through her hair. "No. No, not me. I'm not distracted."

Yeah, right. Madeline gave a sly smile. "So where are you going to stay?"

She shrugged. "I'm not sure yet."

"Are you taking your bags with the intent of sleeping on the street?"

Frowning, Celise eyed her mother. "Of course not, Mama. I'll find another hotel."

"Oh, I see. You know I had something I wanted to ask you earlier, but you left in such a hurry."

"Really? What?"

"This is purely a personal question. No business involved, either mine or yours."

Celise nodded. "Ooohhkay."

She'd exaggerated the word in the hopes of speeding up the conversation, Madeline presumed. She didn't like talking to her mother about her personal life, never had. And generally Madeline had kept a safe distance from Celise and whatever man she was involved with. Now, in retrospect, she thought that may have been a mistake where Nigel Bingham was concerned. That's why she intended to get to the bottom of this new matter immediately.

"What do you think of Jason Carrington?"

"I want to know how Pamela got in here, man." Jason paced the floor in his first-floor office. After Celise left him standing half naked in the doorway he'd decided that if he stayed in his suite a minute longer he was going to go crazy. Why? He wasn't quite sure, but he was almost positive it centered on Celise Markam and the time they'd spent together there.

"It's a free country, Jason. You can't just make her disappear because you're pissed with her." Clive fixed himself a drink at the mini bar then took a seat in the leather chair across from Jason's desk.

"This is *my* hotel," he roared.

Clive nodded. "Yes. It is. And I've already spoken to the staff downstairs, and they don't have her registered as a guest here. If she's seen on the premises again, she'll be escorted out. But other than that, there's really nothing we can do."

"That's comforting," he said sarcastically.

"What's really eating you?" Clive asked.

Jason was pacing again, trying to work off the tension that had built and the clutter that filled his mind. "What?"

"Pamela never had this effect on you before. Not even when you were involved with her. So I'm assuming that something other than her impromptu visit has you upset."

Dragging his hand over his face Jason took a deep breath. "Yeah, you're right. How about the fact that she was on her knees about to pleasure me when Celise walked in? Is that enough to upset me?"

Clive whistled. "Yeah, I'd say that was a dozy."

Dropping down into his chair, Jason closed his eyes, then opened them toward the ceiling. "What am I doing, man? One woman is just the same as another, right? I'm trippin'."

Clive watched his longtime friend, wondering if that was what he was doing. At one point in both their lives they'd shared the same philosophy about women. As they'd grown older, little had changed. But in the span of two days Jason seemed different.

"What did Celise say?"

Jason rubbed his temples. "I think it was more what she didn't say."

"Huh?"

"She didn't say much of anything. Something like she didn't mean to disturb me and that she was canceling our dinner date. Then she just walked away. I mean, she just walked away from me like I wasn't even there."

Jason sounded flabbergasted.

"Really? Maybe she doesn't care," Clive suggested.

Then he could only sit back and watch what was definitely a historical event. Jason was always calm. He never let business or his personal life stress him out. Yet, here he was looking pretty damned stressed by this new development.

"Fine," Jason snapped. "She doesn't have to care. We had a good time, but I'm not up for all this drama. She's just one woman out of a million."

The phone rang, and Jason threw his hands up in the air before reluctantly taking it. Clive took that as his cue to leave. Once the office door was closed behind him he made fast tracks to the fourth floor—to the room of the woman who in two days had slipped inside his friend's heart.

Bags by the door, purse in hand, Celise prayed she'd make it out of the building before her mother returned with her father. Madeline had asked her a lot of strange questions when she'd been there. Why did she care what she thought of Jason? She couldn't possibly know that she'd slept with him, and if she did, was she going to tell her father? The absolute last thing she wanted to deal with tonight was her father's wrath on the subject.

She'd gone to the bathroom after her mother's tireless comments about Jason Carrington and his success, and when she'd come out, Madeline was gone. That was getting over too easily, so Celise packed in double-time and headed toward the door. As soon as she pulled it open, a body fell into her.

"Hey," she said a bit winded by their almost collision.

"Sorry," he said taking a step back and brushing down his tie as if it had been ruffled by his stumble.

Clive Murdock stood at the threshold his ready smile clearly intended to dazzle her, only irritated her instead. From what she could tell from their first brief meeting, this was Jason's right hand. If he were standing at her door with his six plus foot height, pecan skin-tone and diamond studded left ear, it had to be at Jason's bequest.

Remembering Jason's last words as she walked away from him Celise wanted to call him up and ask, now who was being immature.

"What do you want?"

Clive continued to smile even though she wasn't reciprocating.

"Can I come in?" he asked.

"No," was her quick reply. Celise had no intention of listening to whatever lame excuse Clive might have on Jason's behalf. Jason should have come to make the lame excuses for himself.

Regardless of her answer, Clive hadn't moved. Instead, he'd slipped one hand into the pocket of his dark gray suit pants. "Why?"

"Because I'm leaving."

"Really? Where are you off to?"

Folding her arms over her chest, she tapped her foot to show him her annoyance. "None of your business."

"Come on. This is silly. Let me come in so we can talk. You don't want the entire hotel hearing our conversation," he stated.

Her frown increased. Hadn't Jason tried to get her with that same plea? But he wasn't Jason. Expelling a deep breath, she moved to the side. "Make it quick."

"So where are you going? Back to San Francisco?" he asked turning to her the moment she let the door close behind them.

Celise narrowed her eyes on him for a minute. How did he know where she was from? Then she remembered him leaving with Sharrell earlier when she and Jason...never mind. "No. I'm not going back to San Francisco. I'm opening my restaurant here. It would make sense that I live here, correct?"

Clive shrugged. "I would assume. So where are you staying until you find a place?"

Because she was truly tired of the questions tonight and her head hurt and her mind was filled with tumultuous thoughts regarding Jason, she sighed. "I'll find somewhere just as soon as you leave. You're wasting my time."

He seemed to contemplate her words a moment longer than was necessary, looking down at her bags then back up to her. Finally he nodded.

"Let's go," he said, bending to pick up said bags and already making his way back to the door.

"What? Put my bags down. I'm not going anywhere with you," she protested.

"Do you have another choice?" he tossed over his shoulder.

"As a matter of fact, I do. Carrington Resorts is a lovely hotel, but I'm sure in this great city of Monterey there are more."

He put down a bag, opened the door then looked at her as he picked the bag up again. "You are absolutely correct. There are more hotels in Monterey, but none as good as Carrington. That's why your father wants to buy it, and that's why Jason won't sell it. Now, if you'd like to get some rest tonight in the only place that comes close to the Carrington I suggest you follow me."

Celise believed his words, but was still leery. He could be taking her anywhere. She didn't know him. She hadn't known Jason either, but she'd slept with him.

"Where are we going?" she asked following him because he had her bags.

"Look, I know you've been through something tonight, and I'm not about to defend or explain for Jason. That's his job. But it's getting late, and I can't let you wander the streets looking for a place to stay. Now, I know a great beach house that's hardly ever used. You can stay there."

They were at the elevator, and Celise still looked at him with questions. Admittedly, he looked honest enough and he was friends with Jason, so she didn't get the serial killer/rapist vibe from him. Still, this was more than a little weird.

"Why? Why would you let me stay there? You don't know me."

"I know Jason. And if Jason trusts you, then I trust you," he told her in what Celise thought was a very honest tone, for a man.

The elevator doors opened and he motioned for her to step inside. She could have said no, could have made a huge scene, demanded her bags back and went about her business. But it was late and she was tired and if only for one night she figured she could endure staying in a beach house rather than the hotel room she probably would have secured. With resignation she stepped inside the elevator, moving to a corner and watching him step inside behind her. He pressed L for lobby and gave her a small smile before turning his back to her.

He probably thought he'd won this round, for his friend Jason of course. But Celise knew differently and she gave him her opinion in this regard just for good measure. "I don't give a rat's ass about Jason's trust."

CHAPTER NINE

At the end of Cannery Row on a tiny strip of land to the left of what was a popular jumping-off point for the local scuba diving school was a picturesque cottage. To be accurate, it was a cottage the size of two apartments with four bedrooms, two bathrooms, a huge kitchen with all the modern amenities and the most spectacular view she'd ever seen.

Clive had given Celise a quick tour then left her there with a key and minimal instruction. It was nearing eleven o'clock by the time she'd unpacked and fixed herself a snack. The kitchen was surprisingly well stocked, but then the place was spotless so she should have expected nothing less. She'd asked if this was Clive's home and he'd told her no, but she wasn't sure she believed him. How else would he have a key?

It didn't matter. She wouldn't be staying there long. The next day she'd find herself an apartment to rent. On the ride over she realized, spending money on hotels seemed pointless since she was determined to make Monterey her new home. Wandering into the breakfast room she pulled the string to the mini blinds and watched as the indigo seascape came into view. Moonlight danced over small, dark waves. Houses along the coast lit up the night like a Christmas tree. And if she stared long and hard in one spot, she could just see the lights of a boat on a moonlit cruise.

She took a deep breath, let her forehead rest against the window and thought of her parents. She should call them, let them know where she was. Her father would no doubt get a cab and come to get her, or at the very least send DJ to do it. No, she wouldn't call them just yet. Let them think she'd run away. Again.

Closing the blind, she went into the living room. Her body was tired, her mind begging for a rest, but still she fought it. If she lay in bed and closed her eyes, she'd think of him. She knew it as surely as she knew her name. He'd been just on the outskirts of her thoughts for the last couple of hours. The instant she allowed herself a moment's quiet he'd overtake them, and she wasn't ready for that. He was just a man, after all. One man in a world full of the controlling, domineering species.

She didn't need him.

She didn't want him.

And it was a good thing because after what she'd seen, he obviously didn't want her either. That was an all-too-familiar feeling.

He needed her.

He hated that feeling because Nigel Bingham did not need anybody or anything. And yet, here he was, standing outside in the dark of night, staring into the window of a house at the end of Cannery Row.

She was a spoiled, naïve girl stuck in a gorgeous woman's body. A body that never failed to arouse him. She would never have been his first pick as far as a wife would go, but as fate would have it, she was the one for him. Still, Celise Markam needed to be tamed. She needed to know who was in control and how to submit. And Nigel figured he was just the one to teach her that lesson.

What he absolutely would not do is stoop to this stalker personality ever again. It was beneath him. Just as Pamela and her needy personality was. She'd texted and called him more times than he could count in the last hour. As he'd walked up to this house, after waiting patiently for that meddling assistant of Carrington's to leave, he'd turned his cell phone off. Pamela knew how to submit, she did whatever he asked, whenever he asked and she did it well. But she was impatient and unpolished, volatile and sometimes rude. She wasn't Celise Markam, by any stretch of the imagination.

The lights inside the house went out with a sudden blink and Nigel frowned. He walked from the house with a promise on his lips. "You won't walk away from me, Celise. I don't care who your father is or who you think you want to be. You will submit to me."

Jason was stepping off the elevator when his cell phone rang. Reaching to his hip he removed it from the case to answer.

"What's doing little brother?" Jackson asked on the other line.

Jason smiled even though he hated being called Little Brother, regardless of his rank in the Carrington clan. "All is well, Mr. Corporate," he replied using his own nickname for his oldest brother.

It was Jackson's turn to chuckle. "Just thought I'd check in on you since I haven't heard from you in a couple of weeks. You know you could come home to visit your family every once in a while."

Jackson lived in Los Angeles with the rest of the Carringtons. The family business was headquartered there so even with the amount of traveling his parents did for leisure and Jackson did for business, they always ended up back in L.A. at some point. All of them except for Jason.

"My home is in Monterey now. And I'm working, you know how that is," Jason told him moving down the hall toward his suite.

"Yeah, I heard something about you trying to set up shop down there. How's the hotel business treating you?"

Jason thought about telling Jackson about the sabotage and the offers to buy him out. But he didn't. Jackson would only try to help, to fix "Little Brother's" problems for him. Carrington Resorts was Jason's, so if there was fixing to be done, he'd be the one to do it.

"Like I said all is well. No more and no less than what you probably deal with everyday at Carrington Enterprises," he finished hoping to change the subject.

"Nah, I'm into buying and selling, not rebuilding and fixing things up."

"Well, we each have our paths to walk."

Jackson chuckled again lightly at the saying their grandmother used to recite to them.

"I have to get down there to see what you've done with the place," Jackson said after another second or so.

"You'll like it," he replied. "And you need a vacation, you work too hard."

It was true, of all the Carrington's Jackson was the most ambitious. He'd achieved straight A's in high school and his years at Harvard and was considered one of the brightest and most promising minds of their generation. He used that mind to buy and sell companies, read poetry and collect art. It was the only life he wanted, so he'd told his family.

"Money doesn't make itself," was Jackson's response. "But I may be taking a trip in the upcoming weeks, so I'll plan to stop by. You just make sure I get the best suite in the hotel."

"Of course, nothing's too good for you Mr. Corporate," Jason said with a smile.

A few more moments on the phone with his brother and then Jason was alone in his suite. He hadn't bothered to turn on the lights or even stop at the bar to fix a drink like he normally did. Tonight, he moved through the suite until he stood on the balcony enjoying the balmy evening breeze. On second thought, he wasn't really enjoying it. He hadn't enjoyed anything since the moment Celise entered his suite three hours ago. If he weren't the one involved he'd think the situation was funny. But at the moment all he felt was an emptiness that he couldn't quite explain.

He'd only met her the night before, and had just found out her real name and relation that morning. No way was he emotionally attached to this woman already. But then he remembered slipping into her. He remembered her arms going around his neck, her legs wrapping around his waist, holding him tightly, securely inside of her. He took a deep breath and tried to curve his thoughts. Instead they deepened until he could smell her essence on the breeze, could hear her moans with the crashing of the waves. He hardened to the point of pain, even as his mind focused solely on pleasure.

She was smart. She had ambition, goals and dreams. They were so much alike and yet…he didn't know what he could possibly offer her. Every man brought something to a relationship. But what could he give Celise Markam? She had everything: good looks, money, brains. He paused then smiled as the thought entered his mind, *I have all those things too.* Did that make him conceited? Nah, it made him honest with himself, which was something of which he was really proud. He didn't lie to himself about his limitations nor did he lie to others about what he could do.

Could he make her happy?

That depended solely on what her happiness entailed. Opening her restaurant was a huge goal for her. Being successful on her own, outside of the Markam cocoon, another aspiration. But how could Jason make those things happen and should he even try?

With a start, Jason went back into his suite and headed directly for his office. The answer was so simple he almost punched himself for not realizing it sooner. He was looking for his notes. He'd left them on his desk, on the left hand side. He just needed to find them, to look over them and to give his idea a little more thought then he'd approach her.

He wondered briefly what she'd say then wouldn't allow himself to believe she'd turn him down. What she saw between him and Pamela was nothing. He'd get that explanation out of the way first, then he'd spring this on her. His erection strained against his pants as he visualized her eyes glazing over then darkening like they did just before she came.

Damn. He needed to find those notes quick.

Again he could punch himself. "Finding the notes would be a lot easier if you turned the lights on, Carrington." With a frown he reached for the lamp and pulled on the string.

Click.

Nothing.

His frown increased. He pulled the string again.

Click.

Nothing.

"What the hell?"

His cell phone rang again. Abandoning the malfunctioning lamp, he pulled it from the clip and answered. "Jason Carrington."

"Jase, we got a problem." Clive hesitated a millisecond. "A big problem."

WANTING YOU

Part Two

The Carrington Chronicles

A. C. Arthur

CHAPTER TEN

Flashlight in hand, Jason made his way down the stairway. He'd walked down twelve flights and wasn't out of breath but was angry enough to punch a hole in the wall. Luckily he possessed enough common sense to leave the concrete blocks alone. His cell phone rang, and he hastily answered. "Yeah?"

"I'm in the basement at the generator box. Reggie and Abe are with me," Clive announced from the other end of the phone.

"I'm about ten feet away. I'll be there in a few seconds," Jason replied.

All the major fuse boxes as well as the generator that was supposed to switch on if electricity was lost were in the basement. He'd paid a lot of money to have the generator installed in the old building, and he wasn't happy that it wasn't working. It had been approximately forty-three minutes since Clive had called to notify him that the electricity in the hotel had gone out. Forty-three minutes that his guests were left to wonder what the hell was going on.

He found the door and pushed through it to a number of flashlights glaring toward him. Holding up a hand he yelled, "It's me."

The lights switched toward the huge stone-gray box to the far left corner. "What's the problem?" he asked.

"It needs recharging," Abe, the janitor answered.

"Recharging? We've never had to use it," was Jason's slightly confused response.

"That's what I was thinking." This was Reggie, the building maintenance manager. He was a tall, gangly man nearing his fifties.

"How long until it's charged?" Clive asked.

Mike continued to crank something on the side of the box. "Should be just another few minutes."

"Thank God."

Jason had been listening to the conversation, which up until that moment had consisted of only men. But this last voice was that of a female. Lifting his light, he flashed it in the direction from which it had come. His circle of light landed on a familiar face.

"Hey." Sharrell waved.

Jason switched his light over to Clive while mumbling, "Hey, yourself."

Clive shrugged then redirected his attention to the generator. Within minutes they heard a rumbling sound then a low hum. A few seconds after the hum the lights overhead flickered and burned low.

"Finally," Reggie mumbled.

As the brightness continued to build Jason switched off his flashlight. "Clive, round up all the shift supervisors and get someone on each floor to check the guests. Give them whatever they need but assure them that everything is alright, and let's hope they don't want to check out."

He'd begun walking toward the door. Something very strange was going on at his hotel, and he was determined to find out what. He'd almost forgotten that Sharrell Markam was down there until he heard her voice again.

"You're going to hold people hostage after they've endured your self-imposed blackout?"

Jason turned abruptly, and she ran into his tall form. Clive reached out to grab hold of her elbow.

In a low, menacing tone, Jason asked, "What?"

"I think she means we should offer to make them as comfortable as possible." Clive interjected. "Even if that means finding them other accommodations."

Because he felt as if his head would explode, Jason closed his eyes, pinched the bridge of his nose then took a deep breath. "Of course I didn't mean we'd keep any one here against their will. I meant give them whatever they want—including reservations elsewhere." He opened his eyes to see Sharrell staring at him. He gave her a tight smile. "Is that all right with you?"

She shrugged. "Don't mind me. I'm just a guest."

That she was, Jason surmised. But she was a guest who worked for the enemy, who was the cousin of the woman he'd just decided to win over. He'd be remiss if he didn't question the Markams' involvement in what was going on at the Carrington. The flood in the kitchen came right after their meeting at which he'd turned down their offer with finality. And now, the blackout, and Little Miss Markam herself was standing right there witnessing the debacle. Surely she'd run back and report to her uncle.

Dammit.

David Markam and his family were still staying at the hotel. He'd graciously offered them a week's stay on the house in exchange for no hard feelings about the business deal. Crap. What else could go wrong?

He didn't say another word, but turned on his heel and stormed out of the room. The elevators were working by the time he'd made it to the main lobby.

Claire, the front desk attendant on duty, looked at him with wide eyes. "Mr. Carrington, the phone has been ringing off the hook. I don't know what to tell people. Some of them are getting quite rowdy."

Jason sighed deeply. "Give them whatever it is they want, Claire." He needed to get away. His head was spinning with thoughts, and he knew if he stayed in this hotel a moment longer he'd definitely explode. How had the life he'd mapped out so perfectly gone so wrong?

"Jason?"

Reluctantly he turned toward the voice. "What now?"

Clive approached him slowly. "Listen, man, I'll take care of this. I just wanted to let you know that Reggie thinks it was deliberate."

"What was deliberate? You mean somebody sabotaged the generator?"

Clive nodded. "Just like somebody took a sledgehammer to that pipe. We've got a serious issue on our hands. Somebody doesn't want Carrington Resorts to stay open. Now I can think of a few suspects, one of whom we just spoke about earlier, but right now you could use some rest."

Jason was pinching the bridge of his nose again, feeling the pressure building within. "What was she doing downstairs?" he asked his friend.

Clive sighed. "We were having dinner when the lights went out. I couldn't just leave her there alone. She's not involved if that's what you're thinking."

Jason wasn't totally sure what he was thinking right now. "There's nothing else we can do tonight," he admitted.

Clive looked relieved that the conversation about Sharrell Markam was over. "Exactly," he said. "I'll handle the backlash of tonight's fiasco while you get some rest. I'm going to need you bright eyed and bushy tailed first thing tomorrow morning though if we're going to get to the bottom of this."

"I don't know what's going on anymore, Clive. I thought we were headed in the right direction."

Clive clapped a hand on his friend's shoulder. "We are. Carrington Resorts will be a success, regardless of these amateur attempts to stop us. Now go on home and lay down."

Jason shook his head negatively. "I can't stay here another minute."

"I didn't mean your room here at the hotel. I meant your home—you know the one you bought but never stay in."

Realizing that Clive referred to the beach house he'd bought the year before, he felt a small measure of comfort creeping over him. "Yeah, I guess you're right. I might as well put the place to good use." Rubbing his hands over his face, he focused on his friend. "Thanks, man. I owe you one."

"Don't mention it," Clive responded easily. As Jason walked away, Clive thought that either he was going to receive a call from a completely outraged Jason in another hour or the next morning his friend would not only be relaxed but would be more focused on what to do about their hotel.

With a grin because he'd bet money the latter would prevail, Clive moved to the head desk to deal with the complaining guests.

The road leading to the beach house was dark and silent but for the crashing waves against the shore. Stepping out of the car, Jason inhaled the saltwater scent and walked toward the door. Key in hand, he pulled the screened door open and prepared to enter. A soothing sense of relaxation settled over him as apprehension prickled at the back of his neck.

Dismissing the conflicting emotions, he unlocked the door and let himself in. It was dark inside, but then he'd expected nothing less. It was late—the clock in the car had read just after 2:00 A.M. before he'd switched off the ignition. Although he rarely stayed there, his memory of the floor plan was good enough to guide him through the house toward the bedroom farthest in the back without having to turn on any lights. That was the master bedroom, the one with the king-size bed and fresh linens he paid a cleaning service to put on twice a month.

When his knees bumped against the edge of the bed, he stopped and stripped off his clothes, exhaustion pulling at his limbs and muscles. Reaching down, he grabbed the sheets, pulled them back and climbed in the bed. In an instant he was asleep.

He was holding her, whispering against her ear as his erection pressed against her bottom. They lay in his large bed, spent after hours of lovemaking, but eager to enjoy each other again. She scooted back farther, loving the feel of his hot length against her sensitive skin.

He palmed her breasts, squeezing until she moaned in response. He toyed with her turgid nipples until the pounding between her legs became persistent. She squeezed her thighs tightly then gave up and opened them, determined to let him slide home. Instead of his hot length she felt his fingers moving along her nether lips, searching, probing, and exploring the swollen flesh. Sounds of her creamy desire moving against his eager fingers echoed in her head, and she whispered his name. "Jason."

Her voice cocooned him, wrapping itself firmly around his entire being. He could smell her desire, could almost taste the sweetness being emitted from below. He stroked her, loving the feel of her small thrusts against his hand. Sinking his fingers deep inside her, he reveled at the warmth, the tightness around his skin. She was perfect, and he wanted her—now. That night. The next day. He simply wanted her. "Celise." Her name was a ragged cry.

"Yes, baby," she breathed.

With her response he didn't waste another minute but slipped gently inside her, moving with the gentle sway of her hips. They fit perfectly, their bodies responding to silent pleas and requests.

He moved deeply inside of her with consistency until he felt her thighs shaking, her breath coming in erratic spurts. She was so ready to explode and he'd been holding back only to ensure himself that she was satisfied. Now he could let go, he could completely focus on the wonderful sensations her body brought to him. His thrusts intensified, the friction between them rising to higher heights.

Her moans grew louder. His rougher, more pronounced with each stroke. They seemed primal, animalistic with their grunts and strenuous demands, each of them lost in the spinning abyss of pleasure until it was too much for either of them to bear a moment longer and they simultaneously soared into a mindless orgasm.

It was morning. She could tell because her body ached to get out of bed. The birds must have made themselves at home on the windowsill because she heard their bright chatter even before she could open her eyes.

Celise huddled beneath the blankets one last time before pushing them off her. A part of her hated to move because she'd slept so soundly, so comfortably. She hadn't slept like that in ages. Her nightshirt was twisted about her waist, revealing her nudity from the hips down. After her shower the nightshirt had been the only thing she felt like donning. She reached for the material, intending to pull it down then roll out of the bed when the mattress shifted and a long, heavy arm landed over her midsection.

She screeched and jumped out of the bed stumbling into the nightstand. With one hand over her mouth and the other over her frantically beating heart, she looked at the man lying facedown on the bed and yelled again.

"What are you doing here? And what..." Her voice trailed off as she noticed where he was staring. Pulling her shirt down as far as it could go, which wasn't even past her thighs, she looked back at him. She was about to ask him what he was doing there when she noticed a stickiness between her legs.

"What...did...you...do?" she asked slowly, even though she had a sinking feeling that the wonderfully vivid dream she'd had, the one that was the culprit for her exhaustive slumber the night before, wasn't a dream at all.

He rolled over, moving one muscled arm from where it had fallen in slumber over his eyes. Dark brown, very familiar eyes that were now staring at her.

"*I* didn't do anything but come home and get in *my* bed," he said in a voice still muddled with sleep.

Celise was already shaking her head. This could not be happening to her. Why was this happening to her?

"No. Please tell me this is not your house. Tell me he didn't bring me here knowing this was your house, knowing I didn't want to be anywhere near you again," she wailed.

Sitting up, the sheets fell at Jason's waist. She sucked in a breath praying they didn't go further, even though the unfettered view of his bare chest was enough to make her mouth water. A perfectly chiseled six pack revealed itself right along with beautiful pectorals that made her fingers itch to touch.

"Let me guess, 'he' is Clive. And the answer is yes. He knew exactly what he was doing when he brought you here." Jason reached back to adjust the pillows behind him then sat back to stare at her.

He didn't seem particularly alarmed to see her here, or about the fact that his friend may have brought her here without his approval.

"Did you tell him to do it?" She tried to avert her eyes, wanted so badly not to stare at him, but those thick, toned arms and that sculpted chest were just too tempting. He looked like she'd peeled him right off the pages of a *Playgirl* magazine. He was simply perfect with his dark, still sleepy eyes, strong jaw and goatee. Except for the fact that he was an ass for sleeping with her then getting his pleasure from another woman so quickly.

"No. I had no idea you'd be here." But he didn't look the least bit displeased about it either. "Listen, Celise, there's something we need to get straight."

"No." She shook her head and was moving around the bed to find her bag and her clothes. "There's nothing...nothing between us...nothing to get straight."

Before she could pass the bed, he was up, reaching out and grabbing her arms. He was gloriously naked and still she flailed to avoid him. He'd caught her off guard so they both fell back onto the bed—he on his back and she on top of him.

She struggled to break free of his grasp but that only increased their contact, increased the heat building between them. Her response was instantaneous, warmth and moistness pooling between her legs. He must have felt it, too, because when she looked down at him she saw his eyes darken, his lips part slightly. She felt his erection poking into her just as it had the night before and knew she wanted to feel it again. She wanted him deep inside of her, knocking against her walls, searching and finding her spot, releasing her essence.

"I can't keep my hands off you," he whispered and stared at her as if daring her to deny him.

She sighed. "This is crazy."

He cupped her buttocks, pushing the hem of her shirt over her hips. "It's real."

"We can't." She sighed as his fingers sank into her pliant flesh. Then they moved, finding the crease and slipping inside to her warmth.

"Jason." As much as it disgusted her, she was breathless and had to admit that she wanted him again, and again and...

He lifted slightly, caught her bottom lip and suckled. "It wasn't what you thought."

She heard him through the haze of desire and moaned. "That doesn't work. There was only one thing to think." His tongue scraped her bottom teeth, and she opened her mouth, pulling him inside, stroking against his hot tongue the way she wanted him to stroke her. Conflict filtered through her mind, and she pulled back. "Did she return to finish the job?" she asked when her brain fought to overrule her body.

He tried to kiss her lips, but she moved back.

"No. She didn't come back. She's a woman from my past who paid me a surprise visit. I didn't encourage what she was doing and wouldn't have allowed it to go that far."

Celise frowned. "She was on her knees about six inches away from..." her words trailed off. She didn't want to say it, didn't want to think about what had been about to happen in that room with Jason and that woman.

When Jason had grabbed her and they'd fallen to the bed, her arms had been plastered at her sides. Now she moved a hand until she grasped his arousal. Control and doubt battling inside her. "Tell me you would have stopped had she taken you into her mouth."

He closed his eyes and she could see him swallow, a muscle clenching in his jaw. Clearly he was having his own battle with control at the moment.

"I wasn't going to let her put her mouth on me," he told her though his voice was tight and constrained.

"Oh, really? Why? You don't like it?" His entire body was tense. She moved her hand upward then let it slide down his long shaft again, thoroughly enjoying the effect she was having on him.

"I like it—" Jason gritted his teeth—"when it's done by the right person."

His arms had grown slack around her, and she used that moment to lift slightly off him. "Hmmm, I wonder who the right person might be."

He moaned as her finger grazed the tip.

"If you're applying for the job, I'm accepting applications," he offered.

"That's good to know." Smearing the bead of moisture over the turgid head, Celise licked her lips, wanting to desperately take him. He was so long, so hard, so ready for whatever she wanted to do with him. If she thought about it really carefully she'd get up and grab her clothes and get the hell out of dodge, but she didn't think about it, didn't want to analyze what she was about to do. She simply wanted the pleasure.

Slithering down his body, she held him firmly in her hands, positioning him so that his erection was pointing straight toward the ceiling, her hand moving up and down its length with slow consistency. He was gripping the sheets. She literally and figuratively had him in the palm of her hand.

Dipping her head quickly she licked the next glistening bead of moisture from the head and smiled as he closed his eyes tightly. She had him right where she wanted him. Whether or not the mystery woman had come back to finish the job, Celise no longer cared. She was going to make him feel like no woman ever had before.

Tongue extended, she licked him from the base to the tip both on the underside and the outside. He shivered beneath her as her tongue circled the head again and again. She took the bulbous end into her mouth first, holding it tightly then keeping it in the cocoon of warmth while she toyed with him with her tongue. Moving her hands up and down, she continued this motion until tiny grunts came from Jason. His head was thrown back and his eyes were mere slits. When she was sure he couldn't survive another moment, she opened her mouth wide and took him until the head rested against the base of her throat.

"Hmmmmm," he moaned, then sucked in a breath and buried his fingers in her hair.

She lifted until he was completely clear of her lips then took him in deeply again. She repeated this motion over and over until his hands in her hair were directing the movements and his hips undulated beneath her.

"I told you I only like it when the right person is doing it," Jason said as he continued to pump inside her mouth. "You, Celise, are definitely the right person."

Completely aware of the fact that if she continued he'd release his passion into her mouth, Celise pulled back. "The only person," she whispered, her breath brushing over the straining skin at his tip. "Tell me I'm the only person," she demanded.

He let his hands fall from her hair to grab her by the arms. Pulling her up the length of his body, he crushed his lips down on hers then whispered against her wet mouth, "You are definitely the only person."

He grabbed her again by the buttocks, pressing his fingers so hard into her skin she almost screamed. Celise almost stopped him as painful memories tormented her. Then his hands slipped away and she breathed a sigh of relief. He reached over to the table by the bed, pulling the drawer out to retrieve a condom.

He slipped it on then growled, "Now ride it like you really want it." He opened her wide and thrust his manhood into her in one swift motion.

Celise raised up over him until she was sitting down, her thighs straddled over his, his erection embedded deeply inside of her. "My pleasure."

CHAPTER ELEVEN

Jason had slept lightly as outside the sun rose higher in the sky. A golden haze filled the bedroom as the scent of their lovemaking hovered. Now he was awake and being tormented by the feel of her voluptuous body wrapped around his.

Without another thought, and because he simply couldn't help himself, his hands roamed, gliding all over her, feeling her curves, her nakedness. The first time he'd slept with her he'd thought her a wonderful lover, now he changed that assessment. She was beautiful, responsive, accommodating, and dangerous in her assault against his body, his senses. She was everything he'd ever dreamed.

He looked over at her as she lay on her stomach, one leg tossed over his, her arm over his waist. Her face was only partially visible as her hair fell in messy wisps around her. But he could see her long lashes as they fanned along her smooth skin, the curve of her cheekbone and the slight pout of her lips. She looked peaceful and pretty and innocent and fresh. Jason couldn't resist. He reached out and touched a fingertip to her cheek. Gently he pushed the hair aside so her face was free from obstruction. He rubbed the soft strands between his fingers smiling at the thought that she was here with him, in his house, his bed. And he wanted to keep her there forever.

She moaned and shifted slightly, moving closer, her arm hugging him tight while her leg slipped between his. Adjusting to this new position Jason moved so that her head was now resting on his shoulder. Pushing her hair back once more, he kissed the top of her head, and then let his hand slide down her arm.

"Mmmmm. I'm hungry," she murmured against the crook of his neck.

His other hand moved to touch her knee, lifting her leg higher. She was so soft and warm pressed against him and his body reacted instantly. He stroked along her thigh, and then cupped her bottom, slipping between her legs to touch her waiting warmth. She was wet and hot and Jason shuddered. "So am I."

Circling her hips, she grinned up at him. "I mean for food. I didn't have dinner, remember."

He didn't want to stop touching her, didn't want to stop where they were undoubtedly headed, but realized that she was in his house, in his bed. He would have another opportunity to love her again—of that he was certain. On a reluctant groan he slipped his hand out of her and wrapped his arms around her body, pulling her up so that his lips could reach hers. With a loud smacking kiss he smiled up at her. "Goldilocks ate the porridge *before* she climbed into bed."

She grinned. "Your door wasn't open. I had a key and an escort thank you very much."

The only people who knew about this place were his family and Clive. And the only person who had a spare key was Clive. "He didn't tell you it was my house, huh?"

She shook her head. "I wouldn't have stayed if he had."

Brushing strands of hair back behind her ear, Jason looked deep into her eyes. "Remind me to thank him for not telling you."

Half an hour later they'd showered and were in the large kitchen. Jason sat at the island on a wooden stool, a mug of hot coffee in front of him. He'd slipped on running shorts and a T-shirt while she'd donned a sundress that barely capped her knees. He hadn't watched her dress as much as he'd wanted to. She was hungry, and the shower together had been tempting enough. He absolutely could not keep his hands off this woman, so he'd grabbed his clothes and made the pretense of getting coffee started to leave her alone.

Now he stared at her over the rim of his cup wondering devilishly if she'd put on underwear and if so, how soon he could get them off her. On another note—a more sane and mature note—she looked right at home in his kitchen. After a brief tour she'd found everything she needed with ease and had the aroma of his coffee mixed with eggs and whatever she'd sliced and diced to go inside their omelet floating throughout the room.

"Somebody's sabotaging Carrington Resorts," he said in an offhanded manner. He could trust her. He didn't really know why he was so sure of this, but he'd felt that strongly from the moment he'd first met her. She might be David Markam's daughter, but she was *his* lover. He knew things about her he was sure no other man knew. He trusted her, and he valued her opinion.

She'd been stirring the egg mixture about to pour it into the hot skillet when his words stopped her. She tossed him a look over her shoulder. "What?"

He nodded. "Yesterday morning a pipe burst in the kitchen. It was just inspected four months ago. It had a huge gash in it like someone had deliberately split it open."

Butter sizzled in the pan and she turned away from him to empty the egg mixture into the skillet. "Pipes burst all the time. Did you call a plumber?" she asked while she worked.

"Yes. He agrees that it was deliberate. And last night there was a blackout."

She looked over her shoulder at him and asked, "In Monterey?"

"No. Only at Carrington Resorts. The generator didn't even kick in." He took a sip of his coffee, waited a beat for her response.

"Hmph. That does sound weird." She flipped the fluffy omelet and slid it onto a plate. Then carrying two plates filled with their breakfast, she moved to the island to sit across from him. "Do you have any idea who or why?"

He looked down at the plate she'd set in front of him. It smelled wonderful, and his stomach growled.

"I knew food was a good idea." She'd smiled when he looked up at her appreciatively. "And just think if you'd had your way we'd still be in the bed."

Sinking his fork into the omelet, he glanced up at her. "We'll be back in bed shortly. This will give me a little more energy."

He stuffed a forkful into his mouth and was enjoying the taste, the coffee, and the company more than he thought he may have ever enjoyed a brunch with anyone else. Then she asked him a question he'd been expecting last night, but surely not at this very moment.

"Who was she? The woman in your suite last night, I mean."

Jason tried not to frown and replied, "Pamela Walker. A woman I used to be involved with."

"And let me guess: She's looking to rekindle the flame."

He paused a moment. "I don't really know what she's looking for." He reached across the island, grabbing her wrist. "Whatever it is, I'm not a part of it.

Things ended badly between us, but they definitely ended. I don't move backward."

She shrugged. "Your personal life is your business."

Her words caught him off guard, but the fact that she'd easily slipped her arm from his grasp hadn't. "What does that mean?"

"I just mean that who you get involved with is completely up to you, but I don't sleep around, so I'd like a heads-up when you decide to move on. Sharing is not my thing."

But apparently it was his thing, or so she believed.

"I don't sleep with more than one woman at a time. Despite what you might think, I'm actually very frugal in choosing my bedmates."

She arched an eyebrow. "Is that my official title? A bedmate?"

Hell no, he wanted to yell. She seemed a little too at ease with this conversation, like she was the one trying to tell him something. He'd decided the night before that he wanted much more from her, and he'd figured out how he was going to get it before the blackout. Coming here and finding her in his bed had been a pleasant shock. That morning, he knew with even more certainty that he wanted Celise Markam in his bed and in his life. "What title would you like?"

"Whatever, as long as we're both clear on the terms."

"Which are?"

She found his gaze, and for a moment Jason thought she was going to say exactly what he was thinking. Her eyes seemed to say 'I want to be with you and only you forever' and yet the squaring of her shoulders sent a different message entirely.

"This thing between us, albeit as good as it is—" she smiled—"is only temporary. When it's over, we both go our separate ways. No hard feelings, no regrets."

A lump formed in his throat as his anger rose. She was being quite flippant. He wondered if she were doing it on purpose. "Temporary, huh? Is there a time limit on this little arrangement?"

She shrugged again then chewed contemplatively. Resting her elbows on the marble island top she swallowed. "Let's just ride it out."

Oh, and she could ride, he recalled, his thoughts shifting. Her smooth skin called to him. Her breasts, which he knew for a fact were unbound because her nipples had been playing hide and seek with him the entire time they were in the kitchen, beckoned him.

His appetite for food was gone, being replaced by a bigger one in which she was the appetizer, the entrée and dessert all rolled into one. In a quick motion he was beside her, lifting her by the hips until she sat on the island top where they'd been eating. "You really should be careful what you say to me." With a flick of his wrist the top of her sundress was down, releasing her plump breasts. "The thought of you riding something is just too tempting to ignore."

Dipping his head, he took a large, distended nipple into his mouth and suckled.

Her hands immediately went to the back of his head, guiding him as she arched her back for better access. "You're quite tempting yourself, Mr. Carrington."

Cupping both breasts, he pushed them together, tracing his tongue down the crease then pushing both nipples into his mouth simultaneously. Her talk of this temporary thing between them enraged him, pushed him to the point where he had to give her another example of why temporary just wouldn't work. He lifted her legs and wrapped them securely around his waist. He pushed his shorts roughly down his thighs, allowing his burgeoning erection its liberty. She gripped him tightly, and he moaned.

Celise lifted her dress, scooted closer to the edge of the counter, moving as if she were impatiently waiting for him to enter her. "Now," she said, gasping.

Heady with lust and even more excited by her command Jason gripped her tightly. She was passionate and uninhibited, and he was completely taken by her. "You ready for me, baby?"

The tip of his arousal grazed her moistened center, and she almost slipped right off that countertop she was so eager. "Oh, yeah. I'm ready for you to give it to me."

Rubbing his hand up and down his shaft, Jason thought he'd burst with wanting her, but making her beg seemed just a little more alluring. "Tell me what you want, darling. Tell me how to please you."

"I want...I need..." She breathed heavily. "Please, Jason, just do it. I just need you to do it now."

"Fine," he said with a slow grin. "I'll tell you what I want. I want to bury my tongue deep inside you. I want your hands on my head, guiding me, feeding me. Do you want that, baby?"

She squirmed and moaned. "I want your lips, your tongue, and to suck your length until you explode. Then I want you buried inside me, until I'm so full I can't think or breathe or...Jason, please now!"

Drops of his own arousal covered his tip, and he rubbed them off with his finger then brought it to her lips. When she sucked his digit hungrily, he shivered. In the pocket of his shorts he'd stashed a couple of condoms and didn't waste another moment slipping one on.

"Open up and let me in," he murmured as he rammed his length inside of her until his testicles bounced at the base of her core.

He thrust into her hard and deep so that there was barely a breath between them, then he stilled. "Do you really want this?"

Celise groaned. "Oh yes, I really want it." Securing her legs even tighter around his waist, she arched her back and felt his thickness stretching her, filling her completely.

Jason pulled back. "You will always want it." He thrust into her again, stood still again, then pulled out slowly and rammed his throbbing erection into her milky center once more. "Today. Tomorrow. And every day after that, you'll want it, need it."

She had to because that's how he felt about her. He moved his hips in a circular motion as he lowered his head touching his lips to hers. His tongue stroked over hers, masterfully filling her mouth just as his thick length filled her core.

Celise was helpless against him and knew that he was absolutely right. She did want all of him and too much of him. Nobody should want like that. She shouldn't feel as if her life hinged on whether or not he was in it. Yet, she did. The thought bothered her, but the heat building inside her conquered the doubt.

Her nails sank into the skin of his shoulders, and she shifted her hips, trying to get closer, to take him deeper. She heard the smacking sound of her arousal against his, smelled the heady scent and longed to feel just a little bit more. Slipping her hand between them, she felt his damp shaft as it moved in and out of her. Wrapping her fingers around it, she guided him, feeling her own wetness on her wrist and the palm of her hand. Reaching farther, she held his testicles, toying with them until he groaned.

"Who would ever guess there was this side to you?" he said, whispering in her ear.

"It's only for you," she replied honestly as he thrust inside her again.

"It had better be." He cupped her buttocks and lifted her from the island, lowering her to the floor where he directed her onto her knees and smacked her upturned bottom.

The sound echoed in the room, and Celise turned back to look at him. Her heart skipped a beat in that second, memories flashing before her eyes.

"I'm sorry, baby. Did I hurt you?" he asked, concern evident in his voice.

She swallowed, reminded herself that this was a different man, in a different place and tried to smile. "No. It's okay."

He rubbed the spot he'd previously smacked gently then moaned. "You have a great ass. It's so round and so plump. I get hard just looking at it." He continued to rub and knead her cheeks, grasping them harder each time until his fingers dug into her skin.

Celise moaned against the pleasurable sensations rippling through her. Surprised, yet knowing she needed it as confirmation she said, "Then you can smack it all you want."

He did and she moaned again. Shivering as delight rippled throughout her body. There was a sting but it was edged with something else that aroused her immediately. He traced a finger down the crease of her bottom and she grew stiff, waiting, wondering, fretting, until he sank once again into her moistness.

Celise was on her hands and knees, opening herself to his perusal, his assault and loving every minute of it. A few months ago she wouldn't have imagined herself in this position again or demanding that a man touch her the way Jason did. It was at this point that she realized sex with Jason was like nothing she'd ever imagined. He smacked her again, and she felt a fresh stream of warm essence dripping down her thighs.

The next feeling Celise registered was Jason spreading her nether lips wider, his tongue lapping up the moisture. He inhaled deeply and she shook with desire. He licked her up and down and back again, his tongue finding her opening and swirling until she came with a violent shake and a deep, guttural moan.

"Fucking fantastic," he groaned.

Rising over her, he sank into her center then pounded against her as if he were trying to tell her something with his actions.

She bucked back against him, taking in his complete length, feeling him until she'd swear he was buried deep in her stomach. She was so wet, so aroused and so completely into his lovemaking she couldn't think of anything else. He pumped into her fiercely, and she found herself wanting more and more.

What was this power he had over her body? A simple touch, a look, a kiss, and she was melting in his arms. He worked her like she was his prize project, like she'd been made explicitly for this purpose. And she wasn't complaining.

Suddenly, he pulled out of her, shifting them until she lay on her back, panting, breasts heavy and heaving.

"So you think this is temporary, huh?" he asked.

She opened her mouth to speak but he lifted her legs until they rested on his shoulders and pistoned into her once more. She struggled to catch her breath.

Then he pulled out just as quickly, rubbing the tip of his dick over her engorged clit, down the slippery surface to her center and back up again. Celise was gasping, her hands slapping against the floor.

"You want this, don't you?" He smiled down at her.

Was he crazy? Smiling and teasing her like this. "Hell yes, I want it!" she scream. All inhibitions were lost. She wanted him, and she didn't care who knew it.

"Then take it. Take what's yours."

And she did. Wrapping her hands around his thick erection, she slipped him inside of her and lifted her hips to take him completely.

"I said take it," he repeated vehemently.

She shifted, so that her feet were now on the floor. Lifting slightly she undulated her hips, working him as he kneeled above her looking down at her as if she were the only person on earth. His jaw clenched, his lips barely parted. Then his eyes closed, and he gripped her knees, pushing them farther apart. Celise had no idea she was that limber.

"Jason," she whispered his name as her head thrashed from side to side. "What are you doing to me?"

"I'm taking what's mine," was his gruff reply. "I want you to know exactly where we stand. You. Belong. To. Me."

Every word was punctuated by a deep stroke in, a slow pull, out, deep stroke in, slow pull out.

Then Jason began to pump quickly, fiercely, until his passion burned for release. Temporary? She'd said this thing between them was temporary? Hell no, this wasn't temporary! He was taking every bit of her, now and forever. He wouldn't have it any other way. And he was going to mark her so she would never forget that fact or him.

He pulled out of her, grabbed his penis and with one stroke removed the condom. He continued working his stiff rod until his essence spilled onto her belly. He grunted and moaned, even as he guided it to her breasts, watching as the murky liquid swirled over her nipples, slid down the sides of her breasts, beneath the heavy mounds, until it was all over her. He was all over her. He lowered himself, connecting their upper bodies. She dutifully wrapped her legs around him, connecting their lower bodies.

He looked down at her. "Now you know the terms," he whispered before thrusting his tongue inside her mouth.

CHAPTER TWELVE

"So have you thought about staff?" Jason asked as they walked down Cannery Row. They'd left his cottage on McAbee Beach just after five. Celise wanted to finish her exploration, and he simply wanted to be with her.

"I want to start with something small—simple, yet unique." She smiled at an elderly couple who passed them. "Because I want an international menu I'll have to hire at least two additional chefs. A manager is a definite. I went to school with a woman who'd be terrific for that job. I've already contacted her. She's very interested."

"And how soon will you expand?"

"That depends on how well I do."

Jason looked down at her questioningly. "Do you doubt it?"

She looked up at him, then away with a slight shrug. "No, not really."

"Neither do I. That's why I'm thinking you should visualize a little bigger. There's this big cook-off at the hotel in a few days, and I'm sure there'll be lots of chefs and people in the culinary industry. You should definitely check it out."

"Really? That sounds great."

"Not as good as an early dinner," he said, guiding her into the Duck Club. "I'm starving."

Celise smiled and walked through the doors ahead of him. "You're always starving."

"That's because a certain female keeps depleting all my energy."

She didn't blush, but he knew memories of their morning romp glittered fresh in her mind. As he spoke to the host Jason noticed her scoping out the establishment. She would be looking at their set-up, peeping out the menu, inhaling the scents of whatever was being prepared in the kitchen. Determined to make her restaurant a success she was like a sponge, soaking up all the local information she could get. He liked that about her. Another thing Jason liked was when he reached for Celise's hand, she came to him willingly, placing her hand in his without question. He kissed her forehead because words could not accurately express what he was feeling right at that moment.

"The food here is pretty good, especially the Dungeness crab." He rubbed his hands up and down her back, loving the feel of her so close to him. They were having a great day, and he was loath to think of anything that would change that. Besides, he'd called Clive earlier while Celise had napped. After thanking his friend for bringing Celise to his place, Jason found out that things at the hotel were just as he'd thought. A record number of guests had checked out, but then a good amount had stayed, and they'd actually had some walk-in tourists reserve the spots just vacated. News would spread around the community and the next week would tell how bad the blackout had hurt them. Until then, he wasn't going to think about it. Clive assured him that he was doing everything he possibly could, and in retrospect Jason had to admit that there wasn't much more he could have done if he were there personally. So Clive's urging that he take the day off only coincided with the idea he'd had of spending more time with Celise.

She hadn't seemed to mind his company that morning, and he'd proven to her that exploring Monterey was much better with an experienced escort. Now they were seated and he hated that he couldn't continue holding her.

"You know you have to have seafood on the menu," he remarked as he picked up the menu and perused.

She chuckled. "I wouldn't think of leaving it out. With the town's rich fishing and cannery history, I'd be doing a grave disservice if I omitted it. But seafood can be weaved into so many different cuisines."

"I know. I keep telling Peter to bring in more of the fresh seafood. The locals would love it, and they'd tell their family who came down for vacation to stop in and try it."

"Is Peter the only chef you employ?" she asked.

He nodded. "Pompeii isn't that busy during the day. He's only really needed for the evening shift. That's why I had the thought that another restaurant would be a great idea—to sort of fill in the gap."

They ordered appetizers, and she sipped on water with lemon. "I agree. And the penthouse space would be great for it. The view alone is awesome."

Her eyes actually danced as she'd said that, and Jason knew that her comments were his ticket in. "So I'm thinking that with the view and open seating we could really reel them in with signature menus, local cuisine as well as original international dishes. I'd have to find a great chef though."

"I could recommend some for you. You should decide on the specialties you'd like and then start your search. Traditional seafood and maybe complete French and American entrees would be good. Then Pompeii could focus on the lighter menu with an eye towards Greek specialties."

"You're right." *And you're beautiful.* Where had she been all his life? It didn't really matter because she was here at the moment, and he planned to keep her for a very long time.

Her appetizer had arrived, and she chewed plump, slightly seasoned shrimp as she continued to think. "You could have a grand unveiling, maybe have a local contest giving away a free weekend and daily meals at the new restaurant. Good promotion is key too. I took a few marketing classes so I'd be well versed in the industry. If nobody knows about you, they won't come."

His brother Jackson had told him the same thing when he'd first purchased the hotel and since Carrington Enterprises was one of the top mergers and acquisitions companies in the country, he figured Jackson knew what he was talking about. Jason thought he'd done a good job with marketing. The booking of the cook-off was minor proof of that, but she was right, with all that was going on he really needed to step up his game.

When he'd mentioned his brother's advice and how he may have been foolish not to follow it just because he was the younger brother trying to prove a point, Celise began talking about her family. She told him about DJ, the older brother, Isaac, the middle brother who never left San Francisco, and her cousin who was more like a sister.

She talked freely about everything, from growing up the only girl and the youngest child to losing her virginity in college. What she didn't mention was her relationship with Nigel Bingham, and that concerned him. Something had happened between the two of them, something that she obviously wasn't willing to talk about. That meant that whatever had happened couldn't be good.

As if that thought wasn't problematic enough, Jason frowned when he saw one of his biggest opponents in their small, elderly packaging enter the restaurant.

Celise must have followed his gaze. "Oh, the Hampdens. I met them yesterday. They're a very…unique couple."

"You met them?" His attention was back on her. "Where?"

"After I left you in the afternoon. I was sightseeing and shopping, and she sort of ran into me, and began talking."

"What did you talk about?"

She finished off her last shrimp and looked at him thoughtfully. "To tell you the truth I really don't know. I mean it was like listening to a story of riddles. Mrs. Hampden talked more than her husband. He just smiled and nodded. But it all centered around Monterey and how you're destroying their beloved hotel."

She thought that was funny and laughed a bit until she saw his glowering had darkened. "It's not a big deal. They're old and don't like change very much. I told her I thought you were doing a great job with the hotel. I got a scolding look then as she believes I'm smitten with you."

What she left out was the statue of the Regency she'd purchased for him then crushed after seeing him with Pamela.

Still, her explanation seemed to relax him a bit. Celise had noted the immediate tension in him the moment he saw the couple.

"And are you?" he asked.

They were lucky enough to get a patio table and when she looked up at him again she noticed the sun was a bright backdrop to Jason's utterly gorgeous features. He was all man, complete with bulging muscles and superior strength. And then he was a gentleman, opening doors for her, walking on the curbside of the sidewalk, taking her by the hand as they crossed the street. Almost like a prince right out of the pages of a fairy tale.

"Am I smitten with you?" She repeated the question, knowing the answer but wondering if she should reveal so much, so soon to him.

Then they were interrupted when huge crab legs were set before them. Steamed broccoli, fresh coleslaw, summer squash and a bowl of golden, melted butter occupied the rest of the table, and her stomach growled.

"I'm smitten with the way you feed a lady, that's for damned sure," she said picking up her fork and preparing to feast.

And for the next half hour nothing mattered more to Celise than this man and this meal.

"Funny, I thought we were actually going to spend some time together on this trip."

Nigel turned in the chair. He'd been escorted to a large conference room while he waited for the infamous Jason Carrington to return. They'd had a meeting scheduled—a last-minute meeting to which Jason had reluctantly agreed. He'd been waiting for about fifteen minutes already but he didn't mind. The outcome would be worth it.

Her voice held a slight edge, her eyes a dangerous gleam that he'd come to know very well. Pamela Walker was every man's dream. Hot sex on a platter— that's what he liked to call her. She was amenable to all his demands, and Nigel reveled in being the master puppeteer where she was concerned. She was insatiable and eager to please.

She wore a black dress, snug around her hefty breasts, tight at the waist and flaring out to give a man a migraine trying to figure out what was beneath all that material. But he didn't have to worry. He knew full well what was under there and felt an urge to have himself a taste.

"Do I detect hostility?" he said almost gleefully. Pumping fiercely into an angry, aroused Pamela was one of the biggest highlights of his life.

She closed the door behind her.

"You didn't visit me last night." Her voice had changed to that of a pouting child.

Nigel loved to play games. One of Pamela's amazing sexual talents was her ability to role play. Oh, how he enjoyed the roles she played, especially when she was demure and he could take control.

"I had some business to attend to," was his cool reply.

She stopped about a foot away from him, oozing sex appeal and eager to give him whatever he asked. A lesser, inexperienced man would have leapt out of his chair in a hurry to get his hands on all her tempting goodies. Nigel, on the other hand, was a master at waiting, biding his time, until things were just as he wanted them.

Still, he recognized what was going on here. Pamela was feeling insecure after her botched meeting with Carrington. She was feeling undesirable and needed some reassurance. Nigel really didn't have time for this, especially now that he knew Celise was close by. After seeing her two nights ago at that beach house, he decided to focus his energy on making Little Miss Markam see the error of her ways, and then buying this damned hotel. But he acknowledged Pamela might still be of use to him.

Glancing down at his watch, he wondered if he had a few minutes to do her and send her on her way, before Jason Carrington made his appearance.

Without a word, Nigel stood, went to the door and clicked the lock in place, then turned to her. "Get over here."

A finger slipped into her mouth and slid sinuously over her bottom lip as she dropped her purse on the table and took a step toward him.

"I waited for you to come to me last night," she said slowly. "I'll stand here and see if you come to me now." Placing her hands on her shoulders, she slowly slipped each strap down until her breasts spilled from the bodice. Grabbing the heavy mounds, she toyed with her nipples feeling them harden, watching Nigel's eyes glaze.

She was trying to control him. He wasn't impressed.

"Don't touch my nipples," he told her in a low controlled tone. "Drop your hands to your side and stand still."

Pamela looked like she might object. Her dark chin length hair had been pulled away from her face by a black ban. At her neck a diamond choker gleamed, a stark contrast to her deep chocolate skin tone.

"Nigel," she said on a breathy moan.

"Do as I say, Pamela. Now." He didn't yell, but she got his drift because her hands dropped from her breasts so fast they jiggled.

Nigel loved to see her D cups jiggle. His dick was hard, leading him in slow purposeful strides across the room to her. "Take off your dress and be quick about it," he directed her.

She did as he said, looking up to him immediately when she was finished.

"I'm sorry. I just needed you so badly," she whispered, then cleared her throat.

"Your lips are dry. Lick them," he said. One hand moved to his zipper as he watched her tongue snake out to slide along her lips.

He grasped his turgid length, pulling on it with enough strength to cause his eyes to water. Tiny beads of arousal seeped from the tip and he clenched his teeth to keep from groaning.

"Turn around and lay across the table. I want your ass in the air, legs spread so I can see my pussy."

She turned instantly, leaning over the gleaming cherry oak table where she flattened her palms and turned her head sideways so she could look back at him.

"I said spread them," he directed and moved closer to her.

She reached back, red tipped fingers grabbing her thighs and pulling them apart. She wore heels, about five inches high so her ass was lifted just as he wanted. Nigel licked his own lips as he saw her glistening sex waiting for him to get inside.

He took another step, and guided his dick into her moist opening. She yelped as he pushed with enough force to move her along the table.

"Keep still and take it. This is what you waited for last night wasn't it?"

He pulled almost completely out of her, listened as she gasped with the loss.

"Yes, yes, this is what I waited for," was her desperate reply as she wiggled her ass cheeks in an attempt to pull him back inside.

Nigel smacked her ass so hard she cried out, tears welling in the corner of her eyes.

"This is what you want. Say it," he commanded.

She took a deep breath. "This is what I want."

"Then keep quiet and take it. And don't come until I tell you."

Pamela nodded and remained still. Waiting. Needing.

Nigel thrust quickly inside her. Enjoying. Reveling.

A few more deep pumps into her still, but hungry, core, Nigel felt his own release burning at the base of his spine.

"Come for me, now, Pamela. Come," he said control etching every syllable.

She hissed and her body convulsed. He moved deep inside her loving the feel of her essence coating his length. Pressing a palm to the base of her back Nigel pumped wildly until his own release spilled into her warmth.

Then he glanced at his watch once more and pulled out of her quickly. Turning his back to her he adjusted his clothing. When he turned to face her again it was to a deep feeling of disgust. This wasn't the woman he wanted to fuck. She wasn't the woman he needed to control more than he needed to breathe.

"Celise," was the name he whispered as he turned away once more.

Jason hated last minute appointments, but this one had intrigued him. What were the odds of David Markam and Nigel Bingham both requesting a meeting with him in the same week? He undoubtedly knew what Nigel wanted and could have easily instructed his assistant to get rid of him, but he wanted to meet the man who was fool enough to let Celise Markam go.

The appointment was for five-thirty, but he'd taken his time, wanting to test Nigel, to see if he'd wait. Glancing at his watch he noted that he was only a half hour late then only lifted a brow when he was informed that, as of the last time she'd checked, Mr. Bingham was still in the conference room.

With stealth steps he made his way down the hall, completely prepared for what he would do, not the least bit disturbed by the prospect of turning the man down face-to-face this time.

Jason pushed the conference room door open, first seeing only an empty room, then spotting the man standing near the large window. "It's a great view, isn't it?" he asked, closing the door behind him.

Nigel turned, straightened his tie and looked across the room to the man who would make him a millionaire. "That it is. That's part of the reason I'm here."

Nigel Bingham in person was different than what Jason had imagined. While still slim and undoubtedly in great physical shape, the slight graying at his temples and weathered look gave his age away, although Celise had already told him as much. He tried to picture Celise with this man then pushed that thought to the back of his mind. He wasn't here for that. He was here to tell this tenacious businessman once and for all that he wasn't selling.

Extending his hand as he grew closer Jason gave a weak smile. "It's nice to finally meet you in person, Mr. Bingham."

Nigel shook Jason's hand, looking at him as if he'd already sealed the deal to buy the hotel. "Same here," Bingham said smoothly. "Shall we have a seat?

They sat across from each other at the conference room table.

"So you know I want to buy your hotel," Nigel began.

Jason looked at Nigel frankly deciding he really did not want to waste any more time with this man. "And you know my hotel is not for sale."

"For now it isn't." Nigel tapped a manila folder on the table before pushing it in Jason's direction.

"Revenue is down. Your board's not going to be happy about that."

Jason ignored the folder, but he didn't ignore the slimy vibes he was getting from Nigel. "I'm quite aware of our financial situation. Just as I'm aware of what my board of directors will and will not be happy about. But just for the sake of argument, I need you to clarify one point for me."

Nigel nodded. "If I can."

"Who are you making a bid on behalf of this time? I have reason to believe your tenure with Markam is almost over." Jason really didn't know whether Nigel was officially working for Markam Inns and Suites, he'd simply taken a guess that the broken engagement would sever all ties.

A flash of fury shaded Nigel's eyes but he quickly rebounded. "That hasn't become public knowledge, which makes me curious about your sources."

Tension mounted between the two men for two totally different reasons. Jason had to struggle to control his temper as he summed up the man for what he was, a gold-digging opportunist who most likely only agreed to marry Celise because of her familial connections to an empire. The spark of greed was clear in Nigel's eyes. That spark was coupled by an edginess to the man's demeanor that had Jason thinking he might be more dangerous than he'd first considered.

"I only deal with the best of the best," Jason replied nonchalantly.

"Really?" Nigel resumed tapping his fingers on the table. "I wonder how long your little trust fund will hold up."

Jason could have responded. He could have also put his fist in this man's face. But neither action suited him at the moment. No, he was finished talking to Nigel Bingham. He hadn't liked him from their numerous telephone conversations, but he'd dealt with him because Markam Inns and Suites was very reputable in the industry. Once he'd found out his connection to Celise, he liked him even less. He was through tolerating the man. Standing, he looked down at Nigel.

"This meeting is over," he said simply.

"I'll double whatever Markam is offering you. And don't forget that I know what his last offer was," Nigel persisted.

Jason stopped two steps shy of the door and turned back to face Nigel. He was some character. If he had the capital to go double what David Markam had offered, he was sitting on a pretty good chunk of change. He couldn't help but wonder from where his funds were coming. Gut instinct said Nigel didn't intend to play by the rules. Jason decided, he didn't have to either.

"Save your money, Bingham. I'm not selling."

CHAPTER THIRTEEN

Dropping herself onto the couch, Celise lay her head back and sighed. She was bone tired. After meeting with a few seafood wholesalers in the area, she'd met with her new attorney who'd advised her that in this economy teaming up with a local restaurant would most likely be best, unless she intended to capitalize on her name and her father's reputation.

She wasn't keen on either idea. The problem being that this was a small town—a thriving tourist town, but a small town all the same. Accepting something new wasn't easy for the natives whereas the tourist season would promise a better result. But how would she survive in the off-season?

As if this news wasn't bad enough, she couldn't get Jason off her mind. She'd tried like hell to focus on business—to concentrate on the location and the scenery for her restaurant, the menus and the marketing. But try as she might, her thoughts just kept falling back to the man and the time she'd spent with him. And now that she was back at his place his scent filled the air.

So what was she doing here? She didn't know Jason well enough to be living with him. True, she knew his touch, his taste, his feel…but that wasn't the same. He wasn't her boyfriend, and whatever was going on between them had no chance of becoming permanent.

She had her own money. There was really no reason that she had to stay with him.

Except she couldn't bring herself to leave. She liked being with Jason—a lot. Probably too much. He didn't dominate her. He let her speak her mind and seemed to respect what she had to say. And he was a native—his insight and comments regarding the restaurant and the tourists was invaluable. The fact that he was from a very influential Monterey family—his mother had been born here—would help as well should she need a reference, although she didn't intend to use his family name anymore than she would use her own.

So she was still stuck on what her next step would be concerning both the restaurant and Jason.

Jason toyed with the hair on his chin, his gaze focused on the sun's rays reflecting off the slate-blue water. He'd been closed in his office for more than an hour, initially with thoughts of Nigel Bingham and what the man was really after.

It hadn't taken long for those thoughts to shift to Celise. What had she seen in the man? Opportunity? Escape? No, Celise didn't seem like the type of woman to stay in a relationship for either of those reasons. He remembered her conversation with her father, remembered her reaction to David Markam's harsh words. She loved her father that was obvious, and, like Jason, had probably spent the better part of her life trying to please him. But she couldn't do that if that wasn't what she wanted for herself. Jason admired her for having the strength to stand against family. He knew that wasn't an easy decision to make.

He wondered if Nigel had touched her. If he'd kissed her and made love to her. Closing his eyes to the thought, he knew that the possibility was almost definite. How could a man resist? He hadn't been able to. Even now he wanted nothing more than to sink inside her velvety warmth. With Celise he didn't feel this heavy weight pounding down. He didn't feel like he had to prove something. They met on even terms, blending together to create something he wasn't sure he'd ever find with another woman.

And what did all that mean?

He hadn't a clue.

Deciding it was better to deal with facts, with things he could control or at least understand, Jason concentrated on Nigel Bingham and David Markam. The two men were definitely interested in the hotel. But were they interested to the point of sabotaging his efforts to get the property for themselves? He wouldn't put it past Nigel. But for some reason felt that Markam was more on the level. Maybe because he was sleeping with the man's daughter. He wasn't really sure.

Curious, Jason swiveled in his chair until he faced his desk. He called his secretary and instructed her to find Clive. Settling back in his chair, he waited with thoughts running quickly through his mind. It was almost eight. He wanted to speak with Clive about his earlier meeting with Nigel, then he wanted to head home.

Home. He thought with a warm sensation forming in the pit of his stomach. For the past few years his home had been the penthouse with its dark, sort of foreboding furniture and the businesslike atmosphere. However, that day he was thinking of his beach cottage. He was thinking of the king-size sleigh bed across from wall-length windows. Of the fluffy white sheets and the bronze-skinned beauty laying atop them.

There was a knock at the door seconds before it opened, and Jeffrey Carrington entered. Closing the door behind him, Jeffrey walked in the slow, confident gait his sons had inherited. His dark suit accented the golden tone of his skin while the slight graying at his temples gave him a more mature, astute look—a look, his sons would undoubtedly inherit as well.

"Hi, Dad." Jason instantly stood and circled his desk. Reaching out a hand, he shook his father's and gave him a brief hug. "I wasn't expecting you."

Jeffrey loosened his tie and took the seat offered by his son. "I know. I didn't have an appointment," he said gruffly.

"That's not what I meant." Jason smiled and took his own seat. "You're my father. You don't need an appointment."

"That's what I told that little secretary of yours when she tried to announce me." Jeffrey chuckled.

Jason eyed the man he'd loved and respected all his life. He remembered trying so hard to be what his father wanted and then finally giving up. He also remembered the day his father gave him his blessing and told him he was proud that he'd raised such a good man.

"I'll cut right to the chase," Jeffrey began. "Your mother's worried about you."

Jason sighed. His mother always worried, if not about him then about his other two brothers. It was just her way. "I'm fine. I'll call her tomorrow and tell her that." Somehow he sensed that wasn't going to be enough.

"No. It's not just you. She's worried that her boys won't give her grandsons, that you'll spend your years alone." Jeffrey waved a hand. "You know all that crazy stuff she spouts."

"Yeah, I know."

"Anyway, she was talking about you this morning while I tried to have breakfast and read my paper, and then I saw the article about the hotel and the board of directors."

Jason sighed heavily. He'd seen the article as well. The board wasn't happy. But then he'd known that for quite some time. "They're a little impatient. You know how it is waiting to turn a profit."

Jeffrey nodded. "I do indeed. That's why I'm here."

Leaning forward Jason propped his elbows on his desk. "Really?"

"Yes. I'd like to offer to buy the hotel," his father said simply.

Jason couldn't help but chuckle, although he knew his father was perfectly serious. Lowering his head, he shook it negatively then returned his gaze to his father. "Dad, we've had this discussion before."

Jeffrey held up a hand. "Your board of directors wasn't threatening to sell out from under you before, son. Now the situation is a bit precarious to say the least. I don't want to see it end like that. If I buy you out, you'll make a good profit. The board will make a good profit, and you can go find yourself another hotel to turn around. Everybody wins."

Jason shook his head. "But that's not what I'm in business to do. I want to run a five-star hotel, not buy up every squandering resort I can find, fix them up and then sell them. I want the opportunity to build something great." Jason stood and looked out the window. "Like you did."

If anybody could understand Jason's drive and determination, it would have to be Jeffrey.

"Son, I know what you're trying to do, but you have to face the facts that this might not be the place for you to do it."

"It is the place," Jason said adamantly. Monterey was his home. It was beautiful, and it was prime for the type of hotel he wanted. And, if he let himself be totally real for just a minute, it was where Celise was planning to lay her roots. That alone had him digging in his heels with a little more gusto. "I'm not selling. Not to you. Not to David Markam and not to Nigel Bingham."

Jeffrey let out a low whistle. "You've had that many offers, huh?" Stroking the heavy beard at his chin as his son had done moments before, Jeffrey stood and paced the office. "Somebody must know something's up."

"Markam Inns and Suites have been trying for the last year to buy me out. His key man was Nigel Bingham. Today, Nigel made me an offer on his own." Jason turned from his father, knowing instinctively what he was thinking.

"Divide and conquer?" Jeffrey asked.

Jason shook his head negatively. "Nah, I doubt that." He thought of Celise again and of David Markam. The man loved his daughter, regardless of what she did or did not do for him, of that Jason was sure. If Nigel Bingham was still on Markam's payroll, Jason suspected it wouldn't be for long. Something happened to break up Celise and Nigel, and Jason was willing to bet that David Markam was working to find out what. There was no way the two men were in cahoots.

"Then you're in the middle of a war," he stated plainly.

Slipping his hands in his pockets, Jason nodded again. "I think I am."

The door opened and Clive stepped into the office.

Both Carrington men nodded in greeting and waited for Clive to state what had put such a glum look on his face.

"The cook-off people are threatening to cancel. They're nervous about the bad publicity."

Jason swore, dragging a hand raggedly over his head.

"We need to meet with them and reassure them that it's all good. I've set a meeting for tomorrow morning at nine."

The cook-off was one hundred plus guests, media attention and marketing possibilities beyond compare. They'd been working on this event for months.

Jeffrey sighed and looked at Jason pointedly. "You need an ace in the hole where they're concerned."

Clive nodded his agreement. "What we need is a big name that will guarantee a large turnout and sway the committee in our favor. Play up the media attention, the visibility of the hotel that will certainly boost revenue."

Jason listened to their words as he gazed out the window. The sun was just beginning to set, golden rays resting heavily on the sea. He knew what he needed. The heated sensation in his groin had been telling him all day.

"I need an angel," he whispered.

Her bags were packed.

She'd gone over this decision only about a million times and still came to the conclusion that she was doing the right thing. She wasn't ending their affair. And she wasn't running away from yet another issue in her life. Celise was simply establishing boundaries, giving herself the space she knew she'd need in the end. The one thing she could not deny was that each time she made love to Jason Carrington a part of her was forever lost to him.

She was a realist, and so the thought of love at first sight didn't sit well with her. But there was no doubt that she was experiencing some strong lust where Jason was concerned. She'd tidied up the cottage that afternoon, all the while squelching thoughts of coming to this quaint little house every evening after work. It was different from the mansion in which she was brought up. However, there was no doubt that money was not a problem for Jason Carrington. And not a necessity in her life. Independence and freedom were.

Jason didn't deny her either. The more she thought about him, the more he seemed perfect for her and the more conflicted she became.

As if the comparison were necessary she thought of the other men in her life. Nigel was a serious businessman. Nigel didn't give two nickels about whether or not she was pleased in or out of bed. His pleasure was all that mattered. And his pleasure usually caused her physical pain.

And her father, for all that he was a great man, was focused on business and appearances. Although there was no doubt he loved his wife, her mother hadn't had much of a life, taking care of three children and being a trophy wife had been her duty for as long as Celise could remember. And she was determined not to go down that road herself.

What she was doing quite successfully at the moment was giving herself a headache and, she finally admitted, stalling.

His keys rattled in the door, and Celise jumped up from the couch. Suddenly her heart was pounding, her palms sweating like a nervous child. Taking a deep breath she rubbed her hands down her jean-clad thighs, smoothed her hair back and prepared to tell him she was leaving. While she was going over her list of pros and cons, the thought occurred to her that she could have been gone before he returned. That could definitely be construed as running, and Celise was determined not to run away from problems in her life ever again.

"Hi," he said in that deep, sexy voice that melted her heart.

She managed a nervous smile. "Hi."

Without another word, he crossed the room, grabbed her by the waist and pulled her to him. He'd buried his face in her hair, inhaling deeply. His hands splayed over her back spreading warmth as he held her tightly to him.

"Hey," she said, struggling to breathe. "You act like you didn't just see me this morning." The embrace had been intense, a little too intense for an affair. It made her nervous, and she tried to pull away.

Jason reluctantly loosened his grip but continued to hold her. "This morning was hours and hours ago. I've missed you."

Could her heart dance a jig? Or was she having a heart attack at such a tender age? Celise didn't know. What she did know was this was not the type of affair on which she'd planned. A part of her wanted to believe that Jason missed her while another part—the smarter, realist part—wanted to brush him off and get going.

"You did not," she said trying for a joking tone.

He cupped her chin and directed her gaze to his. "That's not just something I toss around, Celise. If I say it, you can believe it."

If there was one thing she didn't doubt about Jason Carrington, it was his integrity. "You don't even know me," she whispered.

He looked at her closely, as if he sensed something was wrong. It almost felt like he could see right into her head and knew what she was thinking and feeling. Her heart hammered and she tried to pull out of his grasp once more, but he held her steady.

"How was your day? Did you speak with your banker?" he asked with tender concern.

Work was a safe subject, she thought. It would kill more time until she had to tell him she was leaving. But she was definitely going to tell him.

"I did," she replied finally.

Jason took her by the hand, moving to the couch where he led them both to sit.

"So what did he say?" he asked when he had her comfortably tucked in the crook of his arm, his hand rubbing absently up and down her arm.

"He said that my business plan was solid, that my ideas were great and that money was definitely not a problem," she repeated almost verbatim from her earlier conversation.

"But?" he asked instantly.

Because she couldn't resist the comfort zone he'd offered Celise dropped a hand to Jason's thigh as she talked. "He thinks I should team up with a local name, something that will convince the citizens that I'm planning to stick around for a while. He feels that tourist towns get a lot of here-now, gone-tomorrow businesses and that the people of Monterey may not readily patronize an establishment if they think that's the case. I don't agree."

Somehow he knew she wouldn't, but Jason was profoundly thankful to her banker for bringing up the subject and opening yet another door for him. "You're Celise Markam of Markam Inns and Suites. Your family has resorts and hotels all over the world. Why wouldn't you open a restaurant here in the picturesque town of Monterey? It's a goldmine."

"I'm not out for money. I have enough of that." She tried to sit up, but he held her arms tightly.

He offered her a smile, even as his fingers found her hair and released the thick mass from its binding. "I know you're not in it for the money, baby, but just put yourself in their shoes. You could have a restaurant anywhere in this world and most likely will one day, so what makes this one in Monterey so special? What are you offering that the citizens should not be able to refuse?"

She thought about his words, even though it was hard while his fingers massaged her scalp.

"I'm offering them good food in a nice atmosphere," she said, realizing that even to her own ears that sounded kind of mundane.

"Both of which they already have." Jason continued to massage her scalp and stroke her hair.

Celise was having a hard time thinking straight, his touch soothing and relaxing her until she wanted nothing more than to cuddle up and fall asleep. "The international cuisine will be different."

Adjusting them both slightly, Jason's hands moved from her hair to her shoulders where he began to knead. "I've got an idea that I think might begin to sway the locals." His voice had lowered to a rich timbre, gliding over her as smoothly as melted butter.

"What's the idea?" she murmured.

Her head lulled to one side. Jason dropped a soft kiss just beneath her ear, and then stroked his tongue over her sleek skin.

"Remember I told you about the cook-off at the hotel?" he began before nibbling along the line of her neck toward her shoulder. She wore a tank top, with thin shoulder straps that slipped off easily as his tongue claimed that spot with slow circles of torture.

"Mmmm hmmm," she said, moaning. What was going on with her? One minute she was ready to tell him she was leaving, the next he was asking her about her day, and now…now he was seducing her with his mouth.

"I want you to enter."

At that her head shot up. "What?" She turned to face him. "You want me to enter a cook-off? What will that prove to the town? That I can cook?"

"The proceeds from the cook-off go directly to the town. The exposure is phenomenal. Your name, your food and the idea of you opening a restaurant here will be all over the place."

She'd been frowning, but as he continued to talk, understanding set in. "They'll get the impression that you're serious about helping the town financially while sampling your food. You're getting to them on two counts at one event."

Celise narrowed her eyes. He had a point.

"And don't forget the fact that the event is being held at a historic Monterey resort now owned by a member of one of Monterey's most influential families," she stated.

Jason feigned surprise. "Is it really? I didn't even think of that."

"Yeah, I'll bet you didn't." She playfully pushed at him. He grabbed her wrists before she could completely pull away.

She felt safe with Jason. Why, she had no idea. But she didn't feel like she had to be anybody but herself. She didn't feel like he wanted anything but what she gave him. And that was a good feeling, one she never thought she'd have again. "Thanks for mentioning it to me. It does sound like a good idea."

With one quick tug he had her on his lap. "It is a good idea and a good opportunity," he told her. He lifted her arms, locking them around his neck after she'd shifted so that she now straddled him.

He continued, "And when you win, it'll give your restaurant hundreds of customers before you've even opened." Then he kissed her on the tip of her nose.

Celise could do nothing but smile. His thighs were strong and muscled beneath her. Her hands rested on his shoulders, and she felt the beginnings of arousal. In the last six months she'd avoided sex, avoided the chance to be criticized and used, but with Jason she longed for the intimacy, the connection they shared when they were stripped of everything except their sexuality.

She positioned her now throbbing center over his growing arousal and watched his eyes darken. Questions of whether this thing between them was right or wrong, temporary or otherwise, fled her mind.

She focused on the physical. The tangible facts. Sex was primal. Natural. And absolutely amazing with Jason.

Jason had driven as fast as the law would allow, in a hurry to see her again. The knowledge that she was there waiting for him had sustained him throughout the day, until the moment he'd walked through the door and saw her and her packed bags in the corner. Then there was only desperation to hold her.

All day he'd thought of sinking deep inside her warmth again, of her riding him until he exploded. He gripped her hips then thrust his straining erection upward to meet her core. His thickness brushed against her, and she shivered. "What did you have in mind?"

"Hmmm, I think I'd like to give you something," she told him. She sat up straight and grasped the hem of her tank top then pulled it over her head to reveal her naked breasts.

Jason sighed and rubbed his hands up and down her bare back. His gaze fell to the heavy globes and puckered nipples. His mouth watered, but he restrained himself.

"I should give you something—" she shimmied closer until her right nipple was only inches away from his mouth—"something that really shows you how grateful I am."

His hands went still on her back. He willed himself to remain still. This was her show, and he was curious to see where she would go with it.

"I...don't...know," he said, exaggerating each word so that his breath fanned over the ever-tempting nipples. She shivered, and he smiled. "I'll gladly take whatever you want to give me." And he meant exactly that. She called this an affair. He didn't agree. And he was determined to prove that to her.

Celise lifted her breast and fed Jason. He opened wide, taking in as much of her as he could before pulling back and nibbling hungrily on her nipple. She arched her back and with her free hand squeezed the other breast.

"Give them both to me," he whispered.

She obliged, pushing her breasts close together so that he could suckle them simultaneously. When Jason figured she couldn't take the torture another minute, she rose from her position on his lap and undid her jeans, slipping them down along with her underwear. He watched her with a heated glare. She saw him watching and slowed her actions. Then she put a finger in her mouth. She pulled the finger out, letting it slide slowly down the length of her naked body until it rested amid the triangle of dark curls between her thighs.

Jason shuddered. He swallowed as hard as he could and prayed he could hold on.

"Do you want some?" she asked coyly.

"After you," was his rugged reply.

She lifted her leg, resting her foot on the chair beside him. With fluid movements she opened her nether lips, spreading her arousal until a smacking sound echoed in the room.

Jason had removed his shirt and was now unbuttoning his pants to free his erection. Reaching into his pocket, he retrieved a condom and smoothed it down his length, all while keeping his eyes fixed on her finger—its in-and-out motion, the sight of it appearing and disappearing between her legs. Grabbing his erection, he stroked himself along with her ministrations. "Is it good?" he rasped.

She licked her lips and let her head fall back. "Oh, yes, it's good."

She was absolutely beautiful. Her bronzed skin was illuminated by the waning rays of sunlight peeking through the blinds. Her head thrashed wildly, her hair like a sheet of ebony satin. She worked intensely, fervently, trying to bring on her own climax. In that moment he admired her, he adored her, he wanted her so very much. He knew that this was her show, and she was supposed to be thanking him, but he couldn't take it any longer. Rising from the chair, he lifted her and lay her down in the spot he'd just vacated. Pushing her thighs apart he said, growling, "Don't stop."

She acquiesced. He watched her for endless moments before inserting a finger of his own alongside hers, groaning once more as she bucked and thrashed.

In and out, out and in, his finger moved with hers. His penis swelling until the point of bursting, Jason watched as her essence illuminated her core, the scent filtering through him like a powerful aphrodisiac. And then it was too much. Abruptly he pulled both their fingers out then lifted hers to his lips and suckled.

"I've never tasted anything sweeter," he whispered.

She sighed and moved her hand down to touch his chest. Jason slipped inside her with one hard thrust that left them both gasping. He pulled out and rammed into her again, some distant part of him wanting to punish her for the foreign feelings coursing through him. Another woman might have complained at the roughness, but Celise wrapped her legs around his waist and met him thrust for thrust.

Her voice, her body, everything about this woman was driving him mad until he couldn't think straight. He pulled out of her quickly then bent over to satiate the craving he'd been having all day. Cupping her bottom in his hand he pulled her center closer to his face. His tongue did not miss a spot as he licked and devoured every drop of her pleasure. She bucked against him, her breath ragged and distraught while he feasted.

Celise fell against the pillows of the couch like a rag doll, the intensity of her climax having depleted her. But Jason wasn't finished. Slowly she opened her eyes and watched him standing over her, stroking his still-hard arousal as he looked down at her center, her breasts and then finally her face.

"You said before that you weren't into sharing," he spoke slowly.

She only nodded in response.

"I'm a very jealous lover, Celise. I *won't* share you, in any way, with anyone." He was thinking of Nigel Bingham and of what Celise still held close inside regarding their relationship. He'd seen it in her eyes whenever they spoke about the man, and he'd felt it the first time he'd touched her. Whatever had happened between her and Nigel was still there between them, and he wanted her to know that he knew it.

She lifted up slightly, cupping his cheek in her hand. "I'm with you. And only you."

Jason turned slightly, kissed her palm and let the fact that he could easily love this woman wash over him. Then he slipped inside of her again, his racing emotions calmer, quietly humming with the anticipation of their culmination. He stroked her slowly then, pulling almost completely out of her only to sink into her creamy heat again. She sighed, rubbing her hands up and down his back, cupping his buttocks as he moved. He kissed her, long and deep. Finally, dragging his mouth away, he nipped along her jawline before resting at her ear. Inhaling her all-woman, sexy-as-hell scent, he whispered in her ear, "You are a part of me."

"Yes," she whimpered.

Jason felt himself nearing completion and knew she was once again close as well, but as badly as he wanted to watch her receive her pleasure, he wanted to hold her more. He pulled her closer, kissing her ear and making his way back to her lips. His heart hammered in his chest as he stroked her long and slow. He kissed her, his tongue stroking over her lips, then dipping inside one last time. "Celise," he said, groaning before the telltale sensations began and he felt himself spilling deep inside of her. "You are mine," were his last words before they both succumbed.

CHAPTER FOURTEEN

"I can't believe she agreed to do it," Clive said from his seat at the bar.

"What's that supposed to mean?" Jason frowned then took a sip from his glass. "I asked her, and she agreed."

Clive lifted a brow in question. "Just like that?"

"Yeah, just like that. I mean, you know, I gave her all the pros to why something like this would be good for her image toward the town of Monterey. It'll be great exposure for her and her restaurant."

"Sure it will," Clive agreed. "And it's saving your ass as well. Did you mention that?"

Jason smiled. "That didn't come up."

Clive chuckled. "You're playing a dangerous game with her, Jase."

Jason instantly sobered. He didn't like Clive's tone, and he didn't like what his words implied. "I'm not playing any game with her."

"No?"

"No. I'm not. All our cards are on the table." More so than even Clive knew. Clive was his best friend, but there was no way he was about to tell him that he was falling for Celise and she was stuck on keeping their dealings strictly sexual. That was his problem—one with which he needed to deal on his own terms.

"What happens after the cook-off? And after this fascination with her wears off?" Clive asked.

Jason was so beyond being fascinated by Celise he couldn't even explain it. "Everything is going to work out. We're all going to get what we want in the end."

"I sure hope so," Clive said, looking away from his friend toward the attractive female heading their way.

"What the hell is this?"

Clive's smile shifted as a bright-colored sheet of paper was thrust in his face. Jason leaned in the opposite direction to give her room as she began her tirade.

"This is not funny. We can sue you for slander or defamation or for whatever. My family is not an advertising tool for you two or this dwindling hotel you're trying to save," Sharrell ranted, looking back and forth from Jason to Clive as she did.

"Whoa. Wait a minute," Clive said, clasping her wrist and finally taking the flyer from her hand. He looked at it briefly then placed it on the bar so Jason could see it as well.

Jason frowned but decided since Clive looked pretty familiar with Celise's cousin he'd let him handle it.

"I know my cousin did not agree to headline this little cook-off thing for you. And where is she? Are you holding her captive?" She tossed this question at Jason.

Jason held up both hands in mock surrender. "I'm not in the business of keeping women who don't want to be kept," he said with a shrug.

"Just what are you in the business of, because your hotel is going to hell in a hand basket," Sharrell spat.

Jason stood. Clive did the same, putting a hand on Jason's arm unnecessarily. It wasn't his personality to physically lash out at any female. But he would put the other Miss Markam in her place.

"What goes on in my hotel is my business. I didn't ask you or your family to come for a visit," he said, staring the smart-mouthed vixen down. "And as for your cousin, it's high time your family respected her wishes and let her be an adult."

Sharrell was not one to be cowered. Jason had figured that much since she ran a five-star hotel in the biggest tourist town in the United States. He also presumed she'd handled bigger and meaner men than he. Still, he had a point to make and he was determined to see that she understood that fact.

She'd squared her shoulders and stared up at him in the same manner that Celise probably would have. "You don't have the right to tell me about my cousin when you've known her all of five minutes. I know Celise wouldn't put her name to such an insignificant affair for a hotel that—"

It was at that point that Clive decided to intervene. He stepped between Jason and Sharrell, putting his back to his friend and taking Sharrell by her shoulders.

"Just hold on a minute. If we're advertising Celise's involvement it's with her full permission. Furthermore, you're way out of line with your remarks about the Carrington. If it were as bad as you say, your uncle wouldn't be ready to sell his life away to get his hands on it," Clive told her.

Sharrell pulled out of his grasp. "As a part of Markam Inns and Suites it would definitely be a five-star hotel. But with him running it," she said, looking around Clive to Jason.

Clive intervened once more. "With him running it, Carrington Resorts is already a four-star hotel and can only get better with time. You can report that back to your uncle."

Jason stepped from around Clive. "I see why Celise is in such a hurry to get away from you people. You think that everything has to be your way or no way."

Sharrell took a deep, steadying breath. "Where is she?"

"If she wanted you to know, she'd tell you," Jason answered matter-of-factly.

Jason Carrington was handsome as sin. He was arrogant and too damned sure of himself. And he was defending Celise. This had Sharrell wondering just how involved the two of them were. "But she told you?" she asked.

Jason shrugged. "I can't run a hotel, but I can garner Celise's trust. Go figure."

"Look, I'm just worried about her. When I saw this flyer in the hotel, it made me worry even more. Can you tell me where she is? I need to talk to her."

"Do you want to tell her how to live her life too?" Jason asked.

Sharrell chuckled. "You may have her trust, but you obviously don't know her very well. Nobody tells Celise what to do. We give her suggestions and pray that she takes them."

"Maybe she's tired of all the suggestions."

Because Sharrell believed that Celise was finally at her max with living her life the Markam way, she conceded. "I just need to make sure she's all right."

Jason looked at her seriously, not with the simmering anger as he had a few moments ago, but with a guarded look instead.

"She's fine. I wouldn't let her do anything that I didn't believe was good for her or good for her career. She really wants to open this restaurant. I thought it'd be good exposure for her to do the cook-off so the people of Monterey would get a glimpse of what's to come."

Sharrell folded her arms over her chest and surveyed both men. They were both fine, successful black men. A woman would be proud to claim either one of them. While she leaned more toward Clive's quiet charm than Jason's arrogant charisma, she could certainly see why her cousin was spending her time with him.

"Just be careful with her. Her last relationship didn't end too well, and I think she's still a bit hurt by it," she warned.

Slipping his hands into his pockets, Jason looked as if she'd hit on a subject that interested him.

"What happened between her and Nigel?" he asked.

For a minute Sharrell looked shocked that he knew with whom Celise had been involved, then she took a seat on one of the empty bar stools and waited for the two men to join her. She ordered a ginger ale and sipped from the glass when it arrived.

"All I know is she was trying to do what her father wanted. Celise loves her family very much. A lot of times she loves them beyond herself. She's always known her father's plans for her, and while she still manages to do most of the things she wanted, in the back of her mind she still wants to please him."

"That's why she hooked up with a man as old as Nigel?" Clive asked.

Sharrell nodded. "Uncle David had been impressed with Nigel's business during his time with the company. He was grooming him to take over the western division of Markam Inns and Suites, but since the ultimate goal was for the company to be run by family he thought it would be a good match if Celise and Nigel married."

She watched as Jason took a sip of his drink, his fingers clenching the glass as he set it down again.

"Why didn't he just make Celise head of the western division?" he asked without looking at her.

"Celise has never really been into the business. Don't get me wrong, she could probably run a better hotel than you and I both, but that's because she's smart and she's observant, even to things that don't really matter to her. She's grown up in the business, but she's always had her own goals. Over the years they've shifted a bit, that's partly why Uncle David doesn't take her new venture seriously."

"So he figured if he married her off, that would settle her down," Jason finished for her.

Sharrell nodded. "Nigel was older, more mature, and steady—boring as hell, as Celise put it. But she gave it a try. They were engaged for a little over a year before she broke it off."

"And why did she break it off?"

Sharrell shook her head. "She really didn't go into details with me, which is unusual. That's how I know it really hurt her. Leaving Nigel broke her father's heart but she did it, so it had to be serious."

Jason simmered. Sharrell was only confirming what he'd suspected. Celise loved her father enough to become engaged to a man more than twenty years her senior, then she dumped him. Going against her father wasn't easy, and he could see her trying to deal with that. Nigel did something to her, of that he had no doubt. "If he put his hands on her…"

"Jase, calm down, man. We don't know what happened. Whatever it is, Nigel's still real interested in getting his hands on the hotel, and I'll bet Markam doesn't know that," Clive stated.

"No. I'm sure my uncle doesn't know. He hasn't officially fired Nigel yet because he was hoping that he could get Celise to come around, but I think Uncle David suspects something bad happened between them now as well. I heard him talking this morning to DJ about finding Nigel and getting to the bottom of this."

"Nigel is trying to make the deal behind Markam's back. He offered me double what your uncle did," Jason admitted.

Sharrell drummed her fingers on the bar. "Something's definitely going on. I know Uncle David doesn't know about Nigel's offer to you. Did Nigel call you directly?"

"Better than that," Jason said his temples throbbing either from the drink or the growing concern where Nigel Bingham was concerned. "I met with him yesterday. I believe he's staying at the hotel."

Sharrell looked surprised. "He's here in Monterey? He's supposed to be in New York."

"It seems there are quite a few unexpected guests at Carrington Resorts this week. Isn't that a coincidence?" Clive asked, giving Jason a knowing look.

Jason took another swallow of his drink. "There's no such thing as a coincidence."

"She's staying with who?" David Markam yelled.

Maddy waved a hand in his direction. "David, calm down. DJ, get your father a drink. She's staying with Jason Carrington at his beach house," she repeated.

Celise had just called her telling her where she'd gone and that she would probably stay there until she found an apartment. She also mentioned that Jason was advising her on the restaurant, but Maddy didn't see any reason to mention that at the moment. Her daughter had sounded quite calm and just a tad happier than Maddy had heard her in a while.

David continued to bluster. "Is she trying to kill me?"

DJ handed his father a drink. "Just take it easy, Dad. I'm sure Celise knows what she's doing."

David took a drink then slammed down the glass. "How the hell can you say that? She's made one impulsive decision after another all her life. And now she's broken her engagement and is shacking up with a man she hardly knows."

Maddy had a feeling that Celise knew Jason Carrington a lot better than any of them realized. "David, I think it's time you accepted that Celise is very serious this time. She's going to open this restaurant with or without your approval." She knew those words hurt her husband, but he had to understand that his little girl wasn't going to bend to his will this time.

"Okay," David breathed a little more calmly. "Fine. She's going to open a restaurant. I can help her with that. Why is she with this Carrington guy? She doesn't know him. And why is she staying with him? There are plenty of hotels around here, or I can get on the phone with my real estate agent and get her an apartment if that's what she wants."

"I think she wants to do this herself," Maddy said quietly.

"That's ridiculous. Why wouldn't she want my help? I'm her father. It's my job to take care of her."

DJ gave a slight chuckle. "It seems that Jason Carrington has taken over that job."

Maddy smiled knowingly at her son then sobered as she looked at her husband who didn't take that statement as well.

❧

"Jason Carrington wants to play hardball," Nigel said the moment he entered Pamela's suite. She'd told him about her encounter with Jason, and he was grateful that he'd had the good sense to put her room under an alias. He removed his jacket and sat on the edge of the bed. Pamela didn't say a word but came to him rubbing her hands over his back.

"I made him a good deal. He should have been wise enough to take it. Now, I'll have to take what I want," he said adamantly.

"Do you think he's considering Markam's offer?" she asked.

Nigel stood abruptly and walked over to the table. He didn't look back at her, didn't care what she was doing or really saying for that matter.

"He said he wasn't, but David Markam is a very persuasive man." Nigel remembered how David had convinced him that marrying Celise would be a good business deal for all of them.

Upon first glance her age and naïveté had been an issue for him. Then he'd settled into the idea of grooming her to be the perfect mate. In the very beginning she'd acquiesced for the most part. Then once he'd begun to fully disclose what he needed from her sexually, she'd begun to shy away. Or maybe it was that she simply wasn't capable of giving what he'd asked, either way the entire process began to be more tiring that he thought it was worth. Now, in retrospect, Nigel wondered if he'd made a grave error in the courtship of Celise Markam.

Without her he would not obtain any controlling shares in Markam Inns and Suites, but he'd reconciled with that fact. Jason Carrington was new to this business, sure he seemed strong and smart on the outside but Nigel was convinced he could wear the young pup down. And when he did he would start his own line of resorts and build the fortune that should rightfully be his.

As for Celise...

Pamela was talking, but he hadn't been listening to her. A moment ago she'd begun touching him, and while a couple hours in the bed with Pamela could surely clear his mind, he wasn't in the mood. He had pressing matters with which to deal, and he needed to figure them out. Slamming his fist down onto the table, Nigel clenched his teeth. Then realizing that his hand hadn't met the hard surface of the cherry wood table, but had been cushioned by something else, he looked down. Today's paper was folded so that he could only see the headline.

HOTEL HEIRESS TEAMS UP WITH LOCAL MILLIONAIRE

Curious, he lifted the paper to scan the rest of the article.

His temples throbbed instantly, his hands balling even with the paper intact.

"Nigel? What's the matter?" Pamela asked, moving from the bed to stand beside him.

He didn't want to hear her voice, didn't want to see her face. Nigel thrust the paper at Pamela and tried like hell to resist slamming his fist into the wall.

Pamela gasped, catching the paper, then turning it around so she could read it. "Well, isn't this something?"

Nigel reached into the jacket he'd placed on the back of a chair and pulled out a cigar. Lifting it to his nose to savor the smell, he was determined to settle his mind. Anger wasn't going to bring him results, only complete control would do that.

"It's something alright. Something we're going to use to our advantage," he told her.

"What? How does this help us?" she asked.

Nigel turned to her, letting his gaze rest on her plump breasts and ready mouth. He took a step closer while rubbing his finger along the length of the cigar. Then holding the tip to her lips, he moved it slowly across their fullness. His mood had definitely changed.

"It gives us ammunition."

Pamela didn't have a clue what he was talking about, she'd been still trying to wrap her mind around the fact that Jason and Celise Markam were truly a couple. But then Nigel moved the cigar from her mouth and was tracing it over her cleavage. Desire rippled through her, and she shivered. "How so?" she whispered, already growing wet between her legs.

"Jason and Celise are linked together for this so-called cook-off. We both know how society works. This picture of the town's most eligible bachelor and a newly single woman will start tongues to wagging. They'll be touted as the next royal couple in Monterey."

Pamela didn't like the sound of that, but she loved the feel of Nigel plunging that cigar between her breasts, which were fitted tightly together in her bra and blouse. "I still don't get it."

"But you want it, don't you?" Nigel asked in a low, raspy voice.

"Yes," she whispered.

"And you'll do anything for it?" He removed the cigar and pulled on her blouse and bra until they both gave, freeing her heaving breasts. Dropping the cigar to the table, he bent and bit one distended nipple until she screamed.

"Yes! Yes, I will!" She breathed heavily.

Nigel looked up at her, squeezing each breast. "I want you to seduce Carrington." Pamela's head lulled back, and he licked each nipple. "And then I want him to get caught. The scandal will be horrific, and he'll beg to sell this hotel. Then I'll be there. Waiting."

He squeezed her breasts once more, but she didn't move. Tracing a line over her lips had her opening her mouth, dutifully sucking on his finger the same way she liked to suck on his penis.

"You will seduce him, won't you? You're so sexy and so good. He'll want you. Just like I want you."

She was sucking his finger so hard as he talked, knowing his erection was growing at the same time. Nigel got off on this type of foreplay. Anger aroused him, fury pushed him to the point of restrained control and that made him a powerful lover for her. She needed that right now, needed the pain of Nigel's loving, and the intense pleasure that blinded her to everything else in the world.

"Say you'll do it. Say you'll do Carrington for me."

She wanted more than just to seduce Jason. She'd wanted him as her husband, even felt like she could love him with her whole heart. But that dream had faded just as all the others in her life. Nigel was her future. If he wanted her to sleep with Jason, to wrap him and his stuck-up girlfriend in scandal, she would do it. Gladly, because loving someone who didn't love her back was pointless.

"Yes," she said in a breathy voice. "I'll do it. Now I need you to do me."

Before she could speak another word, Nigel had turned her away from him and pushed her over the table. Pamela hiked her dress up over her hips displaying her bare chocolate-brown buttocks. She wore no underwear, and Nigel panted as he freed his burgeoning erection. Grasping each plump cheek he opened her wider then rammed himself into her with a blissful sigh.

But as Nigel rode her fiercely, Pamela had other thoughts on her mind. She remembered Jason, remembered the steamy nights of passion they'd shared and felt heavy waves of jealousy wash over her. He had a new toy now, she thought then pinched her nipples to speed up her own release. Celise Markam was an amateur. There was no way she could give Jason what he needed from a woman.

Nigel moved faster, and Pamela knew he was about to finish. She also knew he was just as distracted as she was. She kept one hand on her breast and moved the other one between her legs to rub her clit, both actions Nigel would never normally allow. He alone was in control of her release, each and every time. But tonight she was in control. Her release was coming...coming...

Nigel reared back and growled as he spewed inside her.

Pamela screamed, willing herself not to say the wrong name as she did.

And the fate of Carrington Resorts was sealed.

CHAPTER FIFTEEN

"I hope you know what you're doing," DJ said to his sister.

Celise let her shoulders relax. She'd come to the hotel to follow up the phone call she'd made to her mother. They deserved more than words over the phone, and Celise hoped that seeing her would convince them that she was doing just fine on her own. She hadn't anticipated catching DJ alone because he was always at their father's side, but it had turned out to be a good thing. DJ hadn't yelled or chastised her. On the contrary, he'd seemed almost happy to find out that she was okay and more than a little interested in her plans.

"I'm doing what I think is right for me. That's all I know. So what are you guys still doing here?" The last time she'd spoken with Sharrell she'd told her of David's offer to Jason. Celise knew that Jason wouldn't sell his hotel, but she'd wisely kept that fact to herself. Whatever she was doing with Jason was between him and her. The hotel business was between Jason and her father. She planned to be especially careful in steering clear of that.

"You know Dad doesn't give up that easily. And with the blackout and the bad press, he thinks Carrington will come around."

Celise nodded. That would be her father's game plan. "So how much longer do you think you'll stay?"

"I have a meeting with Carrington this afternoon. I'll wait and see what happens before I decide. Mom, however, is not leaving until she talks with you again. And, Sharrell…it's funny, I haven't seen her anymore than I've seen you."

"Really?" That had Celise wondering, but something else had piqued her interest. "You requested a meeting with Jason, alone?" DJ rarely did business without their father. It seemed weird that he'd said "he" had a meeting with Jason and not "they." Unless he was meeting with him for another reason, in which case Celise wanted to know for sure so she could tell him to mind his business.

DJ apparently followed her train of thought. "Calm down. I didn't call the meeting. Carrington did."

"Jason? Why?"

DJ shrugged. "I'm not sure, but I'm guessing it has something to do with the fact that Nigel is here."

"Nigel's here?" Celise sighed. She didn't want to talk about Nigel Bingham, and she certainly didn't want to see him. It was a good thing she was staying with Jason. Her time at the hotel didn't have to be much except now she was registered for the cook-off. "Why would Jason want to talk to you about Nigel?"

DJ tweaked her nose, something he'd done since she was a little girl. "I don't know, but I don't want you to worry about it. I'll meet with him and see what's going on."

"Will you tell me about it?" she asked skeptically.

"If it concerns you directly, I'll let you know. If it's just business then—"

"If it's business I don't want to know," she finished for him.

DJ nodded. "I thought that's what you'd say."

Celise had waited in the suite for her mother to return, but Sharrell came in first.

"Well, well, well, I hear I'm not the only one who's been missing in action," she said, smiling from her seat on the couch.Sharrell startled at the sound of her voice then re-routed herself to go into the living room instead of to the room in which she was staying. "Hey, stranger," she said, plopping down beside Celise. "You've been pretty busy, huh?"

"Not as busy as you, I suspect. Where have you been, and why doesn't anyone know about it?"

"I could ask you the same questions, but I already know your answers." Sharrell smiled.

"What? How do you know?"

"I saw your boyfriend at the bar a little while ago."

Not even questioning to whom Sharrell referred, Celise asked, "And he told you I was staying with him?"

"As a matter of fact he told me that he was taking good care of you." Sharrell watched as Celise fought off a smile. "That was after I'd threatened to sue him for misusing your name."

"What? Why did you do that?"

"Considering I haven't seen or heard from you in almost two days, I had no idea you'd agreed to do this cook-off thing at his hotel. I thought he was using your name to get some positive publicity, so I called him on it."

Celise chuckled. "I'm sure you did. And I'm sure he didn't like it."

"Hell no, he didn't like it. Got real uptight about it and his friend Clive had to calm both of us down. It was about to be on in that bar, you hear me."

Celise continued to laugh, imagining Sharrell and Jason going at it. "I'm sure it was. But really, I did agree to do it for my own reasons. It'll be a great introduction into the community, don't you think?"

"Yeah, I agree, but that was after Jason had pointed that out. He's damn fine, girl. You've made yourself a good catch."

"I haven't caught him," Celise said quietly.

"Don't even try it. That man looks whipped, caught and strung out over you. You should have seen the way he defended you and then had the nerve to tell me we should stop telling you what to do."

"Jason said that?"

"Mmmm hmmm. But by that time I was cooling down so I didn't tell him that I was always rooting for you, even if it was in the background."

"So wait a minute, you were talking to Jason and Clive? You've made friends really quick." There was definitely something Sharrell wasn't telling her.

"Not really. Jason and I have been butting heads each time we meet. But Clive, he's a different story."

"One you need to tell me about," Celise said anxiously.

The door to the suite opened, and their conversation was cut short as David and Madeline Markam entered.

Celise stood quickly, taking a deep breath in preparation for the confrontation. Sharrell stood, too, taking Celise's hand and giving it a gentle squeeze. "Just tell them what you're doing and go do it. Don't let him stop you," she whispered before David and Madeline were close enough to hear.

"The prodigal daughter returns," David said.

Maddy eyed her daughter cautiously as David looked on with barely restrained anger.

"I'm going to go and change. I have an appointment later," Sharrell said then quickly made herself scarce.

Celise waved at her then turned to face her parents. "Hi. I wasn't sure you guys would still be here," she said tentatively.

"My business here isn't complete," David said gruffly.

"Sit down, Celise. You look as if you have something to say," Maddy said.

Celise sat. She watched her parents sit across from her and remembered Jason telling her about his parents, about how he, too, went against the grain career wise. He'd made a stand, and his family respected him for it. He'd encouraged Celise to do the same. With his voice echoing in her head she took a deep breath and spoke.

"I'm staying at Jason Carrington's beach house, just until I find a more permanent spot of my own. He's giving me some tips on the area and what it's like to own a business here." They really didn't need to know the other things he was doing for her. "I signed on to be in the cook-off here at the hotel so that I could get some exposure and as an introduction into the community. My business adviser thinks it's a good idea."

David said nothing, only watched her.

Maddy gave her an encouraging smile. "And Jason is staying at the beach house with you?"

Of course she'd already told her mother this, but Celise sensed her mother wanted her to tell her father. She couldn't lie. She could omit some facts, but she couldn't lie to her parents. "Yes."

"Dammit, Celise. You're engaged," David yelled.

"I am not engaged anymore. I told you that several months ago."

"Yes, you did, dear. What exactly happened between you and Nigel?" Maddy asked, hoping her daughter would give more details this time.

"Nigel and I were incompatible. He wanted a different type of relationship than I did, so I ended it."

"Did he do something to you?" David asked through clenched teeth.

Again, Celise was faced with whether to lie or to tell only parts of the truth. What Nigel had done to her was awful and too humiliating to repeat. She couldn't say those things to her parents. "He didn't beat me if that's what you mean," she answered.

"But he did do something?" David asked, standing over her.

Maddy rushed to her husband's side, putting a hand to his shoulder. "Darling, maybe she doesn't want to talk about it now. It's over, and that's all that matters."

"It's not all that matters. If he did something to my daughter, I damn sure want to know about it. I haven't heard from him in weeks, and I'm sure he's up to something." David walked over to the bar to pour himself a drink.

Celise was a little stunned. It was close to five in the afternoon. She'd never seen her father drink this early. She thought about telling him that DJ said Nigel was there at the Carrington but she refrained. She really didn't want to be involved in their business dealings. She simply wanted her parents to accept her decisions and to give their support.

"I'm sorry things didn't work out between Nigel and me, Daddy, but I don't regret breaking up with him. I'm doing important things with my life now—things that mean a lot to me."

David Markam sighed. "I'm glad you've found something to be passionate about, Celise. And I'm very proud of the stand you've taken. I guess I have to let you grow up now."

Celise smiled nervously, relief washing over her. "I'm still a Markam, even though I'm not in the hotel business."

"You're still my baby girl, no matter how grown you think you are." He pulled her to him then, pouring all the love he had for her into the embrace.

"I know. I love you, Daddy."

"I love you, too, darling."

Maddy dabbed the tears away and put a hand to both her husband and her daughter's back. "Now that you two have had your moment, can I talk to my daughter? Alone."

Celise didn't like the sound of that.

"So you think Nigel is up to something?" DJ asked Jason while they sat in his office.

Jason steeped his fingers and stared at DJ Markam seriously. He had no concrete evidence to prove that Bingham was up to no good. All he had was his gut instinct, and Jason always followed his gut. This could be partially due to the fact that he knew something more had happened between Nigel and Celise, but the bigger shadow of doubt was cast when he'd met with Nigel. Something in the man's eyes told Jason he could not be trusted. That and the fact that he was now dealing behind David Markam's back. "I'm positive he is."

DJ nodded in agreement. "My father hasn't seen or heard from him in weeks. The issue with Nigel and Celise has been bothering him."

Jason decided not to share his opinion in that regard. He hadn't called this meeting with DJ to discuss his relationship with his sister, although he was sure she was a big part in what Nigel had planned.

"He has a room at the hotel, and he's not scheduled to check out until next week. I plan to watch him closely in that time."

"You think he had something to do with the blackout?" DJ asked.

This was another thing Jason hadn't planned on discussing with DJ. The fact that each instance of sabotage in the hotel had happened after the Markams had arrived hadn't escaped him either. Although, Jason was finding it increasingly hard to consider this family as low dealers who would do something like that to gain control of his hotel. And because he was growing closer to Celise, he wanted to give her family the benefit of the doubt.

"I don't know for sure, but I'm exploring every option," Jason said.

"I'll speak with my father. We'll find out what we can about Nigel and what he's up to." Then DJ looked Jason directly in the eye. "I'll keep you posted."

Jason knew that was as close as he was going to get to the man's blessing where his sister was concerned. From the moment DJ stepped foot in his office Jason knew he was sizing him up, seeing if he was worthy of Celise. And while they hadn't discussed his relationship with her out in the open, he knew what was really on DJ's mind. "And if I find out anything new I'll let you know."

DJ stood. Jason followed suit, coming around his desk to walk him to the door. When DJ extended a hand Jason readily clasped it.

"I appreciate what you're doing," DJ said. "*Everything* you're doing."

Jason nodded. "Thank you."

DJ walked away then turned back. "I hope you know how special she is."

"I do," Jason replied seriously.

When DJ was gone Jason walked back to his desk and sat down. There was no doubt in his mind how special Celise Markam was. And as he thought of her again, the familiar throbbing in his groin began. Laying his head back against the smooth leather chair, he remembered waking up next to her that morning. She'd curled her back against him, and his hand had readily slipped between her legs. She was hot and wet, waiting for him. He'd fingered her until she climaxed then slipped his pulsating erection into her and stroked until his own release had escaped.

Every time he entered her, she took another part of him. There wasn't a minute in a day that he didn't think of her. She'd come into his life and filled a spot he was beginning to doubt would ever be filled. And he loved her for it.

Yes, he loved her. He wasn't afraid to admit it, to himself at least. To Celise, well, he'd wait a while on that. She still seemed convinced that they were having an affair, and although she didn't talk about it as much, he knew she expected to move into her own apartment and for them to never see each other again. It was his goal to change that part of her plan.

On his hip his cell phone vibrated, jolting him from his thoughts. "Jason Carrington."

"Hello, Jason Carrington."

Heat spread throughout his body instantly at the sound of her voice. "Hello, Celise Markam."

"I'm missing you terribly," she said in a sultry tone.

"Really? How terribly?"

On the other end, she sighed. "I'm on my way back to the house, but I couldn't stop thinking about you."

She spoke in that same breathy tone she used when he was inside of her, when she whispered all the things she wanted him to do to her in his ear. Jason's body was on full alert, his erection snaking along his thigh. To afford himself some semblance of relief he unzipped his pants to release the throbbing arousal. "What are you thinking about?" he asked gruffly.

"I'm thinking of how much I'd love to have you in my hands. I miss the feel of your skin, the scent of your arousal."

Jason moaned. "Tell me what you'd do if you had me in your hands right now. And talk slow."

She gave a soft chuckle then another breathy sigh that made him groan.

"I'd hold you tight, right at the base. I'd squeeze until you gasped, then I'd stroke you upward, pushing your skin toward the tip then pulling it back down again."

Jason grabbed his penis, performing the motions she described and grunted with pleasure.

"Do you have something for me, baby?" she asked.

Gritting his teeth, Jason looked down at his burning erection to one tiny white drop. "Yeah, baby. I've got something for you."

"I want to lick it, Jason. I want to lick all of you. Oooooh, Jason, I want you so bad."

His temples throbbed. His penis ached while his hand moved fiercely up and down. "Celise, if you don't stop, I'm going to make a mess."

"I'm getting out of the car now, Jason, and going into the house where I'm going to run a nice hot bath."

Images of her naked flashed into his mind, and Jason sat straight up in his chair. "I'll be there in fifteen minutes." He disconnected the phone, fixed his pants and left the office.

After talking to her mother, Celise had been on an emotional roller coaster. Maddy hadn't pulled any punches when she'd questioned her only daughter about why she was staying with this man she'd just met. And Celise had been defenseless. But it was what her mother said just before she'd left that had pitched her emotions into overdrive.

"I never thought you loved Nigel, and I never saw the spark in your eyes I see now when you were with him. There's something strong between you and Jason Carrington. I can tell."

Celise hadn't wanted to accept that so she'd brushed her mother off as being overdramatic and quickly left the hotel. But once she was alone, the impact of her mother's words coupled with the sensations she'd been feeling lately began to overwhelm her. Each time Jason touched her, she came alive. Each time he brought her to climax, she shattered only to have his words, his simply being there build her up again. And each time she was rebuilt he was closer to her heart.

This was an affair. That's what she kept telling herself. It was temporary. She had other things to do. Jason was not a part of the plan. Another disappointment in her personal life was not a part of the plan.

But Jason had yet to disappoint her. He'd been perfect in every way. He listened to her. He respected her thoughts and opinions. He encouraged her. And he sexed her like crazy. Nope, there was no disappointment where he was concerned.

Just thinking of him had her heart pounding, her body demanding release. She'd climbed into her car, wanting nothing more than to feel him touching her anywhere and everywhere. It didn't matter what he did to her physically, she seemed to enjoy every minute of it. Her thighs quaked as she'd sat in the driver's seat, and the moment she started the car, felt the engine purring beneath her, an overwhelming urge to ride him surfaced.

She'd retrieved her cell phone and called him hoping that the sound of his voice would somehow soothe her ache. Instead it increased the tempo of her need, and she found herself doing something she'd never done before. She'd been on the brink of having phone sex with him. Had she not been in that car she would have continued. She knew he was stroking himself just the way she described herself doing. But for the fact that she'd have crashed and most likely killed herself, Celise would have taken her free hand off the wheel and brought herself pleasure as well.

Now she was in the house stripping off her clothes as she made her way to the bathroom, her body humming with sexual awareness. Switching on the water, she hurriedly pushed her panties down and unclasped her bra. She sank into the heated water and sighed. Her skin tingled as she laid her head back, her thoughts centered on Jason.

Her breasts were heavy, thumping slightly with the need to be touched. Without another thought she grabbed them both in her palms, kneading and squeezing until some of her edginess dissolved. Her tongue stroked her bottom lip, and she pinched her nipples, hard, just the way Jason did it. Her center throbbed, and she let one hand slide down the length of her water-slick torso to the nest of dark curls between her legs. She wasn't a pro at masturbation and in truth hadn't touched herself until the moment she met Jason, but her fingers separated her moist folds with expertise then marched up and down her center, rubbing her puckered clit and slipping down into her opening.

She gasped at the sharp spikes of pleasure prickling her skin and continued her movements. Simultaneously she worked her fingers in and out of her opening and squeezed her breast until she felt as if she were milking it. Her moans grew louder, echoing in the large bathroom. Luckily she'd turned off the water a few moments earlier because at that point she couldn't move a muscle, she was so taut with desire.

Her breathing increased as she felt herself nearing completion. Amazed at the fact that she was doing this all by herself and heady with arousal, she worked herself harder, pulling her fingers out to rub enthusiastically against her clit. Sensations rippled and consumed her. She panted wildly, begging for that sweet culmination.

That's what Jason saw the moment he entered the bathroom. He'd walked into the house picking up each piece of clothing from the trail leading to the bathroom. His erection throbbed and threatened to split his pants. Tiny beads of sweat dotted his forehead as he'd broken all speeding records to get there. The needy sound of her voice echoed in his mind as he drove.

He stopped when he heard her moan, his gaze fixing on her naked body in the tub, her hand between her legs. Her eyes were closed, and he could tell she was really into it. Without taking his eyes off her, he pulled his shirt over his head and threw it to the floor. He undid his belt and removed his shoes. In one sweep his underwear and pants lay on the floor beside her. Her clothes, which he'd collected, were dropped since seeing her. He was now as naked as she. He grabbed his jutting sex and worked it, all the while watching as Celise worked herself. He'd never been this aroused in his life.

She whimpered, and he moved closer to her holding his arousal. Drops of pre-cum filled his tip and he stood beside the tub, touched his free hand to the back of her head and whispered, "I have something for you, baby."

Celise opened her eyes slowly, her gaze immediately falling to his erection, to the white drops threatening to spill over its head. Without hesitation she came up onto her knees, leaned forward and flicked her tongue over him, lapping the salty-sweet mixture greedily.

"Ahhh," Jason moaned. "Keep touching yourself, baby. You're almost there." He pumped his hips as she took his shaft completely into her mouth and watched her hand driving deeper and deeper between her legs.

"Yes, Celise. Yes!" He pumped harder, faster matching the rhythm of her hand.

When he could take the sweet torture no longer, Jason pulled slowly out of her mouth and lifted her from the tub. He didn't speak as he lay her on the thick rug that covered a good portion of the tiled floor. She eyed his erection hungrily, reaching for him once more. Moving out of her reach and bending, he grabbed a condom from his wallet and ripped the package open then smoothed the latex down his engorged penis.

"Oh no, it's too late for foreplay now," he said, growling, then entered her in one hard thrust.

She arched to receive him. Jason grabbed her thighs, spread them even farther as he pumped into her fiercely. "Look at us, baby. Look."

Celise lifted up on her elbows and looked at their joining. His long, erect penis moving in and out of her, his balls tightly slapping against her buttocks. He was on his knees holding her legs apart. Jason reveled in the slick sound of their bodies joining. She reached down then and touched him, pulled his hot shaft into her faster and faster.

"Yes. More, Jason. I want all of you. I need all of you," she said, heaving.

Pumping wildly Jason tried to give her everything she needed and more. They were so beyond sex at that point. His feelings for her, his yearning for her were more than just a primal act. Even their joining, the way she'd licked him, touched his penis, his sac, it was with a delicateness, a meaningfulness that was not just desire filled. Jason was almost afraid to hope she'd felt what he did, but when he looked down into her eyes he knew it without a doubt and when her legs began to shake, his name on her lips became a muttered whisper he let himself go, allowed all the emotions to take over and spilled deeply inside of her.

CHAPTER SIXTEEN

The Grand Ballroom of Carrington Resorts could be considered nothing less than glamorous and elegant. It was evident that Jason had spent a good deal of time and money in this particular area of the hotel. Gilded moldings traced the ceilings illuminating spectacular chandeliers, while crystal wall sconces dazzled on silver leaf panels and windows were adorned with silk embroidered drapery. The leafy design and rich, dramatic gold, burgundy and ecru colors in the rug pulled the entire design together in a stunning fashion that left Celise breathless the moment she entered.

Now, half an hour later, Celise hummed while moving around the tiny makeshift kitchen that had been designated to her early that morning. There were ten chefs competing in three categories: seafood entrees, appetizers and pastry, all of which were her specialties. She'd already planned precisely what she was going to make, and with the help of her Sous chef, Cheyenne, whom she'd called in from New York, she was sure to make a good impression on the citizens of Monterey. And who knew, she might even win the competition, although that wasn't her reason for being there.

Jason had told her just the night before that the hotel was sold out for the event and that even his parents had booked a room so they would be close by for the festivities. News media, the local paper as well as food critics from New York, Los Angeles and San Francisco were there. She'd met with the critic from San Francisco the previous night over dinner. They'd discussed her accolades in New York as well as her aspirations in Monterey. Celise felt good about the event and was already claiming the victory for her restaurant.

She was also feeling quite satisfied with where things were headed with Jason. Over the last few days they'd grown closer, sharing more about their plans for the future. Jason spoke a lot about the restaurant he wanted to bring to the hotel, and Celise found herself giving more suggestions. At one point she'd even jokingly stated that if she continued giving him so many ideas there would be no point in her opening her own restaurant. He'd kissed her then, effectively taking her mind off the subject.

That's how things were between them, comfortable and easygoing, so why was she waiting for something bad to happen?

"Allow me to properly introduce myself," a female voice interrupted Celise's thoughts.

She looked up from the carton of eggs she was inspecting and found herself staring into a face she'd almost forgotten about.

Almost. Big, stylish curls framed the familiar face while makeup attempted to cover the lines of age and stress around her eyes. She gave a phony smile. Celise had to struggle to present one of her own.

"Yes, the first time we met I believe you were a bit preoccupied." She kept to herself the remark about the woman being on her knees like a tramp.

"I'm Pamela Walker." She extended a hand.

Celise accepted the hand without any hint of her reluctance. "Celise Markam."

"Miss Markam, I should say it's more than a surprise to see you here. I mean, with your family owning a huge chain of hotels themselves, for you to make an appearance at this humble establishment is such an honor."

"I pride myself on recognizing great properties." She didn't know why this woman was at the contest nor did she have time to play this game she'd started. Jason had already told her all about his past with Pamela—how he'd first thought they were a good couple and that she might be worth settling down with, but then she'd lied to him. There was no love lost on Jason's part, but it was obvious that Pamela had another agenda. Although Celise distinctly remembered Jason saying he'd banned her from the property Pamela seemed perfectly comfortable in the main ballroom of Carrington Resorts.

"And this is a wonderful property. I've stayed here frequently," Pamela added.

"Really? Would that be in your own room or in someone else's?" Celise asked in a sickeningly sweet voice.

Pamela's smile wavered a bit as she took a step closer to the table. "Since we're obviously dropping the pretenses, I have a question. Don't you think that sleeping with the owner of the hotel is in direct conflict with you being in this contest? I mean, if you have no other means of employ and you need the money, something like this is fine, but you seem to be working both angles. How does your father feel about that?"

Celise didn't flinch, and she didn't reach across the table to slap the woman either, which was very tempting. She'd never had a high tolerance for cattiness.

"Actually that was two questions. But never mind the specifics." She waved a hand and continued. "Who

I sleep with is my business. And what I do with my time is my business. Now, I have more of a request than a question."

Pamela arched a perfectly waxed eyebrow in response.

"Don't beat around the bush. If you have something you want to get off your chest, just do it. We're both adults," Celise said.

Pamela looked as if she were about to take Celise up on her offer but one of the judges walked up to her table and she remained quiet.

"Ten minutes to start time, Miss Markam," the stout woman said.

Celise smiled. "Thank you, ma'am."

Cheyenne came up behind her. "Are the eggs okay, Celise? Do we need to send to the kitchen for anything else before we get started?"

Celise lifted the container of eggs and handed them to Cheyenne, never once taking her eye off Pamela. "They're fine, Cheyenne. Everything seems to be ready for us to start."

"I guess I should wish you luck, but then that wouldn't be sincere," Pamela remarked.

"I'm sure that won't be the first time you've faked it." Celise smirked.

With an audible gasp Pamela rolled her eyes and stalked away.

Celise took a moment, counted to ten and released several deep breaths before hearing the buzzer sounding the start of the first round of the competition.

"She's a very pretty girl, Jason," Lydia Carrington stated when she'd joined her son at the head table in the ballroom.

Dressed in a champagne colored pantsuit, her silver hair neatly curled and resting on her shoulders, diamonds sparkling discreetly at her ears and on her fingers, his mother was the epitome of grace and style and set the stage for everything Jason had ever wanted in a woman.

He stood, kissed her on the cheek and held out her chair as she sat down. "Thanks, mom, I think so too."

The cook-off had officially ended ten minutes earlier. Everyone was taking their seats while the judges tallied their votes. Celise was still cleaning up her kitchen and would be making her way to the stage with the other contestants shortly. The day had gone splendidly, and Jason was proud. He was more anxious to have a moment alone with Celise, but he was happy with the turnout.

Clive and Sharrell seemed inseparable as they made their rounds. The Markams were there as well. DJ and Madeline had made a point of seeking him out and congratulating him on such a fine event while David Markam had given him a stern look and reluctant praise. Jason wasn't deterred. He'd been thinking that morning that it was time the two families got together to dispel any hard feelings. After all, he planned on a long future with Celise, and it seemed only right that their families get along. Of course, he hadn't mentioned any of this to Celise yet. While she hadn't spoken of their temporary affair in a couple of days, he hadn't decided when he was going to push things to the next level.

Talk about his restaurant had gone just the way he wanted the other day, and she'd actually mentioned the fact that she seemed more involved with his new business venture than her own. He didn't miss the fact that she wasn't too pleased with that prospect, so he'd decided to back off. If Celise thought for one minute he was maneuvering her she'd be livid and would definitely pull away from him. He had to work slowly and precisely with her, that was no doubt. But in the end they would both get what they wanted.

"She seems competent in that kitchen," his mother continued. "I passed her booth several times just to see how she worked. It's evident that this is a passion of hers."

Dragging his thoughts back to the present, Jason looked at his mother and smiled. "She's really a very talented chef. I believe she'll do well in this competition."

Lydia nodded. "I heard some of the judges commenting on her dishes. You're probably right about her doing well."

Jason watched as Celise made her way to the stage, his heart swelling with both love and pride. She was pretty and she was capable, and she took the stage without an ounce of conceit. In this competition she was a chef only. Her family name or her connection to Carrington Resorts wasn't important. She'd told him this the night before, it was all about her talent. This competition might tell if she would sink or swim in Monterey. Jason was sure that whatever the outcome Celise's goals would not be deterred.

And as he watched her move to the seat designated for the contestants dressed in black slacks and white jackets, he felt a burst of pride.

"You really care about her, don't you?"

Jason didn't hesitate in answering. It was so much more than caring, so much more than words could accurately explain. "Yes, Mom. I do."

"More than you care about this hotel?" Lydia pushed.

That was a different question, one he hadn't quite considered. "Why do you ask?"

Lydia shrugged and accepted the glass of champagne a waitress had just set on the table in front of her.

"She's the daughter of one of your biggest competitors. That could prove to be a very sticky situation."

He nodded. "I've thought of that. But Celise isn't a part of her family business. Kind of like I'm not a part of ours."

"You're still a Carrington, Jason, no matter where you work," she told him.

He smiled. "I just told Jackson something like that the other day."

"Your brothers are very proud of you. And so am I and your father. You're doing what you need to do to live your life."

Jason nodded, loving the sound of those words from his mother. "I wish you could tell her family that about her."

"Do they know how you feel about her?" Lydia asked after a moment of silence.

Jason looked across the room to all the tables filled with guests. He heard the clinking of dishes as the wait staff took away old glasses and replaced them with full ones. He watched as a couple stood near one of the large windows that looked out to quaint shops nestled comfortably across the street.

His fingers toyed with his napkin as he contemplated his mother's words. "They don't know, and it's not really any of their business. What Celise and I have doesn't involve anyone but us."

Lydia was not inclined to let the conversation end with that statement. "I met her parents," she continued. "They love her very much. They gave the impression that they're a very close family, just like ours."

Jason didn't like where she was going with this. "Okay, so what's your point, Mom?"

Lydia placed a hand over his. She'd done this with him as a teenager whenever he was worried about an exam or a sport's competition. The act never failed to calm him and fill him with the type of support he one day hoped to give to his own children.

"My point is that whatever you feel for her has to be stronger than your feelings for anything else. Relationships aren't easy. Ones that begin with family conflict are even harder. If she's what you want you should be prepared to do whatever you can to keep her."

He'd been braced for a more critical assessment of his relationship with Celise. He hadn't anticipated his mother's sincere advice. For so long his goal had been to run the best hotel in Monterey and to expand all over the world. Even when he was with Pamela he'd thought of nothing else. Over the last few days, however, he'd thought less of Carrington Resorts and its impending problems and more of Celise and how to make her happy. But was he prepared to make a choice if need be?

"Ladies and gentlemen. If I could have your attention please," Russell Branch, the chairman of the cook-off, requested.

A hush settled over the room as everyone stared at the podium expectantly. Russell was not only in charge of this competition, he also owned FFT, the Food For Thought Network based in Chicago. As such, two of the station's top hosts, as well as full camera crews were also present today.

"I would first like to give a hearty thanks to Jason Carrington and Carrington Resorts for hosting this year's event. He's done a splendid job in offering us hospitality and a terrific stay in Monterey. Let's give him a hand," Russell stated giving a nod to Jason.

Jason stood, did a mock salute to Clive and then to Russell before taking his seat amid the applause. His father had joined them and shook Jason's hand with pride. Jason's gaze found Celise and watched as she clapped exuberantly, smiling happily at him. That smile gripped his heart, and everything else seemed to fade.

"Now we'll get right down to the business at hand," the chairman continued. "There were three categories in this year's competition. Each chef was rated separately, and the scores were tallied. The overall average determined the winner."

As the chairman spoke Jason noticed an empty seat on the stage to Celise's right. He wondered which chef was missing and looked around the room. Near the door he saw Nigel Bingham, his gaze set on Celise. Trying not to give in to simmering anger, Jason looked away. At a table closest to the kitchen sat several members of his board, including Mr. and Mrs. Hampden, his biggest contenders. They were smiling, so Jason assumed they were pleased with the turnout.

The second runner-up was announced and applause sounded for the Miami chef. Jason clapped absently sensing that something was wrong. He continued to watch his surroundings. Clive must have picked up on Jason's feelings or had some misgivings of his own, because he stood and looked around the room as well.

The first runner-up was announced, and again the sound of the two hundred or so people who had gathered for the event clapping echoed throughout the room. Jason looked back at the door to where he'd just seen Nigel and noticed the man was gone.

"Jason, are you okay?" his father leaned over and asked.

But Jason was standing, signaling to Clive to meet him.

"And the grand prize winner of the Food Festival's Annual Cook-Off is Celise Markam of San Francisco."

Everyone in the room stood with applause. Jason continued his walk toward the center of the room where Clive was also heading. As if on cue, the moment Clive and Jason met someone yelled, "This is an outrage! I've been sabotaged!"

The statement was repeated as the chef who had been missing from the stage made his way from the kitchen. Thankfully the applause continued and only a few heads from the guests closest to the kitchen turned in the disgruntled chef's direction. Both Jason and Clive stopped and looked toward the man.

"My supplies were tampered with. It's a fix. This whole contest was fixed!" he yelled, his cheeks red with agitation.

It seemed the crowd picked that exact moment to stop clapping because the man's words echoed throughout the ballroom.

He was a short, thin man with a strong accent, and overstated mustache. Jason tried desperately to remember his name. All he could latch onto was the man's accent that sounded strangely like Nigel Bingham's.

"I've been cooking for twenty years, and I've never had something this underhanded happen to me," the chef said vehemently.

Clive had managed to get close enough to the chef to grab the sleeve of his white jacket. "Sir, what seems to the problem?"

"The problem is that someone has sabotaged my food. I found this." He held up a potted plant that looked similar to the ones in the lobby of the hotel. There was shovel in the pot, and the plant itself looked as if it had been uprooted. "It was near my kitchen. And then as I cleaned I found there was dirt in my spices."

Murmurings encased the room. Jason felt a heated burn in the pit of his stomach, as he was sure the plant had come from the same local florist who had delivered the other ones early the previous morning.

"Sir, let's go outside. We can discuss this there."
Clive tried to diffuse the situation.

"I will not! I demand a new contest. We must do it
all over again. I want satisfaction!" he insisted with a
petulant stomp of his foot. "This contest was a fluke
and I intend to let everyone know about it!"

The chef's tirade continued, to the point where it
was beginning to irritate Jason. Around him guests had
begun to whisper and stare, no doubt hearing the chef's
words and wondering at the possibilities. This was not
how this event was meant to turn out.

Russell Branch had begun speaking again, asking
that everyone remain calm and assuring them that they
would get to the bottom of the situation. He went on to
conclude the day's activities. Jason, while thankful for
the man's quick thinking, couldn't seem to gather his
words.

A touch to his arm stole his attention. "Nice job,
sonny," Mrs. Hampden said as she positioned her purse
on her shoulder. "The board isn't going to like this.
We've had enough of your bad publicity." She stomped
off without another word, dragging a bewildered and
tired looking Mr. Hampden with her.

He hadn't a moment to digest her words when a
female hand snaked around his neck, strong perfume
permeating his senses and quickly inspiring a headache.

"Hello, Jason. I said I'd be back," Pamela cooed.

With exasperation, Jason moved beyond her reach.
There seemed to be so much going on around him. In a
matter of seconds everything had spiraled out of control
and he felt as if his entire world had shifted and turned
upside down.

"What's going on here?" Jeffrey Carrington was at
his son's side concern marring his chiseled face.

Then came, DJ Markam dressed in dark slacks and a
white polo, questions clear in his eyes. He looked as if

he were about to voice those questions, to ask Jason what had happened, and possibly how he could help. It didn't matter because everything and everyone seemed to be swirling around him. The minute someone spoke to him or asked something of him Jason thought he might actually explode with anger.

But then he heard her voice.

"Why don't we clear everybody out and then we can get to the bottom of this? Sharrell, you can help me get the guests settled while the men gather the chefs and the judges in the other room," Celise said with gentle authority.

She'd walked up to their small group, coming to a stop directly in front of him. She stood with her back to him as if she were somehow protecting him from the onslaught.

Sharrell had already nodded and set out to work with the guests, Clive following her.

Jason didn't speak but touched a hand to her shoulder. When she turned she looked up at him. There was no pity, no questions, and no accusations. Just love, he thought with a start.

"Is that okay with you?" she asked.

Everyone around him seemed to wait for his answer but he only had eyes for her. "That's fine," he finally managed and watched as the others around him moved to do Celise's bidding.

An hour later, Jason, Clive, DJ and Jeffrey were seated at a table in the ballroom. Staff members still milled about removing dishes, taking down the booths and clearing off the stage. But the four men sat off to one corner, talking in confidence.

"So who are the suspects?" Jeffrey asked.

"Nigel Bingham for sure," Clive offered.

"I think it's someone closer to the hotel than Nigel," DJ offered, shaking his head. "This seems personal to me. The flood, the blackout and now this. If Nigel wanted to take you down he'd go right for the jugular."

Jeffrey drummed his fingers on the table. "But if he wanted a smoke screen he'd be on the right track."

Jason sighed. "Pamela is still in town," he said grimly.

"Your ex-girlfriend?" Jeffrey asked. "But she wouldn't have anything to do with the hotel."

Clive looked at Jason expectantly. Jason sighed, his relationship failure had been a private one. He hadn't told anyone about what happened with Pamela, but Clive. Now it appeared more people were about to find out.

"One of the reasons Pamela and I broke up was because I caught her going through my desk. A week or so before that I noticed that some of my financial reports were out of order in the files. I never did figure out why she was snooping around because I tossed her out before asking any questions."

Jeffrey harrumphed, not looking at all surprised. "I don't blame you."

DJ looked contemplative. "So you think she's a player?"

Jason rubbed a hand over his face. "I don't know what to think."

Clive, who had already ditched his tie and sat with his suit jacket on the back of his chair, shook his head. "She's up to something, and we need to find out what right now."

"I agree. The food people are all squared away, right?" DJ asked.

"Yeah. They crowned Celise, and Chef O'Hurley will get an honorable mention. Since the dishes he claimed were tainted weren't the ones to receive his lowest scores it wouldn't have mattered anyway. Celise still would have won hands down." Jason couldn't help but feel pride at that admission. He hadn't seen Celise in the last hour. She'd been busy speaking with guests and taking care of damage control with the press and he'd been busy with this latest catastrophe.

"I don't think too many of the guests realized what was going on. Sharrell and Celise did a great job hustling them out of here before they could ask questions." Clive sat back in his chair as he spoke.

Jeffrey nodded. "That was some fast thinking on Celise's part. You've got yourself a good woman there, Jason."

DJ looked at Jason. "Celise has always been good under pressure. My dad was really proud to see her taking charge of the situation today."

"Even though it was for the competing hotel?" Jason inquired.

DJ shrugged. "He figures you must not be that bad if Celise is hanging out with you."

The men chuckled, albeit stiffly.

"I guess I should be thankful," Jason said attempting to rub away the tension building at his neck.

DJ sobered. "You should. Celise is a good woman. If you've won her trust you must be doing something right. And my dad...well the Markams aren't in dire need of this hotel. It was just something he wanted. We all know how hard it is to let go of something we really want."

Jason smiled, thinking of Celise. "Tell me about it."

"Anyway, I'm sure he's waiting in his suite for an update." DJ stood, and Jason followed suit. "I'm going to stick around until we find out what's going on. Sabotaging a hotel isn't good business for any of us."

Jason nodded, pleased to have DJ and the Markams finally on his side. He extended his hand to DJ. "Thanks, man. I appreciate all your help."

DJ grasped Jason's hand and smiled. "Don't mention it. You might be family soon, and we've got to look out for each other."

Jason didn't speak. The fact that DJ thought he and Celise were that serious meant a lot to him. He only hoped Celise would share those feelings.

"This could not have worked out better."

Nigel smiled as he entered Pamela's suite.

Pamela didn't share his good mood. Jason had brushed her off again, and after meeting Celise Markam she hated her even more. Things were not working out the way she'd planned. She was beginning to rethink her position in this game.

"Don't you agree?" Nigel asked her as he roughly fondled her breasts.

She was even getting tired of sex with Nigel. She usually enjoyed sleeping with him, but he was obsessed with the hotel. She wanted to suggest they leave Monterey and take what money and experience Nigel had in the industry to buy a hotel someplace else, but she knew Nigel wouldn't hear of it.

He squeezed her breasts hard. "Are you listening to me, Pamela?"

"Yes."

"Then answer me, dammit," he roared.

Pamela wanted to scream her breasts hurt so bad. Instead she lifted her dress and straddled him. The last thing she wanted was Nigel upset and horny. She'd learned long ago that the two didn't mix well.

"I don't want to talk about business anymore, Nigel. Can't we just spend one night without worrying about this hotel?"

She was unbuttoning his shirt, making sure her nails scraped over his exposed skin as she did. Nigel liked a little pain with his sex. Actually, he liked a lot of pain. He liked inflicting it as well as receiving it. This particular aspect of sex, Pamela had never latched onto, but for Nigel she'd given it a try. He'd complained of all his previous lovers not enjoying his adventurous loving, and she'd been eager to please him...in every way.

Nigel ripped the top of her dress then viciously tugged her bra free. Her breasts jiggled, and he buried his face in their plumpness. "What do you want to talk about?" he asked in a muffled voice.

Despite what she knew would be a long, tortuous night Pamela felt her body responding to his touch. "I don't want to talk at all." She ground her center into his erection and moaned.

Nigel bit her breast and felt sheer ecstasy as her scream echoed throughout the room. He pulled away, watched pain flash through her eyes and smiled. He licked the spot lavishly then pushed his hand between her legs, inserting four fingers roughly into her center. She bucked, and he felt the first spurts of cum seep into his pants.

CHAPTER SEVENTEEN

Jason flopped down onto the couch after entering the house and making sure the doors were locked. After his meeting with the guys at the hotel he'd gone to his office and reviewed his latest financial report. Surfing the Internet he'd seen that Carrington Resorts' stocks were down, which was never good because another hotel could begin buying until they had enough to take over. He wondered if anyone on his board would be willing to sell their stocks. As it stood at the moment, he had forty-nine percent of the shares in Carrington Resorts. The remaining five members of the board held percentages of the rest.

He decided to speak to Clive the following morning about making some of the members a deal to sell to him. He couldn't lose his hotel. He'd worked too hard to get where he was to let it go. When he'd finally had enough business for one day he shut down his computer and was about to leave the office. That's when Celise came in.

He'd thought she'd left a long time ago with either her cousin or her parents. Surprise, however, did not override the joy he felt in seeing her.

"Let's go home," she said and took his hand while they boarded the elevator and went to the car.

They hadn't spoken much on the ride home. Jason wondered what she was thinking, but despite his earlier resolve couldn't keep his mind off the day's events.

He was tired, and he was stressed. He had to find out who was sabotaging his hotel and get rid of them. Then he had to focus all his energy on this restaurant and anything else that would build up his hotel. Closing his eyes to all the wildly running thoughts in his mind he tried futilely for a moment of relaxation.

Celise had been watching him. From the moment they'd gotten into the car he'd been tense and distracted. She knew this business with the hotel and someone continuously trying to make him look incompetent was bothering him. Truth be told, it was beginning to bother her too. That coupled with the fact that his ex-girlfriend had paid her a visit had made this a pretty stressful day for her as well.

She vowed to make things a little easier for them both.

Moving over to the couch, she bent over and placed a kiss at each of his temples. He opened his eyes slightly, and she smiled down at him. He gave her a small smile in return. Her hands roamed over his shoulders and down his arms, then to his chest where she felt the tautness of his muscles. Sliding down sinuously slow she felt his tight abs then undid the snap of his slacks. He watched her from half-closed lids as she continued on her course.

Removing his flaccid manhood, she dropped a quick kiss on the tip then slipped her hand to the base, slowly working her way up and down until his thickness grew. With her other hand she held his sac, moving the heavy mounds between her fingers then cupping them in her palm. Jason remained still.

Staring down at the now pulsating veins on his penis made her mouth water. She loved the sight of him aroused—his long, hot shaft, a honey-toned rod thrusting from a thick nest of dark hair. Her breasts grew heavy with arousal, and she bent, taking only the bulbous head between her lips. She sucked, enjoying the soft silkiness of his skin against her tongue. She heard his sudden intake of breath and was encouraged.

Because Celise knew he watched she pulled away a bit then extended her tongue, stroking from the base of his penis to the tip as if she were indulging in an ice cream cone. She licked then slurped at the head. All the while working his length steadily with her hand.

"Harder," Jason whispered. "Hold me tight in your hand while you lick."

Celise did as she was instructed, grabbing his penis tightly and stroking him faster. When the head of his manhood was covered with his pre-juices Celise moaned and smoothed her lips over the creamy fluid.

"That's right, baby. Lick it up."

She raised her head so he could watch her lick his essence from her lips. He clawed his fingers through her hair until they scraped her scalp, then guided her back down to his erection. "More. Suck me some more."

She took his entire length into her mouth, waited until his tip hit the base of her throat then moaned. Closing her lips completely over him she sucked, lifted until he was almost completely out of her mouth, then dove in and sucked him once more. Again and again she sucked and devoured, pulled and stroked him, titillating his balls between her fingers.

Jason thrust his hips faster, his fingers moving fiercely through her hair. Celise knew he was nearing his climax. She heard it in his breathing, felt it in the way he gripped her hair. She could have stopped then, but she didn't want to. She wanted Jason—all of him— so she continued to work her mouth over his thick, pulsating erection until he was gasping and chanting her name. Slipping her hand just beyond his sac, she used her thumb to press against the spot holding his penis tightly, securely in her mouth as she did.

His hands tensed on both sides of her head as he held her steady.

"Celise," he said, growling.

Celise focused only on him, only on his pleasure as she swallowed his release.

Jason carried her to the bedroom where he stopped her from immediately undressing and climbing into the bed. The night wasn't about sex.

It was about what she'd come to mean to him. For years all he'd been able to think of was his hotel and his future success, and in one day she'd breezed into his life, changing that forever.

He pulled her shirt from her pants and lifted it slowly over her head. Dropping a kiss to her shoulder, he smiled as she shivered. "Relax, baby. We've got all night."

He moved his fingers along the soft skin of her collarbone down the center of her chest into the deep cushion of her cleavage. He paused, felt her erratic heartbeat and willed himself to go slow. Reaching behind her he unclasped her bra then let it slip from her arms to fall to the floor. Her breasts were heavy with desire, her nipples already beginning to pucker. He stroked each one with featherlike caresses, looking deep into her eyes as he did.

He saw so much in her eyes—a yearning for something she didn't quite understand. A need to reach for even more.

With both hands, he spanned her waist then knelt in front of her, dropping a tender kiss to her navel. She rested a hand on his shoulder as he removed one shoe then the other, massaging the arch of her foot briefly as he did. Dragging his hands up her legs he paused at her hips, reached around and kneaded her butt, giving in for a moment to his own growing desire. When her fingers dug into his shoulder, grabbing fistfuls of his shirt, he stopped and moved to unfasten her pants. Sliding his hand into the band of her panties, he pushed both garments down her legs and let her step out of them.

Then he stood.

She looked up at him expectantly.

"Get on the bed," he said in a voice laced with barely there restraint.

She did as he asked.

"Show me what you have for me, baby."

Celise lay back against the pillows, grasping first her breasts then moving her hands down her torso to her hips and her thighs. With her eyes on him she spread her legs, letting her hands slip along the inside of her thighs.

Jason swallowed deeply. "Lift your legs."

She lifted her legs until her feet were flat on the bed.

The blinds were still open, and moonlight slipped through, casting a sensual glow to her bronze body. Her thighs were slick with her desire, the dewy curls at her center releasing her intoxicating scent. He inhaled deeply and licked his lips.

"It's not fair," she whispered, moving her hands upward to her center.

"What's that?"

"You get a show and I don't."

Jason grinned. "I told you to relax. Your show's coming."

He removed his shirt much quicker than he had hers then stepped out of his shoes. His pants were still undone from her attention in the living room so he simply pushed them down his legs.

When he was gloriously naked Celise stroked her clit. "Magnificent," she murmured.

He loved to see her touch herself, loved the fact that she wasn't ashamed to bring herself pleasure if need be. Only, there was no need that night. He was there and he had every intention of pleasuring her until she couldn't see or think of anyone but him.

Moving to the nightstand, he pulled several condoms out of the drawer. Dropping all but one onto the table he crawled to the center of the bed. "Is this all for me?" he asked, dragging his gaze up and down her body.

Celise replied, whimpering, "Yes."

Ripping the foil packet he smoothed the latex over his erection and climbed between her legs. With slow movements he brushed the tip of his arousal over her clit. She squirmed and reached for him, tried to pull him inside.

"No. Not yet."

"Please, Jason."

"I want you as crazy with desire as I am," he said, pulling back so her hands couldn't wrap around him. If she touched him there he would be through. There was no doubt about that.

"I am, Jason." She moaned. "I need you."

Her hand was between her legs again, her fingers slipping through her moistened folds. Jason licked his lips, loving the sight, wanting to taste her sweetness once more. He bent down, blowing his warm breath over her center.

She undulated her hips, opening herself even wider for him. He licked her then, from her clit to her opening and back again. Then he dipped his tongue inside and grasped her hips to hold her still. For endless moments he worked his tongue inside of her, thrusting deeply then suckling.

Celise was helpless. Her center contracted under his masterful ministrations. Her heart beat frantically as the pressure built. He was pulling her, dragging her into a mindless orgasm, something she'd come to expect from only him. Momentarily her thoughts shifted to her last intimate relationship, to the nights she'd longed to be taken like this but instead had endured a sadistic form of torture. She let go of those thoughts, of that time and focused solely on the man between her legs. He wanted her crazy with desire, and he was doing a damn good job of getting her there.

Jason was a very considerate lover, and because of that, she found it easy to shed any inhibitions. What they shared was a mutual enjoyment of sex, a very strong attraction and...

She shook her head, unable to think straight. His mouth working over her was just too much to bear. Screaming his name and thrashing about on the bed didn't seem to be enough. She needed another release, a more powerful discharge of emotion.

He held her hips and her thighs quaked, clamping around his head, trapping him there as her way of continuing the pleasure. She was almost there. He pressed a thumb to her clit, his tongue darting in and out of her opening. Her panting increased.

"Yes," he whispered over her, wanting her even more frantic, more wrapped up in the sensations he was bringing her.

As her entire body tensed, her legs stiffened then released their hold on him, the folds of her vagina swelled and dripped with essence, and he moaned as if savoring this blissful moment. Rising above her, Jason lay alongside her, wiping the wisps of hair away from her face and kissing her mouth softly. "You are so beautiful when you come," he said, propping himself up on his elbow and looking down at her.

Celise heard him speaking but took a few more steadying breaths before daring to respond. "You are so evil."

"What? Me?" Jason feigned innocence.

"You should have told me in the beginning you were into torture." The moment she said the words, the realization hit and she tensed.

"What is it, baby? Are you hurting?"

Celise shook her head, attempting to clear the unwanted thoughts from her mind. The last thing she wanted between them, in this bed, was Nigel and his sadistic ways, but she'd brought him there. She'd spoken of torture during sex. That thought could only have come from what she'd endured with him.

"No. I'm fine." Regrouping, she turned on her side and cupped his face. "I just meant that you were really mean to have teased me like that."

He didn't believe her, she could tell by the way he continued to stare at her.

"Celise, if something is wrong, you can tell me," he said seriously.

She leaned over and kissed him lightly on the lips. "Nothing is wrong with me," she said, moving a hand down his chest, past his stomach to his still throbbing erection. "But I think you still have an issue that needs to be handled."

"I think you have issues you're denying," was his response.

She shook her head then wrapped her fingers around his heavy erection. "Not now. I only want this now. I only want us."

Jason pulled her to him, and she continued to stroke his shaft.

"Do you trust me?"

Celise nodded. She did trust him, more than she ever imagined she could trust a man. This wasn't supposed to happen. It was just supposed to be an affair. And now...now, she felt like it had blossomed into so much more.

"Then tell me what's wrong," he implored, his warm breath fanning over her face.

She kissed his chin, his jaw, and his lips. Her tongue played over his lips then sucked them into her mouth. He responded, reluctantly at first. The kiss was wildly erotic with their tongues dancing around each other, retreating and scraping over lips and teeth. Their need for each other echoed throughout the room in the form of their moans and panting.

There was no doubt that he wanted her, the tautness of his body, the rapid beating of his heart all confirmed this fact. And yet, he pulled back. He nibbled on her ear and Celise closed her eyes.

"You said you only want us. That's what I want too. But there's something between us, something that's stopping you from giving me everything. Please, tell me what it is," he whispered.

With his turgid erection in one hand and his deep, sexy voice in her ear Celise knew without a doubt that there was only one thing she wanted at the moment. "Make love to me, Jason. Please. Now."

He hesitated and Celise held her breath hoping, praying that her past didn't destroy her future.

Finally, pushing her onto her back Jason slipped into her in one smooth stroke. She gasped. He looked down at her and waited until her eyes were on him. "Think of only me. Only me, Celise."

Lifting her legs, she clasped her ankles around his back and whispered, "Yes, Jason."

His strokes were long and slow, deep and tender. How did he know this was just what she needed? He bent down to kiss her, and she hugged him close. His thickness filled her, completed her. Tears streamed down her face at that realization.

Jason pulled back and looked down at her. He kissed one tear away. "Just you." He kissed the other tear. "Just me."

Her eyes fluttered, and more tears fell.

"That's all, baby. It's just you and me."

Celise couldn't help it, the feel of him so deep inside of her physically and invading every part of her emotionally was overwhelming. "For how long?" she asked.

Jason didn't hesitate, but on the next down stroke ground into her deeper than he'd ever done before. "Forever."

Warning bells didn't go off in her head nor did chimes of happiness, but her heart filled with an emotion she hadn't thought possible. And when he kissed her again all the feelings she'd been holding at bay spilled out and into him.

She grabbed his bottom, pushing him deeper and deeper still. She wanted him so much, the desire for them to be one surpassing anything else.

"That's right, hold me, baby. Hold on to me." Jason lifted up until he was on his knees. She moved her hands from his bottom and he grabbed her wrists, put them back in place. "No. Right here." She clasped him, and he pounded into her. "Now look at me."

She opened her eyes. "Don't ever think of him again." He thrust his hips, plowing into her center so deep his testicles slapped against her bottom. "Not when you're with me." He thrust again. "Not ever."

She moaned, focusing on the wondrous sensations. Then he touched her clit and her eyes shot open.

"That's right, look at me. Keep your eyes on me." He rubbed the tightened nub and moved his hips in a circular motion.

She kept her eyes open although it was a task. God, he was handsome. Even in the throes of passion he stopped her heart. His face was tense, his movements concentrated, and she marveled at the fact that he was so focused on her. "Jason." All she could do was whisper his name. There was something else on her mind at that moment, something she wanted to tell him. Something she was afraid would change them both from that point on.

She bit her bottom lip.

"Oh, yeah. Come for me, baby. Come for me." His movements quickened.

The words fumbled around in her head, the thought of saying them or not saying them blurred by the intense pressure building inside of her. She screamed his name again just as her release burst free like remnants of a broken dam.

"He hurt me," Celise said quietly as her back rested against Jason's front. They were in the tub, hot water relaxing the muscles they'd used during lovemaking. He hadn't said a word to her since they'd both come to their release. He'd simply scooped her up into his arms and carried her into the bathroom.

She felt him tense beneath her and decided to keep going before she lost the nerve. "He didn't beat me or anything like that. His abuse was on a deeper level. The most intimate moment two people can share is when they're having sex. That's because it's when you're most vulnerable."

His hands were folded over her chest as he held her. She moved hers to be on top of his and rubbed his long fingers. "Nigel was my first serious relationship. You already know that we were supposed to get married, so I thought that I should give myself to him totally. But after the first few months Nigel made it clear that I was lacking in the sex department. I wasn't afraid of sex. In fact, I've always been curious and eager to try new things. But Nigel was older, and I wasn't sure how he'd feel about my adventurous sexual thoughts. Anyway, I decided to just come out and tell him. That was the first time I saw that smile.

"Nigel looked at me as if I had just said some magical words, and he wasted no time taking me to bed. I had no idea what his intentions were." She stopped speaking and dealt with the wave of shame and embarrassment that washed over her.

Jason kissed the top of her head then her temple. "Take your time," he whispered.

Celise took a shaky breath. "I guess I wasn't as adventurous as I'd previously thought. He wanted to do things…he did things…that I didn't like."

Jason's tone was strained. "Did you tell him to stop?"

"I tried, but it seemed like the more I complained, the more I tried to break free of him, the more aroused he grew. He kept telling me that I was doing a good job, that he loved it and he loved me. Eventually, I just kept still and let him do what he wanted."

"For how long?"

"I stayed with him another six months after that. I began to dread the nights he'd want sex. Then one day I was cleaning out a closet in his bedroom and I found this box. It was full of all sorts of things. Sex things. Things that he hadn't used on me. Things I was afraid that one day he would want to use on me. I confronted him. We argued. And he basically told me that I should get used to it, that once we were married I'd have no choice but to do whatever he told me. I believed him and I tried to do what he wanted. I tried to do what my father wanted. I tried but then there was another woman and he suggested we all get together. I just couldn't do it." She shook her head. "I just couldn't."

"So you broke it off with him?" Jason asked in a strained voice.

"No. I still stayed. About a week after that I heard him on the phone talking about wanting to move the wedding up sooner and needing to hurry up so that my shares in the company would become his. And it dawned on me that I was just a pawn in his game—a pawn he planned to use in every possible way." Celise took a deep breath, knowing without a doubt that she'd done the right thing both now and then. "That's when I left him."

Jason was quiet. She wasn't sure what he was thinking about what she'd told him or about her. When she couldn't stand the silence any longer she prepared to get out of the tub. He grasped her around her waist and pulled her back against him.

"Don't run from me."

She sat stiffly between his legs, willing him to either say something or let her go.

"I wondered why you continued to hold back from me. I knew there was more to your breakup with Nigel."

Celise relaxed a bit because there was no anger in his voice. She didn't think she'd be able to handle it if Jason were angry with her over this. Nigel blamed her, told her it wasn't his fault she was timid and afraid to try anything knew. He told her there were plenty of women who would gladly do what he wanted when he wanted them to. For a brief period in her life she'd let him chip away at her self-esteem. "I knew that if I didn't leave him I would lose myself."

Jason held her tightly. "But you did leave him. And it wasn't your fault."

Celise closed her eyes to the memories. "I tried. I really did. It just didn't seem right. The things he wanted me to do…I just couldn't."

"Shhh. Don't give it another thought."

"I guess I'm not as sexually uninhibited as I thought I was."

"That's not true. You said yourself that sex is about intimacy. And intimacy is about trust. If you don't completely trust the person you're with you won't feel it's okay to let everything else go and just concentrate on what's between the two of you."

Celise listened to his words. That explained why she'd done things with Jason she'd never done with anyone else. Why she'd allowed him to do things that when Nigel did them repulsed her. And why she enjoyed sex with him so much. "I could never relax with him. I felt so insecure, so incapable. Like I didn't have an ounce of passion," she admitted.

Jason smiled. "Baby, you're the most passionate woman I've ever met. It's not so much the act but the emotion that goes into it that makes it passionate and explosive. You've got that and then some."

She smiled. "You think so?"

He gave her a loud, messy kiss on the neck and chuckled. "I know so."

She squirmed and cuddled closer to him. His words made her feel good, confident. Jason was definitely unlike any other man she'd ever known, and she wondered what that really meant. She admitted to wanting this thing between them to only be temporary in the beginning. But now knew she'd be heartbroken if it ended.

"If I weren't afraid of losing you, I'd kill him," Jason said thoughtfully.

"Hmph, he doesn't deserve death."

"If you say so."

"Castration would be much better." She giggled.

Jason laughed with her, then he turned her so that she straddled him. Water sloshed around them, but neither of them seemed to notice. "Seriously," he began, lifting her chin with his finger, "I meant what I said about you not thinking of him anymore. It doesn't matter what he thought or what he said to you. He was wrong."

Celise nodded.

"You are a gorgeous, sensual woman who needs to be loved just right." He traced the line of her jaw with that finger.

Oh yeah, this was so much more than an affair. She knew it without a doubt and wondered if he could feel it too. "I...there's something between us," she began, not sure how to put her thoughts into words. She'd just come out of a bad relationship. Would he believe her if she told him how she felt about him?

"There is something between us, Celise. I've known it since the first time I laid eyes on you." He cupped her face. "You're very important to me. I care about your goals and ambitions and your pain." He leaned in, taking her mouth in a soft, measured kiss.

She shifted above him, melting into his embrace like she always did. She should tell him how she felt. But she wasn't sure. Was it love? She cared about Jason a great deal. That was why she'd stepped in when catastrophe struck that afternoon. He meant a lot to her and as such his hotel meant a lot to her. She hadn't stopped to think how her father would feel about her helping the enemy nor had she asked Sharrell before volunteering her help too. She'd simply done what needed to be done to relieve some of the stress she knew Jason was feeling. That was something people did for a person they loved.

The kiss deepened, and she lost her train of thought, another thing she seemed to do frequently when he touched her. He shifted a little, never breaking their kiss, and plucked a condom from a basket on the floor. They'd decided days ago that it made more sense to have them all around the house since their lovemaking was not restricted to the bedroom.

"Put it on. Now." He growled and handed her the condom then dipping his head to suckle her breast.

She obliged then lifted her bottom from the water and sank down onto his stiff rod, loving the feel of the hot water and his thick arousal stretching her, filling her. This was the type of completion she thought she'd never feel. He was the type of man she thought she'd never find. He didn't dominate her, didn't profess to know what was best for her. He simply let her be who she was.

They both gasped with the entry then settled into a slow, comfortable pace guaranteed to bring them both to supreme release.

Celise sighed and rested her forehead against his. They didn't speak, just moved. Slow and sensuous, deep and seductive. Intimacy was about trust. She trusted Jason's business advice as well as his personal observances. She trusted him to touch her in the right spot, to bring her to the most powerful release. And at that moment there was no doubt in her mind that she'd fallen in love with Jason Carrington.

CHAPTER EIGHTEEN

Jason was in his office reviewing sales statistics and ignoring the newspaper to his left with the headline:

HOTEL HEIRESS WINS COOK-OFF BY SABATAGING OTHER CHEF'S WORK

He'd called Celise the moment he'd arrived at the hotel and saw the paper on his desk. He hadn't wanted her leaving the house and being approached by the citizens of Monterey who actually believed she'd done this.

He also had his secretary call the paper and ask for the editor to whom he'd advised that if he didn't print a retraction his attorneys would be in touch. There was no proof that Celise had sabotaged anything. The paper had implied she was libel, and he wasn't about to stand for it. After some choice words and the threat of lost advertising dollars, the editor agreed to run a series of interviews, one with him, one with Celise and one with Russell Branch. That satisfied Jason, and Celise had agreed it was a fitting solution when he'd spoken to her.

She'd seemed undaunted by the prior day's activities and was actually meeting with her friend from New York whom she wanted to hire as a manager for her restaurant. Jason was sitting back in his chair thinking of when the right time to ask her about running his restaurant would be. They'd definitely made strides the night before, coming really close to defining this thing between them as a serious relationship. Celise, for all her candor and bravado, was not at ease with expressing her emotions. He sensed that was Nigel Bingham's fault and reminded himself to punch him an additional time for doing that to her. Jason was almost certain she had feelings for him, feelings with which she wasn't entirely comfortable. And until she was comfortable, he wouldn't push her. He still felt guilty as hell not telling her of his plans.

His office door opened, and he looked up thinking it was his assistant. But it wasn't.

"Hello, Jason."

He scowled. "Funny, you never struck me as a person who liked to play with fire," he said through clenched teeth.

Pamela closed the door and walked to his desk. "If you're talking about my ban at the hotel, you can't ban a paying guest."

"I can and I have."

"Obviously your staff doesn't listen to what you say," she quipped.

"It doesn't matter. The police will know soon enough," he told her as he picked up the phone ready to dial.

Pamela sat on the edge of his desk, her already short skirt riding higher up her thighs. She leaned over, slightly pressing a finger on the phone's release button.

"Do you really want to call the police, Jason? The press is already camped out front. Imagine what they'd think if a police cruiser pulled up," she stated.

Jason sighed hating the logic in her comment. He placed the phone back into the cradle. "What do you want, Pamela?"

"That's a simple question," she said with a smile. "I want you."

Jason leaned forward in his chair, dropping his elbows onto his desk. "I have a simple answer. No."

"Is it because of your new little toy? If so, she's hardly worth it. I can do so much more for you than she can." Pamela leaned over the desk, her cleavage almost spilling from the rib of her dress. "You remember all the things I did for you, don't you, baby? She's not into those things."

The sight of her was making him sick. He remembered being with Pamela, remembered the hot, unadulterated sex they'd had. But only now did he realize how little feelings had to do with their relationship. The sex was hot and out-of-this-world kinky, but it wasn't nearly as moving as his time with Celise. There had been no intimacy with Pamela because there had never been any trust.

"I remember you lied to me. You stole from me, and you betrayed me," he told her succinctly.

"That's over now," Pamela said as she glanced at her watch then stood to move around his desk.

Jason watched her come closer. She licked her lips nervously as she approached.

"Who booked your room at the hotel, and what name are you using?" he asked, suddenly very curious about why she was really there. Pamela was a beautiful woman. And while he knew he was a good guy and a thorough lover, he had no misguided ideas that she was sweating him just for sex.

"I want you back, baby. I told you that." She leaned forward, pushing him back in his chair. "Don't you miss me, Jason?"

She held out both arms and attempted to hug him. Jason grabbed her by the wrists and stood, pushing her away at the same time. "No. I don't miss you, and I don't want you."

Her eyes flashed with anger.

"What, you think because you're screwing Little Miss Hotel Queen her daddy's going to let you join his company? That's not even going to work. You were better off teaming up with me. David Markam is never going to finance your hotel unless you sell it to him outright."

Jason was taken aback by her quick change in demeanor, but he didn't let her see that. "I don't want or need David Markam to do anything for me. You know that. This is my hotel, and it will stay my hotel. Just as who I sleep with will remain my business."

Pamela looked down at her watch again then swore. "I don't care. I'm sick of this game. I'm sick of him, and I'm sick of you!" she yelled. Then as if to show him how serious her words were, she swung an arm, knocking stuff off his desk before turning and heading toward the door.

In two swift steps Jason caught up with her, grasping her arm to keep her from leaving. She hissed in pain, her eyes closing, her face tensing.

In all his life Jason had never hurt a woman and had no intention of starting. He quickly released her arm then looked at her closely. He hadn't grabbed her hard and he hadn't thrown her against the door with such force that she would hurt herself, so why was her face contorted like she was about to cry?

"What's the matter with you?" he asked.

Pamela straightened then glared at him. "Nothing. You don't want me so let me out of here." She brought her right hand up to massage her left shoulder. "I'll leave your hotel because like I said, I'm sick of all this drama."

Jason watched as she rubbed her shoulder then on impulse he moved her hand and pushed the rim of her shirt down until he saw a violent bruise.

Pamela shrugged, trying to move out of his reach, but he held her still, pulling the shirt almost completely off her shoulder. The bruise was big and ugly and looked strangely like a handprint. The thoughts rushing through his mind were too insane to consider, but so was everything else that had been happening at the hotel lately. And just as he'd told Clive, there was no such thing as a coincidence.

"What happened to you? Did somebody hurt you?"

"Like you care," she spat then moved away from him.

"I don't. I just want to know." If what he was thinking had any shred of truth he was definitely fit to kill. He paused, remembering her words from earlier. "How do you know what Celise is into?"

Before she could answer him, there was a knock on his door. She turned her back to him, and with a sinking feeling Jason touched the knob and opened the door. Cameras flashed and microphones were thrust in his face. He didn't have a moment to speak before a reporter blurted out, "Who's the new babe? Are you cheating on Celise Markam? Is there a wedding in the future?"

"What the hell are you talking about?" he asked then looked back at Pamela. "What did you do?"

Myrtle Hampden was the last person Celise expected to see as she sat in a coffee shop sipping her dark chocolate latte. Her meeting with Samantha Kent about managing her restaurant had gone well, and she promised to call her as soon as things were up and running. She'd endured the stares and the polite smiles knowing that everyone had read the paper and was trying to figure out if they should believe the story about her sabotaging the contest or not.

When she looked up to see Myrtle and Ralph approaching, she actually steeled herself for their assault. "Good morning," she said in as cheerful a voice as she could muster.

"Is it a good morning, dear?" Myrtle asked then took a seat. Ralph, as he always did, soon followed suit.

"Every morning you're alive and breathing is a good morning," Celise said brightly.

"That sure is true," Ralph added with a smile, the extra skin at his neck bobbing with his head.

Myrtle rolled her eyes in her husband's direction then plastered on another smile as she looked at Celise. She wore another very expensive suit but this time she had white gloves on her hands as she held her small black purse. Atop her head was yet another one of those old time hats that she seemed to love.

"I was at the cook-off yesterday so I know what happened," Myrtle informed her.

"Really?" Celise asked. "Then maybe you can tell me. I was so busy preparing my dishes that I don't have a clue."

Myrtle gave her a stern look. "Did that boy put you up to it? Did he make you cheat? 'Cause you don't seem like the type of girl who would cheat her way through life."

Celise's calm was wearing thin. How dare she interrupt her to accuse her and Jason of misconduct? "I don't know what you mean. And who is that 'boy'?" Whether or not Myrtle Hampden liked it, Jason was the owner of Carrington Resorts, and he deserved some respect.

"Oh." Myrtle sat back in her chair. "So you're in cahoots with him now? I knew there was something between you when I saw you buying him a gift. It's a shame though, you coming from such a good family and all. I mean, he comes from a good family, too, but he just doesn't know what to do with himself. I hear you don't either."

"Mrs. Hampden, I'll have you know that I'm perfectly sure of what to do with myself as is Jason. We do what we want without asking permission. That tends to ruffle a few feathers every now and then. That's life." Oh yeah, she was definitely getting tired of Myrtle Hampden.

"With that attitude I can see why the two of you are together, but you'll be packing up and leaving town together before I get through." Myrtle stood.

"Before you get through?" Celise stood with her. "What does that mean?"

Ralph stood a few inches away from his wife, a look of pure guilt and regret on his face. Celise looked from Myrtle to him and back to Myrtle again.

"What have you done?"

Ralph and Myrtle made a hasty retreat, and Celise pulled out her cell phone to call Jason. If what she was thinking were true, he needed to know right away.

"He's in a meeting, Celise. Is something wrong?" Clive asked when he picked up the phone in Jason's office after his secretary had announced that Celise was on the line.

"I need to talk to him about the Hampdens."

"What about them?"

"I think something's going on with them. I don't know anything specific but they're acting stranger than usual, and Myrtle seems pretty sure that Jason won't own the hotel much longer."

Clive was quiet for a moment. "I'll talk to them as soon as I can."

After Celise arrived at the hotel, Clive called a couple of officers with whom he'd spoken the day before at the cook-off and asked them to come over. He then called the Hampdens to set up a meeting.

"It's about time. Are we voting on the sale?" Myrtle said the moment she'd entered the conference room.

"Not exactly. Have a seat, Mr. and Mrs. Hampden." Clive pulled out a chair and waited until Mrs. Hampden was seated before sitting on the other side of the table next to Celise.

"Where's the rest of the board?" Myrtle asked before looking at Celise. "And what's she doing here?"

Ralph touched her hand. "Give him a chance to tell us what's going on, Myrtle."

Clive nodded. "Thank you, Mr. Hampden. I apologize for your assumption that this was a full board meeting. Celise and I really just wanted to talk with the two of you."

"Just us? Why? We're not supporting your friend anymore. This has got to stop. He's not keeping his promises." Myrtle slammed her weathered hand on the conference table.

The woman seemed overly excited, but then if what Celise suspected had any bearing, she had reason to be. "I was just wondering if you actually knew of a buyer since you seem so adamant about Jason selling the hotel," Clive said.

"No. But I know there are many buyers out there. This hotel has a reputation, you know," was Myrtle's quick retort.

Again, Clive nodded. "Yes, the money."

"It's a treasure, hidden somewhere in this hotel," Myrtle corrected him. "In the early years I searched and searched but never found anything, but they say it's here. Anybody would want to get their hands on the hotel for that reason alone."

"I don't believe there's any treasure here," Clive said. "And if you believe it why do you want to sell?"

"Because I'm tired of all the crap Carrington's been selling us. I've been telling him to sell this hotel for months, and he's too stubborn to listen."

"But you're determined to make him see reason, aren't you?"

Ralph grabbed Myrtle's hand as he looked at Celise and Clive carefully. "We just want our share of the proceeds. If you're selling then we're with you."

"And if we're not selling…" Clive paused and looked from the man to his wife, "are you against us?"

When neither of them spoke Clive stood and opened the door. Two uniformed officers came in. To their credit, neither Ralph nor Myrtle showed a moment's concern.

"I'm sure you've heard about the mishaps at the hotel in the last few weeks. The officers here are investigating those incidents," Clive announced.

The first officer, the one standing closest to Ralph asked, "You two have a room at the hotel—one that you keep as a perk to being a shareholder. That's strange since you also own a house near the beach."

"It's not strange. It's a perk like you said," Myrtle stated and rolled her eyes.

The officer nodded. "You also have free reign of the building. That's a perk too."

Ralph narrowed his eyes. "What are you getting at, son?"

Clive who looked tired of the whole interrogation scene decided to get right to the point. "We had all of the rooms in the hotel searched because we figured that whoever was sabotaging us had to be a guest."

Myrtle kept her hard stare. Ralph looked down at the table.

Officer number two finally spoke. "We found some pretty interesting things in your room. A sledgehammer, wire cutters, garden gloves."

"Maybe you could tell us what you were doing with those things, Ralph," Clive said.

Nobody spoke.

"Better yet, why don't you tell us what you two were planning to do next? I mean you added potting soil to one of the contestant's dishes. Were you actually prepared to kill someone in this hotel to get Jason to sell?" Clive asked.

It didn't take five more minutes before Ralph Hampden confessed and as a gentleman tried to take all the blame on himself. But Celise and Clive were certain Myrtle had been the mastermind. She didn't look the least bit regretful, which only confirmed his suspicions. Celise had never heard an elderly woman curse the way Myrtle Hampden did when she was cuffed and escorted out of the building.

"You are not doing this, and that's final," Jason roared through the conference room.

Clive put a hand to his shoulder. "It may be the only way, Jason. Pamela said that Nigel was livid when she talked to him earlier about their plan going wrong again. He's not going to be very receptive to her at this point."

"I'm the last one he would expect to come to his aid," Celise added.

"But why should he trust you? You left him and haven't spoken to him in months. Not to mention the fact that the papers already have you linked to Carrington," DJ said, standing from his seat with a worried expression.

"I could do it," Sharrell offered.

Pamela spoke up after a long silence. "He's least likely to trust you because he's never had any real dealings with you. Celise is the best bet. In the event that Nigel couldn't convince you to sell, his backup plan was to buy enough stock to give him controlling interest."

Celise looked at Pamela questioningly. "You've been a part of his plan all along. How do we know you're not stringing us along this time?" The moment she'd seen Pamela with Jason she'd been ticked off, although she'd remained calm for the sake of their current situation, but Pamela's remark, no matter how much truth it held, made her wonder again.

All eyes went to Pamela.

"I'm sick of this game," she said, crossing her arms over her chest. "Nigel acts like this hotel is a gold mine, and Jason is willing to give blood for it. I just want to be done with the whole mess," Pamela answered.

"Then why not just leave?" Sharrell questioned.

"Because Nigel is a monster and if anybody knows how serious I am about that statement, you should," she said to Celise. "He owes me for the time I've put in with him, and since it doesn't look like I'll be getting that payment in a nice hefty sum, I might as well walk away with some satisfaction."

Jason watched as Celise took a deep breath and expelled it slowly. Pamela's remark would have hit the mark with her, which would seal this deal for her. For Jason, he still wasn't so sure. He stood from the table and walked away while they continued to talk.

He heard them talking, heard the question that he'd asked Pamela himself being asked again and wondered if he really believed her. Then he remembered the bruises on her and decided to trust her.

They'd been in the conference room for the last two hours piecing together the happenings at Carrington Resorts for the last month. From Celise's impromptu meeting with the Hampdens that morning Celise and Clive had managed to reveal Myrtle's plot to sabotage the hotel so that it would receive so much negative publicity Jason would be forced to sell.

Jason and the Markams had been more than surprised by the lengths to which the elderly couple were prepared to go to see him fail. And yet with that behind them a threat still existed. If Nigel got his hands on enough stock he could end up with controlling interest in the hotel.

While Celise and Clive were with the Hampdens, Jason had Pamela in his office, and because he couldn't get hold of Clive, had called DJ instead. He and DJ managed to get Pamela to spill the story on Nigel.

Now Sharrell, Clive, Pamela, DJ, Jason and Celise were holed up in the conference room trying to come up with a plan to stop Nigel. With the minor sabotage attempts accounted for, and taking into consideration Nigel's violent history, as told via Pamela and Celise, they knew they had to proceed with caution and to attack Nigel at his weakest point, which apparently was women. Nigel couldn't resist sex, and he definitely couldn't resist his preferred type of sex.

The mere thought of Celise going into his room and offering herself to him just to get an admission made Jason cringe. His temples pounded as he desperately tried to think of a better way. This hotel was very important to him, the independence and satisfaction he received from buying it and re-building it to match his vision was beyond anything he could have ever imagined.

But this was Celise. It was the woman he loved and they were talking about sending her into a room by herself with an animal. An animal that had already scared her emotionally—he did not even want to think about how Nigel may have scared her physically before Jason they met.

From behind he felt her slip her arms around his waist, laying her face against his back, welcoming the warmth of his body against hers. "I'll be okay, Jason," she whispered.

He didn't move. "No, Celise."

She stiffened at his tone then moved around to face him. "You can't tell me what to do."

"Don't do this," he said, shaking his head. "Don't pick now to get on your stubborn stance and tell me you can make your own decisions because I don't want to hear it."

She began to speak, but he held up a hand to stop her. "He's dangerous. You know that. And you expect me to stand by and watch you put yourself in harm's way? No! It's not happening. We'll think of something else."

"There's no time to think of something else. The board is outraged at the way the hotel is being perceived in the press. You can expect that in a day or two they're going to hold an emergency meeting with plans to sell this hotel. And Nigel will be waiting in the wings to buy it and then what are you going to do?" she asked with a tinge of attitude in her voice. She was challenging him over this situation, this fucking man!

Jason spoke through clenched teeth. "Nigel still won't get his hands on it. My father or your father would buy it first. Then at least it would stay in family hands."

"But it won't stay in your hands," she said quietly.

He knew that. He'd thought of nothing but that for the last year and a half, but now he had something else to consider. His mother had asked him if Celise was more important to him than this hotel and he hadn't answered. At that moment, he realized that she was. He'd pictured a future owning and running Carrington Resorts and then she'd walked into his life, and that picture had been altered. He wanted her by his side, whether he was running this hotel or another one. He wanted her there with him, safe and unharmed. Sending her to Nigel Bingham was not an option. He looked at her seriously, his voice lowering so that only she could hear him. "You're important to me, Celise. Much more important than this hotel."

Celise's heart melted at his words, and her eyes filled with tears. She'd never felt like she was that important to anyone before. Even her father put his business before her. And knowing how much this hotel meant to Jason could only mean that their affair had definitely turned to something else. And it was with that knowledge that she stepped to him, cupped his face in her hands and said, "And you are more important to me than what Nigel Bingham did. I'm not afraid of him, and I'm not afraid to go to him because I know that you, my hero, will be waiting right outside his door. I trust you to protect me. Won't you trust me to help you?"

He'd never wanted anybody's help, was convinced he could do everything by himself, but he was man enough to admit defeat, and as she touched him and spoke those words she put her life in his hands, her trust in his heart. That was worth more than this hotel and more than anything else to him. How could he deny her?

He pulled her to him hugging her and wanting to say so many things but realizing they weren't alone. Pulling back, he looked down into her eyes. "The minute he puts his hands on you it's over. Like you said, I'll be right outside that door. If he so much as breathes too close to you—"

She put two fingers to his lips to end his next words. "Shhhh. We're not going to think like that. I'll be fine.

I'll get him to talk and then I'll walk away—*we'll* walk away."

Jason kissed her fingertips then moved her hand to his chest, placing it over his heart and covering it with his own.

She looked up at him questioningly.

"When this is over we have a lot to talk about," he said.

She nodded, accepting the change and welcoming the joy it brought her.

CHAPTER NINETEEN

The plan was that she would go into Nigel's room, wired with a microphone of course, and get him to talk about his plans to monopolize Carrington Resorts' stock. While the setup wasn't illegal, the way he purchased the stock was. Nigel and his sick, perverted mind was systematically seducing and demeaning the daughters or wives of the stockholders, taking pictures of them in compromising positions then blackmailing the stockholders into selling to him. Besides the Hampdens, who he couldn't touch because they'd immediately turned down his offers to purchase their stock via Myrtle's insistence that she would get Jason out on her own, there were three other members of the board: Christian Bloomfeld whose wife had succumbed to Nigel's charms; Grant Holcomb whose twin daughters had loved Nigel's adventuresome mind and made an X-rated video with him; and Olivia Hansfeld who was a very rich woman who loved to keep a boy toy until she found out that Nigel wasn't the keeping kind.

But he still didn't have controlling shares because Olivia was experienced in keeping her lovers at arm's length. She had yet to sign the final paperwork, which meant that if the Hampdens along with Olivia signed over to Nigel, he would have the controlling shares.

Still, they wanted Nigel out, and the only way to get him out was to beat him at his own game.

Sharrell helped Celise slip into an awesomely tight black dress that barely skimmed her knees. While lacing up the corset front Sharrell looked at her cousin. "You're sure you know what you're doing?"

Celise nodded. "I'm positive."

"You know Uncle David is going to kill us all when he finds out we let you do this," she said nervously.

"Lucky for us he won't find out anytime soon." Celise was a little nervous, but she refused to think about it. Instead she thought about Jason and remembered his heart beating against her hands. The connection she'd felt the first time they'd met had intensified as he created another first in her life. This was the first time she knew real love. She loved him so much she wasn't only willing to see the man she hated but to also chance being alone with him.

A knock sounded at the door signaling that they were ready for her. Sharrell opened the door letting the men inside. Celise instantly locked gazes with Jason who came straight toward her. "Where did you get this dress?" he murmured close to her ear then kissed her cheek.

"In New York," she answered nervously. "Why?"

"After today you are forbidden to wear it or anything like it in public again," he whispered hoarsely.

She'd peeped herself in the bathroom mirror already. Her breasts protruded over the tight bodice, almost to the point of revealing her nipples. Her waist was accentuated and punctuated the round backside she'd inherited from her mother. It was an ultra sexy dress and she felt damned powerful wearing it.

Warmed by his words and wishing they were alone, she smiled. "I'll wear it only for you."

Draping an arm around her shoulders, he said, "You bet your ass you will."

Then a guy she'd never met before came closer to insert the microphone. He reached for her and she took a step back. Jason's arm tightened around her.

"This is Ricky Voe. He's a PI, and he's heavily into surveillance. He's agreed to help us out," Jason explained.

"Oh," she said then stood still as this man she'd just met stuck his hand down the front of the dress to insert the smaller than expected microphone.

Jason watched Ricky carefully, which would have been funny had Celise's nerves not been starting to get the best of her.

"You don't have to talk above your normal range and it'll pick up any voice within ten to fifteen feet," Ricky instructed her then pulled what looked like a necklace from his bag.

It was silver beads with a large onyx hanging in the center. He placed it around Celise's neck. "There's a camera in the center of the black orb. It will show whatever is in your line of vision on the monitors over there," Ricky said.

In the corner another man was setting up two televisions. The screens were full of TV snow until Ricky gave a nod to the other guy who in turn flicked a switch on the keypad. Then they flashed and focused showing Ricky and Clive and Sharrell who stood behind him.

"I feel like a spy," Celise said shakily.

Jason rubbed her shoulders. "Just remember, it's temporary."

She nodded, wanting to get this task over with as quickly as possible. Pamela had called Nigel's suite and endured his extreme curse out just to ensure that he was there. Jason was no longer threatening to have her arrested since she'd told him everything and was now cooperating.

"Get him to talk about the stock and how he obtained it. He can be prosecuted for blackmail. We just need to prove it. The board members will definitely go along with it," Clive told her.

"Okay," she said.

Sharrell took a step closer to Celise. "Start talking as soon as you get in there and don't stop until he tells you something. Keep moving and don't let him get close to you. And if he gets…"

Celise held up a hand. "Sharrell. I know what to do."

"You should go before he leaves the room for dinner. Nigel doesn't like room service." This was Pamela who had taken a seat near the window, her hands calmly resting in her lap. Celise couldn't help but notice how suddenly tired the woman looked.

"She's right," Celise agreed. "I should get going."

Jason walked her to the door, holding her hand until they were out in the hallway. The door to the room closed behind them.

At first he didn't speak, just cupped her face and looked deeply into her eyes. Then he kissed her, long and slow and infinitely sweet. "I'll be right here waiting for you," he said softly.

"I know," she answered.

He pulled her to him, hugging her tightly. Celise released a breath then said in a small voice, "If he touches me—"

Jason pulled away from her, ran his fingers through her hair, holding her head steady, keeping her gaze on him. "If he touches you, I'm coming in. To hell with his confession and to hell with the hotel, I won't let him hurt you again."

Because she believed and trusted him with all her heart, Celise only nodded in agreement. With one last quick kiss Jason turned away from her and went back into the room.

She didn't hesitate, and even though her heart beat rampantly she willed her feet to move and walked toward the other end of the hall to Nigel's suite.

He was hungry. He was angry. He was growing increasingly tired of uncooperative women.

Nigel slammed his palm down onto the table then stood. There was no use being angry with Pamela. She'd tried and she'd failed. He should have expected that from a woman like her. Pamela was an opportunist. He'd known that the moment she'd slipped into his bed two years ago. She hadn't any shame as she'd slept with him and Jason Carrington at the same time. And once the pretty rich boy had dumped her she thought Nigel was going to marry her. She could not have been further from the truth.

Nigel loved a variety of women. Settling down with one was never a part of his long-term plan. While he was going to go through with the wedding to the delectable Celise Markam, it wasn't because of any great love. She was fresh and alluring—like the forbidden fruit that undoubtedly got Adam and Eve into trouble. He'd fallen for her pretty face and sensuous body. But then her true colors had shown. She was a tease—a whining, unpleasant spoiled little rich girl who jumped ship the minute she couldn't have her way.

He'd tried to break her, to mold her to his needs but had been unsuccessful. Celise wasn't what she seemed, and Nigel suspected that very few people knew that about her.

Enough of that. He didn't want to think of Celise or of Pamela anymore. He was so close to getting what he wanted, so close to having it all.

All he needed was for Olivia Hansfeld to make her delivery. He expected her at six. That was only fifteen minutes away. Olivia held his future in her very experienced hands. A grin spread across his face as he remembered his time with the intriguing woman. Unlike Celise and Pamela and his other Monterey conquests, Olivia knew just what to do to a man, and she did it very well. He'd loved every minute he'd spent in her bed and almost hated to muck it all up with the unpleasantness of blackmail. But nothing, not even mind-blowing sex, was going to stand in the way of his success.

A knock at the door interrupted his thoughts. The person standing there was a shock.

"Hello, Nigel." Celise Markam smiled when he opened the door. "It's been a while since I've seen you."

Nigel was startled, and then he took in her outfit and quickly recuperated. "Celise. I seem to remember you making the decision not to see me." His blood was already warming. The hunger for her was still there.

"That's what I wanted to speak to you about. Can I come in?"

He didn't hesitate. Sure he questioned why she was there, but that sexy ass dress was all the answer he needed.

Celise heard the door closing behind her and willed herself not to jump. Taking deep, steadying breaths she walked to the other side of his room. Clasping her hands on the edge of the desk she leaned back, jutting her chest forward so that Nigel would have an unfettered view. For a minute she felt cheap for luring him this way. She felt like she was no better than he was in the tawdry way he treated women. But then she remembered her cause. She remembered Jason and remained focused.

"I've been thinking about the way I ended things between us," she began.

He stood a few feet away from her, slipping his hands into his pockets. Celise remembered he would do that when they were out in public. To everyone around him it looked as if he were simply standing with his hands in his pockets, but she knew that he was fondling himself. Nigel loved to be aroused at all times. He'd told her that sometimes he aroused himself then fought the deep lusting off to prove he had the power to do so. She remembered thinking how weird that sounded then. Now, she knew he was just weird all the way around.

However, this time, his weirdness was going to play in her favor. Keep him talking, she told herself. "Do you ever think of us being together again, Nigel?"

"I think of you often, Celise," he said tightly.

His gray eyes were like pieces of steel as he followed her movements. He was hard now. She could see it through his slacks, and he was stroking himself. She could see the lines of concentration on his face. She slipped onto the desk, crossing her legs as she kept her eyes on him.

"Really? I've been thinking of you too. Particularly since I've been staying at Carrington Resorts." Celise looked around the room and gave an exaggerated sigh. "This could be a fantastic hotel, don't you think?"

Nigel took a few steps closer to her. "This *will* be a fantastic hotel."

She found his gaze again and held it. "When you own it, right?"

He gave a terse smile. "Yes. When I own it."

"My father couldn't clinch the deal with Carrington," she said and uncrossed her legs, letting them fall slightly apart as she did. "Do you think you can persuade him to sell to you?"

Nigel's eyes fell to her legs and didn't bother to return to her face. "I won't have to persuade him."

Celise relaxed. This was going a lot easier than she'd thought. She licked her lips then planted her hands firmly on the desk behind her. "You're going to do such *great* things with this hotel." She emphasized great and watched his eyes darken.

Nigel was rock hard. He was aroused and ready to pounce and she felt the edge of fear creeping along her spine.

"I'm capable of great things. Don't you remember?" he told her, his olive complexion coated now with a light sheen of sweat.

Nigel was a tall, lean man with strong bone structure and a captivating smile. He was the epitome of polished sophistication, with a romantic Irish accent. She could easily see how a woman would be swayed upon first glance. But she knew him better. Her heart rate increased, and she willed herself to calm down. "I remember a lot about us together."

Nigel's hands came out of his pockets, one moving to smooth his hair back while the other cupped his growing erection. "Us together. Hmmm, that's a good memory."

Celise rubbed her hands down her belly, which was covered by sheer black material, then moved them up to brush over her breasts. Her thumb grazed the microphone, and she thought to speed things along a bit. "We could run the hotel together, Nigel."

He was close enough now that she smelled his cologne. It was mixed with a musky smell that she remembered—with a wave of nausea—was his arousal. Her throat was dry so she swallowed deeply and licked her lips.

Nigel groaned and stepped even closer. She wanted to jump from the table and run. Then she remembered that Jason was right outside the door. He would be in this room the instant he thought she was in danger. She was safe. She just needed to hurry the hell up.

"I suggested that to you before, but you weren't interested," he said his voice lowering.

He wanted to touch her, to take her right here and now. But he wouldn't. Nigel always had to have control. Only this time she could see the strain clearly in the sweat that was now beading on his forehead.

"I've done a lot of growing up since then," she said in what she prayed was a calm voice.

"That you have," he said, his eyes falling to her breasts. "What do you want, Celise?"

To run out of here like a bat out of hell. She took a deep breath and concentrated on not saying what she thought. "I want you to tell me how we can take over this hotel. Together."

"If you're serious about us doing it together..." He moaned then gave in and undid his pants.

The sound of his zipper being unzipped echoed throughout the room, and Celise struggled not to cringe. She wouldn't panic. If she panicked Jason would know and he would come and they wouldn't get the information and he would lose the hotel.

"I want us to do everything together, Nigel. I was wrong to leave you." She lifted a leg onto the desk, planting her foot firmly and feeling her dress ride up to her hips, giving him an unlimited view of her thigh highs, garter and black lace panties. "Can you forgive me?"

Nigel smiled and whipped out his erection, pulling on the engorged length with big, strong hands. "You want me to forgive you?"

She fanned her fingers over her inner thigh, watching as his eyes lowered and held. "Yes," she whispered.

He came closer and put a hand over the one on her thigh. She took in a sharp breath at the connection. Hurriedly she released the breath and took another one to settle the waves of nausea. "This will be the greatest hotel ever. Then we can open more, and my father won't know what hit him. Tell me what I can do to be a part of this with you."

"Touch yourself," he said immediately.

She hesitated, trying like hell to send Jason a mental message to stay put. The camera only showed what was in her line of vision. So at that moment the room full of onlookers next door only saw Nigel playing with himself. They would not see her hand inching between her legs slowly then halting just before reaching her center.

"How will we do it, Nigel? How will we get the hotel without Jason selling it to us?"

His eyes were riveted between her legs, his hand moving rapidly at his groin. "I already have it."

"You do?" she asked, unable to mask the surprise in her voice.

Nigel paused and looked up at her.

She froze. Could he tell she was fishing for answers? She wouldn't give him a chance to. She moaned and cupped her center. His gaze dropped.

"I mean, I almost do. I just need…"

He licked his lips and grew quiet. The veins in his neck bulged like the veins in his penis.

"What do you need, baby?" she crooned and cupped her breast with her free hand.

"I need…ah…I need…"

Celise let her head fall back and sighed. The sick bastard needed to hurry up and talk. "Tell me, Nigel. Then we can be together."

He growled. "I need you to touch me, Celise. Now! Put your hands on me! Hard and fast like I showed you. You know how I like it."

Like hell she would. She needed to hurry. Nigel was slipping into that mode. At any moment he was going to reach for her. Her stomach curdled with the deep pangs of fear. He'd grab her first and forcibly wrap her hands around his penis. He'd make her jerk him off. He'd come in her hands, then he'd make her strip and lay on her stomach. He liked to look at her butt, to put his feet at the base of her back and apply pressure. He would come again all over her back.

No! He couldn't touch her.

"I'm going to, baby. I know how much you like it, but I need to know that this hotel thing is taken care of first. I need to know that our future is set," she said nervously.

"Celise, the pain." He groaned.

"You like the pain, don't you, Nigel? You want me to jerk you until all you can feel is the pain." She knew the answer even before he spoke. Nigel got off on pain alone. There were nights when he'd never even penetrated her. Biting her nipples or squeezing her bottom until she screamed could easily make him howl with a powerful release.

"Yes!" he yelled his hands gripping his length then quickly pulling away, as if he didn't trust himself not to jerk off right at this moment.

His control was wavering. She didn't have much time.

"Then tell me how we'll get the hotel," she insisted.

He was breathing heavy and his arms were shaking slightly. The muscles in his jaw twitched as he gritted his teeth.

"Olivia," he growled. "Olivia is bringing the paperwork for her stock."

Celise moaned and gripped her breast in her hand. She hissed then as if she were in pain. Nigel threw back his head and growled louder, like a caged animal. "That won't give you enough stock, will it?"

He'd touched himself again, couldn't help himself since she wouldn't do it for him. His hips were thrusting, his arm working fiercely. "No...no...but I've got all the rest I need."

"Mmmm, baby. Tell me how you managed that. I'll bet you used that." She looked down at his erection and licked her lips slowly, making sure he watched as she did.

"Arrrggh!"

He took a step closer, and Celise was afraid he was going to rip off her clothes at any minute. He leaned over her and bit the lobe of her ear. "I used it on all of them and they loved it. I gave his wife orgasms she'd never experienced before, and I sucked his daughter dry. It was so sweet. Then I threatened to tell the world if they didn't give me what I wanted. I always get what I want," he said those last words firmly, as if to prove his point to her.

"Yes!" Celise sighed grateful that he'd said all she needed to hear. But Nigel thought she was saying yes to something else completely. She felt the moment his erection touched her thigh, and she cringed. Before she could speak his hands went around her waist, and he pulled her off the table.

"No!" she screamed.

"Oh yes! I've got you now. You wanted to play with me, to tease me. You know how I hate that." Quickly he turned her away from him, grabbed a handful of her hair and pushed her over the desk. "Now you're going to give it to me the way I like it."

"No! Nigel, don't," she screamed and remembered the words from the last time they were together. They'd been in a hotel room in Chicago. He'd had a business trip and she'd gone along with him. He'd tried his normal form of seduction and a voice in her head screamed that she fight back. She'd bit him and he'd howled with pain. She'd felt empowered enough to walk away, but then his words had halted her. The pain that would buckle any normal man for possibly hours, only egged him on. He'd thrown her against the wall, lifted her and slammed what felt like his fist between her legs. She'd screamed then but nobody had heard her.

CHAPTER TWENTY

He'd yelled at her, telling her to touch him. Jason jumped out of his chair and headed for the door. Clive stopped him.

"She's doing fine, Jase. Calm down."

"Don't tell me to calm down. You don't know what he's capable of."

Clive nodded. "No. But I trust Celise."

His friend's words held him still, and they walked back to the table where the monitors were set up. Nigel looked as if he were losing control. Celise sounded as if she were too.

Jason doubted anyone else in the room could hear the fear in her voice. But he had. She was deathly afraid of this man, no matter the bravado she'd portrayed. And yet she'd willingly gone in the room with him. Jason felt the sting of guilt prickle his skin.

The moment Nigel admitted to the blackmail they all breathed a sigh of relief. Everyone but Jason. They were shaking hands and clasping shoulders, but Jason kept his eyes riveted on the screen.

Nigel lunged, the picture shifted, and Celise screamed.

Jason would never know if anybody tried to stop him this time as his feet barely touched the ground until the moment he kicked in the door to Nigel's suite. Adrenaline pumped fiercely through his body as he entered the room prepared to tear Nigel to pieces. But he was stopped short by the sight of Celise kicking Nigel squarely in the groin then lifting the chair from the table she'd been perched on and bringing it crashing down over Nigel's head as he doubled over in pain.

The chair broke but she held on to one of the legs and hit Nigel in the back as he fell to the floor. She stood over him then, placed her foot at the base of his back and jumped. Jason couldn't believe what he was seeing. Celise stood on top of Nigel completely and jumped on his back again.

Nigel groaned in pain. Whether it was from the blow to his groin or the chair to his back or the hundred-plus pound woman jumping up and down on him, Jason wasn't sure. And not to spare the man an ounce of the pain he so deserved Jason crossed the room, grabbing Celise by the waist, and lifted her off Nigel.

Clive and DJ entered the room then seeing to the still moaning Nigel. But Jason could care less what was going on with them. Slipping his hand beneath her legs, he picked up Celise and cradled her to him and left the room. He didn't stop until they were in his suite behind a locked door. Carrying her to the bedroom he sat on the bed holding her on his lap.

Her body trembled as she buried her face in his neck. They sat in silence for a long while. Jason stroked her hair and down her arms, kissed her forehead and rocked her back and forth.

She'd done all of this for him. She'd put herself through what must have been a terribly traumatic ordeal for him. There were no words that could describe how he felt about that. And then there were.

He smoothed down her hair, tucking strands behind her ear so he could get a better view of her face. When he could see her almost clearly he kissed her forehead then her temple. "I love you, Celise," he whispered.

Her head shifted, and he kissed her cheek. "I love you."

Her lips. "I love you."

Her chin. "I love you."

Her heart was just settling, the anger at Nigel and what he'd done to her in the past and had attempted to do to her again subsiding. The joy that he'd confessed and that Jason would keep his hotel was rising. The comfort and safety of being enfolded in his arms settled over her, cocooning her with happiness and contentment.

Then he spoke the words.

Maybe she hadn't heard him correctly. Her heart skidded.

He said it again. Her heart plunged.

He said it again. Her heart leaped with joy.

She lowered her head so that his lips were now aligned with hers. Through hooded eyes she watched him watch her and said, "I love you, Jason."

For a moment he had a look of surprise then of relief. He kissed her and pulled away. "I really do love you," she repeated and pressed her lips to his, coaxing his mouth open and slipping her tongue inside.

Their tongues swiveled and caressed in a kiss filled with promise and longing, passion and desire. His hands moved down to her butt, cupping her cheeks. She moaned and quickly shifted so that she was straddling him.

His teeth nipped her jaw and slipped down to her neck. "I want you now," he said, groaning.

Celise sighed, feeling the same urgency she heard in his voice. Grabbing his shirt she ripped the bottom to bare his chest. Her fingers moved frantically over his skin. She dipped her head, placing tiny bites along his pectorals and suckling his nipples.

"Tell me how you want it, baby."

Celise worked at the button on his pants, her heart hammering in her chest. She slipped her hands inside, cupping his hot length and pulling it generously. "I want it hot." She pulled his erection toward her, loving the feel of its moistened tip in the palm of her hand. "And I want it rough."

Jason paused momentarily to grab her by the shoulders. He searched her face for clarity. "Are you sure?"

She nodded then thrust her center into his groin. "I trust you, Jason. I love you." Rubbing her breasts over his chest, she groaned. "Take me now."

With harsh movements he pushed her dress up beyond her waist then reached between her legs and ripped the thin patch of lace that covered her center. Thrusting two fingers into her core he moaned at her already slick state then pulled the fingers out and licked them free of her essence. As if he'd just remembered, he yanked the necklace from her neck and tossed it across the room, then he thrust his hand down her bodice and crumpled the tiny microphone before dropping it to the floor. With another tug of material her breasts were free and jutting forth. He didn't touch them with his hands but lowered his mouth and grabbed one puckered nipple between his teeth. Wiggling his head he heard her intake of breath and felt the plump globe moving erratically beneath him.

More turned on than he'd ever been in his life, Jason grabbed her hips and positioned her over his arousal. "Now?" He looked at her in question.

Celise opened her eyes and looked down at him. Her breasts were heavy with want of his attention. But her core ached, her clit tightening to an almost painful state, and she'd never needed to be taken so urgently before. "Yes, Jason. Now!"

He settled her over him, and at the same time thrust forward entering her forcefully, thankfully.

She rode him like a wild woman, her breasts slapping against his face, her cheeks doing the same to his thighs. She was caught up in her own pleasure, her own sensations, and Jason let her have the lead.

Celise wanted every inch of him inside of her. She wanted to feel him from every angle all at once. She simply couldn't get enough of him. And she needed an orgasm the way a junkie needed a fix.

He was thick and hot inside her, and she moved up and down on him until she thought his heated length would rip her apart. She heard animalistic moans and curses and realized the voice belonged to her. But she didn't care. She wasn't embarrassed. She was in love.

Jason watched as she struggled to find her pleasure, to find that blessed release. Pressing a thumb to her clit, he rubbed then held still. She bucked and screamed. He rubbed again. Her thighs shook. He moved another hand around and let his fingers slip through the crease of her butt. She rode him harder until he thought he would lose control first. With quick precision his hands found her other entrance, and he rubbed there, too, the same way he rubbed her clit.

She moaned then hummed, then bounced on top of him with long, excruciatingly slow movements. He increased the motions of both hands, and she began to chant his name.

"Let me help you, baby," he cooed.

And she bucked over him, taking everything that he was giving her. Thrusting his hips, he pumped her quickly, fingered her and rubbed her clit. Celise was lost. In a mindless state of bliss she floated and drifted, knowing the end was near. Her body shook, her teeth chattered then she erupted in a gush of fluids and a wave of euphoria.

Her head lulled against his shoulder, and for a few moments Jason simply held her there. Then his sex throbbed inside of her, and she stirred.

"You're not finished," she murmured.

"No. I'm not."

He lifted her up then, standing her at the foot of the bed. "Bend over," he instructed.

She obliged.

Jason spread her cheeks and plunged his length inside her, thrusting until his testicles slapped against her. Celise held perfectly still, and he placed one hand at the small of her back while the other snaked around her to cup her core.

She wiggled then backed up against him.

"Yes," he said, growling. "Do that again."

She did, and his entire body heated until he thought they'd both catch fire. When he felt his knees shake, his mind clouding with desire, Jason grabbed her hips and held her still. He pulled out of her until only his straining tip was left inside.

She whimpered.

He thrust into her long and deep.

He pulled out.

Thrust back in.

Out.

In.

Out.

In.

She cried out his name.

He cried out hers.

And then he came like a piston planting his hot essence deeply inside her.

CHAPTER TWENTY-ONE

One Week Later

"You should have told me what was going on," David Markam stated, obviously agitated.

The Markams and the Carringtons were sharing in a full family dinner at the home of Jeffrey and Lydia Carrington located in Brentwood, California. Lydia had suggested the get together after speaking with her son on the phone two nights ago.

"She's the one," Jason had told his mother. He was in the living room of his beach house, while Celise slept in the bedroom.

"I kind of thought so after seeing the two of you together," his mother had replied. "How does she feel about being "the one"?"

Jason smiled. He held the cell phone to his ear as he stood at the patio doors looking out onto the beach as the evening tide rolled in.

"I think she's on board with the idea," he admitted. "Neither of us expected this to happen."

Lydia had chuckled. "And that's usually the way love goes. Your father is not pleased with all the press you're getting," she said after she'd had a second to sober a bit.

He'd hoped he could smooth things over with the announcement that he'd found the woman he wanted to spend the rest of his life with. But true to form, Lydia wasn't having it. His mother was a very intuitive woman. For all that she usually remained dignified and quiet during a dilemma and for the majority of the time thereafter, she did not mince words when she felt like there was something to be said, especially to her sons. The fact that Jason was the youngest son, the one they worried about most for whatever reason, made him an easy target.

"Nobody was hurt and it had to be done. Bingham was going to harass Celise and the hotel industry for years to come if he hadn't been stopped," he told her in defense.

"I agree with you that he needed to be stopped. I just wish you would have let law officials handle it. Jackson and Jerald think you've lost your mind," Lydia continued.

Jason did smile at that. "I talked to both of them who sounded strangely like worried housewives."

"They love you, Jason. They care about what happens to you."

He nodded his concession of her words even though she couldn't see him. "I know that, Mom. And I appreciate everyone's concern. But everything is fine now. Celise and I are moving forward."

Lydia took a deep breath. "And that leads me to the second reason I called."

"You have reasons for calling me?" he asked playfully.

"Nevermind the smart remarks," she admonished. "I want you and Celise and her family to come for dinner. If we're all going to be joined in this union, we should start out on the right foot."

"Because fighting over a hotel and putting a man's only daughter in front of a madman, isn't starting off right enough?" Jason asked sarcastically.

"Because love deserves a chance to flourish in a healthy environment," was Lydia's retort. "Your father and I have had a long marriage, we've raised three children and we're very proud of what our family has become. From our brief meeting at the Cook-Off, I get the impression the Markams are the same. So we should get together, to put the past behind us and move forward into the future. Don't you agree?"

If he didn't she was liable to talk to him for the rest of the night until he did. Jason figured it was wiser to simply agree.

"Yes ma'am," he said.

"Fine. We'll have dinner on Saturday. Extend the invite to the Markams. And tell them don't bother getting a hotel room, everyone can stay at the house."

"We're not the Brady Bunch, Mom," Jason had ventured to complain.

"No," she said with a chuckle, "We're the Carringtons and don't you forget it."

Now, two days later they all sat in the living room of his parents' estate. Dinner had gone surprisingly well and they were enjoying drinks and coffee in the den as the evening came to a close. At least, Jason had thought everything had gone well, until David's comment about the Bingham incident.

"We handled it, Dad," DJ told him from his spot near the bar. Jerald, who had been playing bartender had just slid onto a stool beside him.

"Nigel Bingham is on his way out of the country after returning the Carrington stock to the rightful owners. In light of facing a huge lawsuit and possible criminal charges from one of the victims, he opted to take the easy route. And Celise was great," DJ continued.

"Probably so, but I won't be volunteering for anymore undercover work for a long while," Celise said with a relieved chuckle.

She hadn't been far from Jason's side this evening and was now sitting with him on one of the two vintage leather sofas in the room. A large oak and glass coffee table separated them from the matching sofa where Celise's parents and Sharrell sat.

Clive, who Jason noticed was sticking rather close to Sharrell, was in a chair to the Markam New York manager's left.

"I don't blame you. Has anyone heard from Pamela?" he asked.

Jason took a sip of his drink then nodded. "Last I heard she was headed back east to stay with some family she has there."

"And the Hampdens?" Jeffrey inquired from the love seat he and Lydia occupied.

Clive answered this time. "They moved to Florida with their children since Jason decided not to press charges against them."

"You should have put them in jail," Jackson chimed in. "At least for a day or two to teach them a lesson."

The Carrington men looked remarkably alike, Celise thought as she looked in Jackson's direction. He was the oldest, the tallest and the most formidable of the threesome. His skin was the same buttery tone as Jason's. Unlike Jason, his dark hair was close cropped and he wore no goatee, just a mustache that was as expertly groomed as the rest of him.

Jerald, was the middle child and just like her brother Isaac he played that role by being the voice of reason between the other two.

Right now, he was shaking his head—the head that was full of sandy brown hair that he kept long, in that rugged semi-afro type of look.

"You can't put old people in jail, Jack," he told his older brother. "Jason did the right thing."

Jerald had a quieter voice than the other brothers and his soft green eyes gave him a distinction between the two, even though it was still obvious from the way he wore his clothes to the square of his shoulders that he was all Carrington.

"They were a nice couple," Celise added thoughtfully then frowned when Jason nudged her. "I mean, they probably used to be. Myrtle was just trying to do what she thought was right. But she probably should have listened to her husband's warnings. At least they're happy now."

"I'd like to propose a toast." Jeffrey stood and lifted his glass.

Everyone in the room followed suit by lifting their glasses or mugs as it were and waited expectantly.

"To my son, Jason Carrington and what will soon be known as the best hotel on the West Coast—no offense, David," Jeffrey offered with a smile.

For a moment David looked gruff, then he gave in to a chuckle. "None taken, Jeffrey."

"Here. Here," Clive added, lifting his glass higher.

They clinked glasses, and all eyes rested on Jason.

"Thanks, Dad." Jason stood, pulling Celise alongside him as he did then wrapping an arm around her. "For so long I've dreamed of this moment. I've sacrificed and focused everything for the past few years on this one goal. And then, when I was about to face the biggest challenge of my life, in came a breath of fresh air." He looked down at Celise.

"Without her I wouldn't have found love for the first time," he admitted.

Celise smiled up at him, at his declaration in front of both their families. She felt her mother's eyes on her and didn't try to hide the happiness.

"Without her I wouldn't have Carrington Resorts safe and sound." He leaned forward and kissed her briefly. "I guess it's safe to say without her I would have nothing."

"Awwwww," Clive cooed, and Sharrell nudged him.

"I'd like to propose a union," Jason interrupted.

Maddy's hand instantly went to David's arm, keeping him still while Lydia smiled up at her husband knowingly.

Jason set his glass down and took Celise's from her as well. Grabbing both her hands, he turned her to face him and smiled into her eyes. "I'd like to propose that since you've brought me so much happiness and in light of the fact that you saved Carrington Resorts on two occasions, that we get married and run the hotel together."

Celise blinked and stared at Jason, trying desperately to understand what he was saying. "Are those the two propositions?"

"No." Jason grinned. "I can't get anything past you."

"She's pretty as a picture and smart as a whip. I'd say you've got your work cut out for you, son," Jeffrey added, laughing.

"I'd also like to propose that the very first *Chances* restaurant be opened on the penthouse floor of Carrington Resorts."

Jason watched her closely as did everyone else in the room.

She felt like she was beneath a microscope and everyone was waiting for her reaction. She'd sensed that something had been on Jason's mind these past few days. He'd been more attentive to her than ever and less stressed about the hotel but still on edge about something. She'd assumed it was a result of the turmoil they'd been through. She'd figured things would calm down soon and they'd slip into a normal routine.

Never had she imagined that routine would consist of her partnering with him in the hotel business. The business she'd so adamantly steered clear of. And as if that weren't bad enough, he'd mentioned her restaurant. *Chances* was her idea. Her dream. Her baby. It had to be realized on her terms, in her time. How dare he step in and maneuver her this way?

"Was this your plan?" she asked quietly. "When you were taking me around town and showing me locations and giving your advice, were you planning that I'd run your restaurant all along?"

He quickly shook his head. "No. That's not what I was planning. I listened to you talk about your dream. I believed in it, and I believe in you. I told you once before that you would be a success, and I meant that."

"You meant that I'd be a success as long as I opened my restaurant in your hotel?" She slowly slipped her hands from his grasp.

"Celise honey, I don't think that's what he's saying," Maddy jumped in.

"It's exactly what he's saying," she countered. "He's doing the same thing Daddy tried to do. The same thing Daddy wanted Nigel to do. The same thing I've been trying to get away from all my life, and I'm sick of it." She was out of the room and headed for the door before anybody could say another word.

She'd just stepped outside into the cool night breeze looking up and down at the driveway full of cars. Of course hers was blocked in. To hell with it, she'd walk. Anything to get away from there and all the people who wanted to run her life.

"Running away again, Celise?"

His voice stopped her, and she turned. "What did you say?"

Jason stepped closer to her, but was careful not to invade her space. He wanted her to hear him out, but he also wanted to give her room to decide on her own. He wanted her in his life, but he wouldn't have her believing he'd manipulate her or push her to do his will. He wasn't Nigel, and he wasn't her father.

"Is that how you always solve your problems? You're getting a little too old for that, don't you think?"

"You don't know me," she accused, taking a step closer and poking a finger in his chest. "You don't know what I do or why I do it, so don't talk to me as if you do."

He still didn't touch her, but he felt every spike of pain in her words. "I know that you've convinced yourself that your family has kept you from following your own dreams all your life when the real person stopping you has been yourself. You talk about starting a restaurant when the truth is you're afraid. You're afraid you're going to fail and that your family won't love you anymore."

"That's ridiculous," she spat.

"Is it? You've been in Monterey for two months, and you haven't found a spot for your restaurant. You haven't started the paperwork for your licenses. You haven't done anything except talk about it."

"That's because I've been too busy helping you save your precious hotel," she snapped.

"You stepped in and handled the guests at Carrington Resorts like an experienced hotelier. You told me what should be done to the new restaurant like a person knowledgeable about the guests who frequented hotels and their wants and needs. You confronted Nigel Bingham because a part of you needed to for closure." Because she shivered, he touched her shoulders, rubbed his hands up and down her arms. "And yes, you saved my hotel for me. Because you love me."

"No," she whispered then inhaled deeply. "I wanted to do it by myself. I wanted to prove that I could do it alone."

He moved closer, wrapping his arms securely around her and pulling her against his chest. "But you don't have to do it alone, baby. My offering you the space at Carrington Resorts is just that—it's the space. You'll still make all the plans. You'll run the restaurant as you want. You'll hire and fire. You'll cook. Whatever you want, Celise. It's yours."

"But you knew this was what you wanted all along. You let me talk about finding my own place when you knew you wanted to give me your space. Why did you do that?"

Jason smiled. "Because I didn't want this to happen. I didn't want you to get all testy about me telling you what to do and controlling your life." He turned her to face him.

"Sweetheart, I come from the same type of family you do. I know how it feels to have them all thinking your life should go one way and feeling compelled to live my life another. I respect that, and I respect you, so I didn't tell you right off the bat. But you have to know that I'm doing this only because I love you so much and I want you to be happy. When you talked about your restaurant, you lit up like a Christmas tree. Your eyes sparkled and your voice crackled with excitement. I wanted to give you that same type of feeling, and I thought my proposal was the answer."

Celise looked into his eyes with the intention of searching out the truth, but she didn't have to look long to see something else. Jason Carrington loved her. And he was right about what he'd said. She hadn't found a location because it was much easier for her to submerse herself in him and his world. There was a part of her that was afraid of failing. She'd preached about how grown she was for so long she'd begun to doubt herself. And she had liked getting involved in the business of Carrington Resorts. Not only because she was sleeping with the boss, but because it felt natural, and it felt right.

Maybe she did belong in the hotel business, just not running the show the way her family had always done. Maybe she just needed to realize her place in the hotel industry on her own, without any expectations guiding her. And wouldn't it be a good idea to open a restaurant inside a hotel already made famous for its controversy? Better yet, wouldn't it be nice to go to work and to come home with the man she loved?

"You're right," she said reluctantly. "I don't like it when you're right."

Jason laughed and kissed the tip of her nose. "Then I'll try not to be right so much."

"You're too arrogant for that to be a possibility." She smiled. "Okay. Make your propositions again."

He held her in a loose embrace so that he could look down at her. "Celise Markam, I would be happy if you would marry me and allow Carrington Resorts the honor of hosting your first restaurant."

"Jason Carrington, I would be happy to marry you and to open *our* first restaurant in *our* first hotel."

READ THE NEXT DANGEROUSLY SEXY INSTALLMENT TO THE CARRINGTON CHRONICLES

NEEDING YOU
By A.C. Arthur

Available In Print & Ebook formats

THE CARRINGTON CHRONICLES

Wanting You
Needing You
Having You – *COMING July 2015*

47019327R00155

Made in the USA
Middletown, DE
14 August 2017